COPY   24 94

Fiction Coughlin, William Jeremiah, 1929-
            No more dreams / William J. Coughlin.
    New York : A & W Publishers, c1982.

        299 p.
        ISBN 0-89479-105-2 : $13.95
        SUMMARY: Love and politics mix as an expert
    on Constitutional law is considered for the
    critical swing position on the Supreme Court.

NO MORE DREAMS

DREAMS

William J. Coughlin

A&W Publishers, Inc.
NEW YORK

While the characters in this book are fictional and bear no resemblance to any existing persons, the places are quite real. However, some of the institutions mentioned in this book may find some changes and additions previously denied them by administrators and legislatures.

Published by
A &W Publishers, Inc.
95 Madison Avenue
New York, NY 10016

Manufactured in the United States of America

Designed by Levavi & Levavi

1 2 3 4 5 6 7 8 9 10

3 9082 05924638 2

Library of Congress Cataloging in Publication Data
    Coughlin, William Jeremiah, date.
        No more dreams.

        I. Title.
        PS3553.O78N6   813'.54   81-70461
                                                AACR2
ISBN 0-89479-105-2

To the Spartans . . . we have obeyed

The author would like to acknowledge the guidance, tact, and encouragement of a very talented lady, Ruth Bridget Pollack.

INTEGRITY: **As** occasionally used in statutes prescribing qualifications of public officers, trustees, etc., this term means soundness of moral principle and character, as shown by one person dealing with others in the making and performance of contracts, and fidelity and honesty in the discharge of trusts; it is synonymous with "probity," "honesty," and "uprightness."

In re Bauquier's Estate, 88 Cal. 302; 26 Pac. 178.

Chapter 1

He pushed the worn bell button at the entrance.

A nun quickly answered the door. She was young. Dressed in a light blue blouse and dark skirt, only her headdress, a mixture of black and white cloth, identified her as a nun.

"I'm here to see Sister Agatha Murphy," he said. "My name is Michael Wright. I'm one of her attorneys."

The young woman forced a polite smile. "Of course. Please come with me, Mr. Wright." She led him down an empty hallway to a sparsely furnished sitting room. "Please have a seat. I'll tell Sister you are here."

"Thank you."

This was not his first visit. He had learned the building was the "mother house" of the order of nuns called the Sisters of Help, a nursing order founded in France. The mother house served as the headquarters of the order and also as a refuge for those sisters who could no longer carry out their duties.

He hoped the inner quarters were more cheerful than the

waiting room for visitors. It contained only three hard-backed chairs, a table, and a lamp. A picture of the crucified Christ was the only decoration that adorned the drab beige walls. A worn rug covered a part of the wooden floor.

Michael Wright sat down in one of the chairs and waited. The red brick building was large, four storied, long and wide, of simple institutional design. He had been told that it housed a permanent population of over one hundred nuns. However, he could hear nothing. There was no hint of human life, no strains of music, no squeaking floors, only barren silence. He detected no cooking odors, no lingering reminders of cabbage or other foods, not even a whiff of furniture polish although everything in the room gleamed under heavy coats of shining wax. The still, sterile atmosphere of the room made him uncomfortable.

But she had asked him to come. He was reluctant, but he was handling her appeal and he considered it his duty to at least maintain some minimal contact with the woman. Sister Agatha Murphy had been tagged as Sister Death by the nation's press. She was in residence at the mother house, out on bond pending appeal. Aiding and abetting a suicide was a felony and a jury had found her guilty. It was his job to reverse that outcome.

The chair creaked as he shifted his weight. He welcomed the sound. It broke the dreamlike silence in the stark room.

Wright speculated that prison well might be preferable to entrapment in this brick tomb. If her conviction stood up and she was sent to prison, Sister Agatha Murphy at least would have the solace of sounds, odors, and contact with the hustle and pulse of living humanity. He had never thought that noise in itself might possess any positive quality until he had visited the mother house.

She swept into the room. The hall carpeting had muffled any warning of her approach and despite himself he jumped. He quickly stood up.

"Sit down, sit down," she said irritably. Although she always spoke softly, there was the unmistakable quality of command in her tone. She was accustomed to giving orders.

Sister Agatha Murphy was wearing a modification of the old habit once worn by her order and now forbidden. Stark black with only a starched white piece at the throat, it was unmistakably a nun's habit. Her headdress was full and concealed everything except her round bland face and some stray strands of her graying hair.

She sat opposite him, primly tucking her hands beneath a cloth fold in her habit. She looked at him, her clear blue eyes slightly enlarged by the thick lenses of her plain square glasses. She had put on some weight since his last visit and was bordering on stout. Her skin was smooth and she looked younger than her age, which he knew was fifty-six.

"How have you been, Mr. Wright?" she asked.

"Just fine, Sister. And you?"

She did not reply immediately, but hesitated for a moment. "I have no work to do. I am accustomed to being busy. They will not allow me to even work in the infirmary here at the mother house. However, putting aside the inactivity, I am well."

"Perhaps if I spoke to your supervisor, the . . . the. . . ."

"Mother General," she finished for him. "I rather doubt that would help, Mr. Wright. It is only a rumor, you understand, but I am told she is under direct orders from the Pope himself in this matter." Sister Agatha Murphy smiled wryly, showing her annoyance at the Pontiff's interest in anything so petty.

"What about other work?" he asked. "Surely there must be other things to occupy you besides nursing duties?"

Her blue eyes flashed. "I am a nurse," she said firmly. "May I remind you, Mr. Wright, that I hold three degrees in my profession. I have run hospitals. I doubt very much that peeling potatoes would prove entirely satisfying."

"How are you being treated otherwise?"

She again smiled wryly. "Oh, some of the younger sisters have been kind. The older ones regard me as a murderess. Very few people here talk to me. They are, however, polite for the most part." She sighed. "I miss my hospice."

"It's been closed. Your order closed it right after your arrest."

She nodded slowly. "That, I think, is the only thing I truly regret. Those poor dying people needed the help we could give them in their final hours. I have been able to handle everything, the implications of madness, the silly examinations by psychiatrists, the condemnation by the Church, but I carry a sense of guilt for all those who were in the hospice. They should never have been turned out just because of me."

"I can appreciate your feelings," he said, eager to change what was obviously a painful subject for her. "Now, is there something you wanted to see me about? You did call and ask to see me." He forced a smile.

She looked out the window for a moment, as if gathering her thoughts. Then the cool blue eyes once again swung toward him. "You stated before, Mr. Wright, that one justice seems to control the outcome of many of the cases before the United States Supreme Court, is that not correct?"

"Yes, Justice Howell."

She nodded. "As I recall in our last conversation, you hoped he might rule for us. What was it you called him, the swing man?"

He started to reach for a cigarette then changed his mind. There were no ashtrays in the room. "You have an excellent memory," he said. "And accurate. Justice Howell's vote often decides the issues before the Supreme Court. Sister, I'm sure you realize we don't know what the Court will do, we can only base our thinking on what they have done in the past concerning similar cases. We believe your conviction will divide the Court. If that happens, Howell's vote would probably decide the case."

"And you thought he might vote in my favor, at least that was your guess," she said.

"Yes."

"But that's only a guess." Her voice was flat, a hint of defeat coloring her usual commanding manner.

It would be unwise to give her any false hope. Still, Wright felt pity for the woman. He paused for a moment to choose the correct words. "I suppose 'guess' is the proper way to express it. But we have obtained some additional information. Quite encouraging, at least in my opinion."

Her placid features revealed no emotion, but her eyes expressed some curiosity.

"Sister, I don't want to mislead you. But you're an intelligent woman so I'll just tell you what I know and you can then make your own judgments."

The cold blue eyes narrowed with increased interest.

"There's a professor at the University of Oregon. He's not a lawyer, he teaches political science. However, he has made a study of the Supreme Court and the justices. Over the years he has developed an uncanny ability to predict how each justice will vote, particularly on this kind of case, the kind that attracts wide public interest."

"Sounds like a soothsayer."

"If he is, he is a very accurate soothsayer." He made an effort to conceal his irritation. "The basis for his predictions is quite scientific. He knows the justices' backgrounds and what kinds of attitudes they have displayed in the past. He keeps track of their public speeches and published articles. He knows exactly how they voted on similar cases. He has developed quite a feel for the individual thought and character of each member of the Court."

"And what has all this to do with me?"

"At first, this professor made these studies merely for his own satisfaction. However, he received enormous publicity when he began to call each important decision exactly. He became nationally known, at least among lawyers. He no longer does it for free. He now demands and gets very substantial fees for his predictions."

The nun sighed. "Superstition still plagues the human race."

Wright merely shrugged. "He has a better than ninety-five percent ratio of success, so it matters little if he does it with a study of decisions or chicken bones, does it? The result is the same, and that result is valuable."

"And he has a prediction of how the court will deal with me, I suppose?"

"He does."

"As you know, Mr. Wright, I have no money. Even if I did, I certainly wouldn't waste it on buying the prophesy of some Oregon sorcerer."

The lawyer forced a smile. "The costs of your appeal are being paid by various organizations, people, and groups who agree with your position."

A flash of anger briefly crossed her features. "I don't want their support. I merely helped desperately ill people stop the pain that was tormenting them. Some of the people and groups you mention are Godless monsters whose views are diametrically opposed to my own."

"Still, they do pay the bills."

Her face once again became placid and emotionless. "I did not ask them to do so. That is their choice."

"Well, they got up the money to pay the professor for his prediction."

"Foolish."

Once again Wright had to control his irritation. She had no idea of the huge fee the man had demanded. "As you know, there are nine justices on the United States Supreme Court. It takes a majority of those nine to overturn any lower court decisions. As it stands now, four justices are classified as liberals, and four as conservatives."

"And that makes Justice Howell, the ninth man, the deciding vote. The swing man."

"That's correct, Sister." Wright was desperate for a cigarette. "Our professor has combed over the justices and their stands on such issues as the death penalty, abortion, and similar matters."

"I don't agree there is any similarity."

He shook his head. "It's a matter of opinion, of course. In any event, the professor believes the Court will again split, as it does so often now, and it is his opinion that Justice Howell will decide for you."

She silently regarded him for a moment. He felt uncomfortable under her steely gaze. "And you think you can actually rely on such a thing," she asked.

"I rely on nothing except the brief we are submitting and the argument we will present. This is a contest, Sister, an important contest. I play to win. We not only bought the professor's predictions, but also his study on the background of each justice. How I approach the brief and argument will be influenced by what I determine is the best avenue for success. The professor's data will be of great use to me. Remember, when all is said and done, I must find the means to persuade the majority of the Court to our point of view."

She looked out the window. "If I lose the case I shall be forced to serve the sentence imposed by the lower court, is that not correct?"

He almost whispered the answer. "Ten years. To be served at the state women's prison."

She looked back at him, the hint of an icy smile upon her thin lips. "I shall be one of the few nuns in prison, at least in this country. But I do not consider myself a martyr. I presume I will be assigned to the prison infirmary where I can once again serve as a nurse, at least in fact, if not in name. I also suppose that my fellow inmates, while perhaps not the genteel ladies I associate with here, will talk to me. That, in itself, would constitute an improvement."

"Prisons are not convents, Sister."

The smile vanished and the commanding eyes narrowed. "I

am not afraid. Do you know what will happen to me if you should win my case for me?"

"You'll be free. Not just out on bond, but really free."

"Mother General has made it quite clear that if I wish to remain in the order I shall be required to spend time with a cloistered order. We shall pray together, but we will not be allowed to talk. The Church regards what I have done as murder. It is a time-honored way of exacting penance. Unlike your civil authorities, no time is set. I shall serve in silence until someone designated by the Church believes I have seen the error of my ways and have been sufficiently punished for my transgressions. When that occurs, if ever, I shall be sent back to serve perhaps as a teacher, but I shall never be allowed again to nurse the sick. I am not to be trusted." Her words were spoken without bitterness, but just as a flat, objective statement of fact.

"That is the fate that Rome will demand," she continued. "That is, should I choose to bow to the Pope's authority."

"And if you don't?" He was interested. Wright had never considered the ultimate consequences to the nun if they were victorious before the Supreme Court.

A cold smile haunted her lips. "I shall be excommunicated. That may not mean a great deal to you, Mr. Wright, but I have taken vows of obedience and I still believe in my Church. If I ignore my superiors I shall be cast out."

"I'm in no position to advise you in religious matters. Still, it *is* your choice. You could leave. You have a tremendous educational background, Sister. Surely you could get work. . . ."

She held up a restraining hand. "Of course. But what kind of work? I am quite notorious, am I not? Do not protest. They call me Sister Death. Can you honestly see any reputable hospital taking me on?"

"Well, there are a number of things you could do. You could teach. And there are hospitals, perhaps not quite so reputable, where you would be welcome."

"Abortion mills! I am a nun, Mr. Wright, but I am not naive. Certainly there are a number of medical places where I could be exhibited like a prize freak, perverse places where men calling themselves doctors scrape away the lives of thousands of unborn and innocent children. No, I'm afraid such a fate would be inconsistent with my beliefs."

Wright was confused by her attitude. "You make it sound as if you really want to lose the case."

Her ability to be inscrutable, to conceal her thoughts and emotions behind her placid features was impressive. He sought a hint of her feelings in the cold eyes behind the spectacles but found none.

She seemed to be carefully choosing her words as she spoke. "I have given my situation considerable thought. Believe me when I tell you that I feel completely justified in the eyes of God, despite whatever position the Church may take at this time. I believe eventually my actions will be seen as blameless under civil law. However, what the future may hold is not in my command. I was trained to serve God and humanity, Mr. Wright. I may be serving God here but I feel the need to serve humanity. I need to resume nursing. That is why I called you, Mr. Wright. I wish to withdraw the appeal and begin my sentence."

The attorney knew the shock had shown on his features, but he quickly composed himself. A lot would depend on just how he handled the situation. He paused, then spoke. "Come now, Sister. You can't be serious?"

Her chilly eyes never blinked. Sister Agatha Murphy was a determined woman. One eyebrow lifted slightly as she replied. "Surely you can have no objection to dropping the matter? I would have thought you would welcome it. I understand most of your work on this case is donated. What do you lawyers call it? Pro bono—for the public good?"

Michael Wright sat back in his chair. He was an experienced trial lawyer and quite accustomed to controlling panic. He knew if he reacted too quickly or emotionally she might perceive the true situation. She was intelligent. It would have to be handled very delicately.

"If you want the matter dropped, Sister, I shall certainly do so." His mind raced for just the right words. "However, your case has really gone beyond the fate of Sister Agatha Murphy, hasn't it?"

She said nothing. Her only response was a slight narrowing of her eyes.

"Sister, there are desperate people all over America. They are dying. Slowly. Painfully. There is no hope of recovery. The pain medications no longer work. Surgical nerve blocks no longer work. You know what is happening to them much better than I. They pray for release. If they are comatose and living on life-support systems, even your own religion allows the plug to be pulled. But if they are alive and screaming in pain, they are forced to endure to the very last."

"Young man, I am not a jury and you don't have to paint any word pictures for me. I have spent most of my life serving such people. If you have a point, make it." Her tone was soft but her words crackled with command.

"Look, if you win, the whole law shifts. People in pain, if they desire it, can ask for release. Doctors and nurses can legally do it. Now, as the law stands, a doctor or nurse who helps these people out of their misery stands in jeopardy of ruin and prison."

"Many do it, despite that."

"Of course, but many do not. That's why your case is important, extremely so. It isn't just a matter of whether you get locked away in a jail or a convent. As in so many of these cases, Sister, your personal fate is comparatively unimportant. But the outcome of your case will affect millions. It will change the law and society will be forced to solve a problem it has long feared to face."

She studied him silently for a moment. "Do you honestly think I was right in what I did with my patients?"

He nodded.

For just a moment her features seemed to soften. She looked out the window again. "All right. I can understand the importance of the decision. I suppose I can endure." She slowly turned her head and looked at him. "Perhaps it will ease your burden if you know that I do not care whether I win or lose as an individual. We will continue the appeal, Mr. Wright." She stood up. "Thank you for coming."

He got to his feet. "You are a most admirable person, Sister. I can certainly understand your discomfort here, but it won't be long now. The Supreme Court has accepted the case. My brief is almost finished. The briefs will be submitted and the Court will assign us a date to argue. The professor in Oregon believes that the court will act quickly on this matter because of the importance of the rational suicide issue and the publicity the case has received." He smiled. "Perhaps the words are a bit inappropriate for you, Sister, but as I tell many of my other clients, just try and hang in there."

Her eyes narrowed. "I do not need your sympathy or your encouragement. I appreciate your intention, however. Good day, Mr. Wright. I'll have one of the sisters escort you out."

"I know the way."

"As you wish."

She was gone as quickly as she had come. Once again he was alone in the eerie silence. Quickly he strode down the hallway, opened the door, and escaped into the world outside. He needed a drink and he knew he had to make a telephone call.

Wright stopped at a bar and had the drink first. Then he moved to the bar's phone booth.

Sister Murphy was incorrect. Michael Wright's time was not donated. He was on retainer and well paid. The check came from the Egress Society of America, Incorporated, but it was signed by Herbert Mennen.

It took several long distance calls to trace Mennen but he finally located him at a health club.

"You got me out of the fucking steam room," Mennen said. "I'm freezing my butt off, so make it fast."

Wright quickly recounted his conversation with Sister Murphy.

"Hey, if that menopausal old broad is going stir crazy, get her reassigned. Shit, sue the lady general or whatever they call her. Raise a little hell. I got too much invested. I don't want this thing dropped."

"Sister Murphy won't sue the Mother General. There's nothing I can do legally. So far, everything is all right, but I wanted you to know she's getting shaky."

"Shaky? Hey, that old bitch killed over a hundred and thirty-five people. Shaky! Shit, if that didn't bother her, nothin' ever will. Maybe she wants something, you think? Maybe money?"

"No. She's straight enough. I don't even think she suspects what's on the line here."

"Wha'd'ya mean, suspects? You talk like I was planning something illegal. That's the whole point of this fucking lawsuit. I want everything legal. That's the only way it'll work."

"I know."

"And I want to get in on the ground floor. Hell, there's big money to be made, but you have to do it fast before the market gets flooded. I got everything ready. I got options on the places. I even got the people lined up to work 'em. Shit, I'll have a nationwide network operating before the ink is even dry on the decision. That is, if you win."

"And if we lose?"

"Look, I'm not in the business of losing. But if we did I suppose my accountants could find a way to write off most of it, but I wouldn't be making anything on the deal. That I don't like. You sure about this guy, what's his name, Howell?"

"Nothing is sure. That's just the prediction. I think it's probably correct."

"I damn well hope so. There's millions to be made in this

thing. Christ, I think I may be able to get the health insurance companies to pay. Wouldn't that be something?"

"They'll never pay for people to commit suicide."

"Hey, why not? If a doctor provides the prescription and it's all done in a hospital setting—one of my hospice places—and it's legal, why the hell shouldn't they pay? Hey, Wright, I'd like to go on talking, but my fucking skin is turning blue. See if you can't do something to keep that old broad happy. We can't be stopped now, now that we're so close to pay dirt. Remember, this is going to be a nationwide deal."

Wright hung up and returned to the bar.

The money was good, very good, but contact with Herbert Mennen depressed him. The question of whether it was a criminal act to assist a suicide was a legitimate issue. There was nothing to be ashamed of in representing a side in a legitimate legal controversy. If Herbert Mennen wanted to pick up the tab—how had Sister Murphy put it about such persons—that was his choice. Still, the association with Mennen caused Wright to feel demeaned and tarnished.

He knew Mennen's background. Mennen's methods may have been as crude as the man himself, but like him, they were always legal. Starting from nothing, he had made a fortune, all in the very best American tradition.

He had started his climb from ownership of a single poultry store where he killed and dressed the chickens himself. He had branched out, ending up with a national net of slaughterhouses. Then came his abortion clinics. Despite the battle over Medicaid funding, Mennen made millions before selling his interests in that business.

There was a definite pattern—Herbert Mennen liked to kill things.

Wright took the Scotch from the bartender and sipped. He thought about the upcoming case in the Supreme Court. The oral arguments would be made with calm dignity in that palacelike setting of the high court. The lawyers and the justices would speak evenly of case precedents, logic, and soaring principles of law. Meanwhile, Mennen would have things set up and ready to go.

If they won, Mennen's "hospices" would spring up like May flowers, and a parade of sick, depressed, and defeated people would line up and pay huge sums of money to sip a pleasantly flavored poison that would ease them quickly and painlessly from beneath the crushing weight of their own particular cross. Mennen's public relations people planned to call it "self-deliverance."

He wondered if the Supreme Court justices ever considered the flesh and blood consequences of their actions, or whether they saw everything merely in abstract legal terms. He wondered if Justice Howell knew he literally held the lives of thousands of people in his hands.

Michael Wright sipped his drink. He formed a mental picture of an ancient Roman emperor. The high court's swing man and the emperor weren't so different. The fallen gladiator lived or died as signaled by the emperor's thumb. Thousands of modern lives would be decided on the stroke of one justice's pen. That would be the signal, just a scrawled signature.

But the swing man wouldn't hear the roar of the crowd, nor would he see the death agony. At least the old Romans had to look at the results of their decisions.

Wright left some money on the bar and walked out. He had a lot to do.

*   *   *

Justice Brian Howell eased his car around a slow-moving station wagon packed with clothes and children. The children were gawking at the lighted Washington Monument. As he passed he noticed the woman, presumably the mother, her face illuminated by the street lights. She was young, but she looked as worn as the battered station wagon. He thought they were tourists until he saw the woman. He decided they were more likely a family migrating to a southern state and to a new life. He put them out of his mind as he increased his speed and left them behind.

It was late and traffic was light.

He enjoyed driving in nighttime Washington. It always had a special fascination, a special aura created by its many illuminated monuments and the massive government buildings; structures that surpassed the awesome fortresses of Europe. And like their European counterparts these giant citadels seemed to proclaim impregnability and mighty power. He wondered if the architecture of ancient Rome had spoken so eloquently of its place in the world and history as did these huge limestone houses of American government.

Road repairs forced him to use the Arlington Memorial Bridge. He guided his car past the monuments at the foot of the bridge. The dark Potomac River reflected lights from the opposite shore. He sped toward the Virginia side and the looming National Cemetery. He hated the cemetery. His wife had dragged him to see it and the memory always depressed him. Crossing the Potomac was like crossing the River Styx, and going into that cemetery was like walking into the land of the dead. Acres of countless graves seemed to stretch on forever. They were all there, the presidents, the generals, the heroes of American history. Judging from the daily crowds that thronged aboard the parade of cemetery tour buses, others did not share his feelings of dread. The buses rolled through the sloping land of graves, each bus with a tour guide who pointed out the historic graves and shrines. He recalled being appalled at the time. He felt a sense of special horror because he realized that by being both a veteran and a member of the Supreme Court it was most likely that this would one day be his own gravesite. He had commanded his wife to cut that tour short, and he had never again returned to the place. He didn't even want to look at it.

Exiting from the bridge he turned right and sped past the lighted statue of the Marines raising the flag at Iwo Jima. He followed a course leading to Wilson Boulevard.

Wilson Boulevard passed through the land of the transient. The businesses catered to the ever-shifting governmental population, usually military, and there seemed to be a sense of impermanence about them, as if they were ready to close shop and follow their customers.

He stopped for a traffic light. Howell glanced down at the copy of the national news magazine on the seat next to him. He was on the cover, a good, brooding photograph with half his face in shadow. The large print on the bottom read "America's Most Powerful Man."

He smiled to himself. The beauty of that statement was that it was true. Officially he was just one of nine, an associate justice of the United States Supreme Court, and the most junior at that. But he was the swing man.

The other eight justices split on most issues, especially those wearing the tag of liberal or conservative. It was always four to four on the political issues. His vote decided which side won. He held the balance of power in the Court. His vote had come to be the deciding factor in the nation's law. The law was what Brian Howell said it was. Considering the vast importance of many of the issues soon to come before the Court he was considered by many as being even more important than the President himself.

The light changed and he continued, still thinking about the magazine article.

He knew that his name, Brian Howell, had become a household word. There had been the tremendous fight over Senate confirmation. The Senate had destroyed the first two men put up for the vacancy. He was the third man nominated and he had made it. The publicity at the time had been enormous. Then he quickly became known as the swing man. Now, as he well knew, law professors all over America were telling their students about Justice Howell and how important he had become. Some, he had been told, compared him to Cardozo, Holmes, and Marshall.

He turned toward home but he knew there would be no one there. Martha was visiting the kids in Chicago. He had encouraged her. He had to study every evening, the work was backing up, and he was glad to be free of the distractions of her attentions and attempts at conversation. Most of the other justices relied upon their clerks to do the reading and research. But they could afford to, they didn't hold the balance of power. He read every case, every brief. His clerks worked long and hard but he declined to rely on their efforts. He was in the spotlight. There could be no mistakes. He checked everything.

He was hungry and developing an annoying headache. There were frozen dinners at home but he was growing tired of the same fare. On impulse he swung the car into the parking lot of a small restaurant.

The restaurant was almost empty. Several young men in civilian dress but with military haircuts quietly ate dinner at a corner table.

A young waitress guided him to a small table at the rear of the restaurant. He liked it. It was neat, clean, and inviting. The girl brought him a menu and water as he again read the magazine article about himself.

"Pardon me," she said.

"Yes?"

"Is that you? I mean, the man on the cover of that magazine?"

He smiled. He enjoyed recognition.

"I'm afraid so."

She smiled warmly. "You're Justice Howell?"

He nodded.

His confirmation took her smile away. Her eyes grew wider and her friendliness was replaced by awe.

"My boyfriend," she said haltingly, "is a law student. He's in his first year at Georgetown. He's talked about you."

"Anything printable?" He grinned up at her.

She grew even more serious. "He says you are the law in America."

Howell chuckled. "Well, you wait until he gets to his senior year. Maybe his opinion will be different by that time."

"Before you go, would it be improper if I got your autograph? It would please my boyfriend."

"No problem."

There was an awkward silence as she just stood there. Finally she forced a hesitant smile and spoke. "We don't get many famous people in here. Please excuse me." She blushed. "I'm forgetting my job. Can I get you a drink?"

He wanted a drink, but he wanted to preserve her lofty image of himself. "Just coffee," he said.

The dinner was excellent. Word of the important guest had apparently been passed along to the kitchen. The steak was large and cooked just as he had ordered. He was brought too much butter and too much bread, and his salad would have fed a platoon for a week. The food wasn't fancy but it was tasty. He ate more than usual to please his unseen benefactors in the kitchen.

As promised, he autographed a menu for the waitress.

The headache grew more severe on the drive home. It seemed to be affecting his vision. He had difficulty getting his key into the lock of their condominium. He called for his wife, then recalled she wasn't home. He felt a wave of nausea as he switched on the lights. He regretted having eaten so much. Something was wrong. He wondered if he was suffering from food poisoning.

A young doctor lived a few doors down. A Chinese. Martha had introduced them at a neighborhood party. He recalled the name. It was Chen. He knew that Martha would have the doctor's home phone number. She was very businesslike about that kind of detail. He tried to extract her telephone memo book from its drawer and found he couldn't seem to make his right hand obey him. He felt confused, uncertain as to what he should do. The pain had become an agony.

He had trouble walking. His right leg seemed to drag, but he managed to get out the front door. He knew where Dr. Chen lived. He stumbled up to his door and pushed the button with his left hand. The pain was blinding. He had to lean against the doorway to keep from falling. His right leg refused to hold him.

The door opened and he looked down at the small Chinese woman. She was very pretty and he couldn't understand why she screamed. Then he recognized Dr. Chen, as the equally small doctor helped him into their home.

Howell tried to speak, but the wrong words came out. He was embarrassed and frustrated. He needed to tell the doctor about the pain, it was unbearable.

He collapsed and fell to the floor.

"My God, Charles, what's wrong with him?" Mrs. Chen stared down at Howell's distorted face.

"It's a stroke. Get my bag! Quickly!"

She ran and returned with his medical bag. Her husband was kneeling over Brian Howell. The man was unconscious and seemed to be fighting for breath.

"Is he dying?" She asked quietly.

"Maybe." He rifled through his bag. "Jesus, you never seem to have what you need." He looked up at her. "Call and get an emergency team here. This may be touch and go. We have to get him to a hospital fast."

She obeyed instantly, then returned. Howell had not changed. "He looks as if he is strangling," she said.

"Very common in stroke victims. It looks bad, but it isn't dangerous. It's not his breathing that's the problem. He may have blown a blood vessel in the brain."

"Will he live?"

Dr. Chen monitored Howell's pulse. "You never know with these things. It depends on the damage. Sometimes they can recover in hours. If there's severe brain damage sometimes the people end up dead or just vegetables. We have to do tests to see what's happened." He looked up at wife. "You better go get his wife."

"She's away."

"After we get him into the hospital we'll have to try and contact her. It would be terrible if she heard about this on the radio or the television."

"Television?"

The doctor looked at his patient. "This guy is big news. As soon as they find out what has happened the hospital will be crawling with news crews."

"If he wakes up, he'll be angry about that."

The doctor slowly shook his head. "That's the least of his worries. Some of these people never wake up."

*　　*　　*

"Boss wants to see you." The copyboy's manner grew more insolent the longer he stayed on the newspaper. He was consumed by envy of those staff members who did the actual writing. He desperately wanted to be a newspaperman so he endured the daily humiliations suffered at the hands of staffers, who took great relish in responding to his arrogant attitude.

Abbot Simmons looked up from his typewriter and smiled. "Which boss? Practically everybody here is my boss."

"The head asshole himself. You must'a really fucked up."

Simmons leaned back and studied the messenger. "How the hell old are you now, Eddie? Thirty-two, maybe thirty-four?"

"I'm twenty-three!"

The tall reporter slowly stood up, the same whimsical smile on his horselike features. "When I was twenty-three I was the night city editor on the Jacksonville paper."

The copyboy's face reddened. "Fuck you," he snapped as he strode away.

Abbot Simmons fished through his coat pocket to get his

cigarettes. He had no heart for torturing the copyboy, but it had become a habit. Eddie was too easy. Not only did he have an unpleasant personality, he lacked simple common sense. Abbot Simmons lit a cigarette. "With those qualities he should be an editor," he said aloud and to no one as he walked down the row of desks toward the office door of the managing editor.

He knocked. Simmons always knocked ever since the night he caught the old man humping Kay Cochran, the society editor. That night he had just walked in without warning. It had been embarrassing. He knew and liked Kay's husband, and he knew and liked the managing editor's wife. That night no one moved, they had all just stared at each other until Simmons frowned at the lady and said, "Does this mean we're through, Kay?"

He thought it was a funny exit line, but later Harry Phillips, the managing editor, had a talk with him consisting of half bluster and half wet-eyed pleading. No one had a sense of humor anymore.

"Come in," Phillips called.

Simmons walked into the cluttered office. "What's up?"

"I liked that story you wrote about the Stevens River Bridge."

The reporter sat down in a worn easy chair. "Yeah, it practically wrote itself. That whole fucking thing is going to fall right into the water one of these days."

"I agree, but I can't run the story."

Simmons blinked. "Why not?"

Phillips pushed his eyeglasses to the top of his head. He had seen the gesture in a movie once and liked it. It made his glasses greasy but he thought it gave him a touch of glamour. "It's that new law," he said.

"Harry, there isn't even a hint of libel in that story. Everything is perfectly true. I got a written affidavit from the city inspector. Hell, I don't accuse anybody of being crooked. I don't even blame anybody. Somebody just fucked up in building the thing, that's all. I just truthfully reported the situation."

"I'm not talking about libel law." Phillips, a rotund man, leaned back and put one thick leg up on his desk. "It's that other law, the written negligence thing."

"You mean like in the Booker case?"

"Yeah."

"That's a bunch of crap, Harry. My story doesn't even come close. No mob is going to drag somebody out of jail and hang him over a lousy bridge."

"Maybe not, but out new state statute makes a newspaper liable for reckless or negligent reporting."

"Harry, my article isn't reckless or negligent. It just reports the facts about a badly built bridge."

The managing editor shrugged. "It's a toll bridge, and thousands use it every day, Abby." Everyone called Abbot Simmons "Abby," and he had to endure the "Dear Abby" needle daily from most of his co-workers.

"If thousands use it, Harry, that's all the more reason why we should run the story. There's a real possibility the thing may crumble. That's not too probable, I admit, but it is still possible, at least according to the city inspector. The people have a right to know."

Phillips grunted. "Look, it's a toll bridge. People pay money to cross it. Let's say we run the story and half the people stop using the bridge. Abby, that's thousands of dollars per day. If someday a judge or jury decided we were reckless in printing the story, we'd get stuck for those losses."

"No court would ever do that. We have the facts right."

"That didn't make any difference with the Booker paper and their story about the killings in Marysville. They had everything right, too. But after the paper hit the stands the mob formed at the jail and lynched the defendant, right?"

"The paper didn't editorialize, it just reported the facts, nothing more. They weren't responsible for what that mob did," Simmons protested.

"But they were sued under the new state statute and got hit for four million bucks."

"It's on appeal. The Booker newspaper chain is taking it right up to the Supreme Court. That law is unconstitutional, it violates the First Amendment."

The managing editor leaned back in his chair. "The reason it's going to the Supreme Court is because the newspaper has lost in every court so far, both trial and appellate. Have you read the decisions?"

Abby Simmons crushed his cigarette and absently lit another. "I read about them, the feature pieces and so on, but I never actually read the decisions."

"I have." Harry Phillips picked up a dead cigar butt from an ashtray and knocked off the cold ash. He relit the cigar, puffing up a cloud of acid smoke. "The courts say it doesn't violate the First Amendment because the newspaper can still print what it likes. No one can get an injunction to stop an article. They say it's just like the law of libel. If you injure someone with a story, you have to pay. They say that's perfectly constitutional. According to the courts, printing a news story is like driving a car or using a hunting gun; you can do it but you have to be damn careful you don't hurt anyone. So, if you aren't careful, you pay. I don't know what the Supreme Court is going to do, but I personally don't think Booker has much of a chance. Especially since half of those old bastards on the Court are looking for a chance to stick it to the media."

"It still doesn't apply to my story. We have a duty to inform, that's basic. That damn bridge is dangerous. And that's just not conjecture, that's based on expert opinion. Even if there is a risk, we have a duty to take it."

Harry Phillips snorted. "So suddenly journalism is a noble profession with you?"

"It's just a job, Harry, you know that. But what the hell, it's unlikely we'd get sued, and even if we were, they'd never collect.

That story should run. It's no big deal, it's not Watergate. It's just a routine thing, it's just part of the job."

Phillips shook his head. "You know what kind of profits this rag is making?"

"I get my paycheck. That's all I really care about."

"Well, sport, our beloved publisher is losing money on this little hobby of his. He makes a buck with the family's chemical company, but this is a losing venture. He eats the losses. It helps some with his taxes, and he likes playing the part of the wise and powerful publisher. But this hobby is getting a little steep, even for him."

"So?"

Phillips chewed on the cigar as he talked. "Daily newspapers are dying all over the country. I don't know about you, Abby, but I'm not a wealthy man and I still have to work for a living. And I like newspapering. So, for that selfish reason alone, I want to see this crappy little sheet live on. Get me?"

"Shit, you think my little story about a bridge is going to sink the ship? You can't be serious?"

Phillips shrugged. "Well, if we get sued, the publisher will have to spend money for lawyers. They don't work cheap. Win or lose, he won't like doing that. The newspaper negligence law has complicated my life. I have to go through this paper with an eye to everything now. If it looks like it could draw a lawsuit under the new statute, I kill it. That's what happened to your story."

"You know what the lawyers call that?"

Phillips shook his head.

"Chilling effect. That's exactly what they mean when they say a 'chilling effect.' Look, you're scared that we might get sued under some cockamamy state law, so you kill a harmless little story. Killed and chilled are the same thing. That damned statute has had a chilling effect upon the First Amendment right to a free press."

"It sounds like you read the decisions. Hell, you're using the same language. They discussed that point. The only problem is that the newspaper lost."

Abby Simmons inhaled deeply on the cigarette and blew out a long stream of smoke. "Harry, if this is happening here, with a little story about a half-assed bridge, it must be happening all over the country."

"Nope, just our little state. No other state legislature has had the guts to pass such a law."

"And if the Supreme Court upholds it?"

Phillips shrugged. "Similar laws will pop up all over the nation. There's a lot of people pissed off at newspapers."

"And when that happens, a newspaper will be just a bunch of advertising held together with recipes, sports, and comics."

"That's overstating it, Abby, but you can bet your ass editors will be damn careful what they run."

The reporter stood up. "Well, that bridge story wasn't exactly the culmination of my life's work anyway. As long as I still get my salary, as they say, that's what's important. Still, all this might work out as a pretty good feature piece."

"Oh?"

"Yeah. Something on the courts. Honest to God, until this minute I never really realized just how important they can be. You know, Harry, if the Supreme Court votes to uphold that law they'll change the nature of news reporting completely. It could end the whole concept of a free press."

The editor nodded. "And probably by one vote. Everything has been five to four with them lately. Did you see where that new guy, Howell, ended up in the hospital?"

"No."

"Just a wire service bit. Family spokesman says it's an undisclosed illness. He's in intensive care according to the hospital. Probably had a heart attack."

"Sounds that way," Simmons agreed. "You know, that court feature might be a good idea."

"Don't make it controversial," Phillips said as the reporter started to leave. "Don't step on any toes. Now the sons-of-bitches can sue us."

"At least until the Supreme Court decides the Booker case."

"Yeah. Until then we have to be careful."

Simmons shook his head. "You know, the whole world sucks."

The editor grinned. "Yeah, that's why the universe is a vacuum."

*   *   *

Amos Deering was "assistant" White House Press Officer. Almost all the new faces in the rabbit warren of offices and cubicles in the White House were "assistants." The transition following the demise of the elected president was designed to be smooth. The former vice president, now chief executive, had made a great effort to show a continuity of leadership. However, he disliked and distrusted most of his predecessor's confidants. But with election only a year away he was reluctant to put the boot to the politically powerful members of the late leader's staff. They continued to hold their former titles with the understanding that they would actively seek other employment. The real work fell to the "assistants," the staffers who were part of the new administration.

"Hey, Deering," Harold Baker called as Deering passed his office door. Baker was still the official press officer. He had lost the job and the power, although he retained the title.

Deering liked Baker. They were both professional politicians with similar backgrounds and understood each other, although Baker was a cool, relaxed Californian and Deering was a hard-driving product of Boston's Back Bay.

"How'd he take it?" Baker asked.

"He was upset."

"Coffee?"

Deering nodded.

Baker took the glass pot from the burner behind his desk and poured the steaming liquid into two paper cups. "It's decaffeinated."

"Just so long as it's hot." Deering sipped the aromatic brew.

"Tell me what you can. I'm nosy." Baker grinned.

"You know him. He hardly ever swears, but he was cursing like a dock hand when I told him Howell had a stroke last night."

"Can't blame him. It certainly screws things up. The Court has a lot of big things coming up."

"Like the Electoral College issue," Deering said.

"Especially the Electoral College." Baker took a sip of his coffee. "If the Court says the amendment is valid, the popular vote will decide the next election."

"And my man will lose."

"Our man," Baker corrected him. "I'm still a member of the party."

Deering laughed. "Yes. I sometimes forget that you California people are friendlies."

Baker smiled. "And some of us are loyal. Not all, but some." His expression became serious. "Do you want my appraisal of the situation?" He was older, more experienced and Deering had come to rely on his advice. Baker had graciously gone from boss to advisor and he was careful never to recross that line.

Deering nodded. "I'd appreciate hearing your thoughts."

Baker leaned back in his chair. "He'll have to move fast if Howell dies. That electoral question can decide whether he wins or loses, according to the polls, and it's coming up for decision in the Supreme Court. The Democrats on the Judiciary Committee know that if they can block the President's nominee, the vacancy won't be filled in time. There'll be another four-to-four deadlock and the lower court's decision will stand, which means goodbye Electoral College system and goodbye Mr. President. He'll have to come up with someone very fast, and that person will have to stand up to a hostile committee. I'd suggest an archangel, but they're rather hard to find."

Deering felt the coffee burn his stomach. The doctor had said it was an incipient ulcer, but Deering had too much to do to worry about such things as ulcers. "They destroyed Shiller and Mosgrove. They tore them apart." He spoke reflectively, as if almost to himself. "Christ, Brian Howell was the answer to a maiden's prayer. He was as pure as snow, and even then the Judiciary Committee crapped all over him. But he got through. God, I know the President would hate to have to go through all that again if Howell dies."

"Death changes a lot of things," Baker said quietly. The irony wasn't lost on Deering. The death of the former president had drastically changed both their lives.

"How's the job hunting coming along?" Deering asked, to change the subject.

Baker shrugged. "Not bad. Oh, there's plenty of opportunity to become the director of this and that study or committee, but I'm shooting for something a bit more permanent. I've had a couple of pretty good nibbles lately."

"As you know, anything I can do to help. . . ."

Baker grinned. "Getting a bit tired of doing all the work and having only the 'assistant' tag?"

"Maybe a little," Deering said, smiling. "You know how this town is, it's the title that counts. But don't worry about it. Anyway, I like you. You're one Californian whose brains haven't been addled by too much sun, surf, and funny cigarettes. You're close, you understand, but I think you still possess some basic human qualities."

"That's a qualified endorsement, but I still appreciate it," Baker grinned. He offered more coffee but Deering shook his head.

"Tell me the details," Baker asked. "I'm no longer close to

power, but I still like to hear about it. What exactly was his reaction when you told him that Justice Howell was at death's door?"

Deering smirked. "Pissed," he said. "That's the only way to describe it. There was no pretense of sorrow or any of that crap. It was as if Howell had turned traitor and voted with the opposition. The President was damn angry about him and his inconsiderate stroke."

Baker nodded. "All politicians think of themselves first, at least if they're successful. That's how they get to the top. It's instinctive."

"He took it very personally. But it was a short explosion. You know how he is, he never lets his emotions show. Everything is 'just swell' and everybody is 'just grand.'"

"Yes. That disgusts me, but that's his training. He's strictly an Eastern 'swell.'"

Deering laughed. "Cheap shot."

Baker smiled. "But true. Old school tie and all that. Tennis anyone? Shit, at least my man had a bit of starch in his shorts."

Deering grew serious. "Starch or no starch, we'll have to go like hell to find someone to replace Howell if he croaks. And it'll have to be someone who can get by the knives of the Judiciary Committee."

"How about a fellow senator? They usually afford a free pass to one of their own."

"We thought about that the last time. But the word was passed that the chairman wouldn't bless anyone, not even a fellow member of the Senate club. He prefers a candidate who's a cross between a convicted Nazi and Attila the Hun. Anyone else, he believes, is a flaming liberal."

"Well, that tends to narrow the choices."

Deering nodded. "I'll say. Of course, if they had nailed Howell, we did have a couple of hot prospects waiting in the wings last time. And that hasn't been so long ago."

"Who?"

Deering hesitated. "A couple of good people. The President said if Howell dies and we have to move fast, he'll probably pick one or the other quickly."

Baker sipped his coffee. "What the hell's the matter with you, Amos? I'm not going to leak anything. As a matter of fact, I may even be in a position to help. Who are these two paragons of virtue?"

Deering thought a moment before replying. "It's not a state secret, I suppose. The President is considering Judge O'Malley of the Second Circuit Court of Appeals and Roy Pentecost."

"I know O'Malley, but who the hell is Pentecost?"

"Dean of a law school."

Baker tapped his lips with his forefinger as if he were trying to test his recollection. "Pentecost. Pentecost. Sure, I remember now. He's the guy who started that law school up in the midwest. I've forgotten where."

"Michigan State University School of Law. He's the founder."

Baker started to smile. "Sure, I place him now. He's the guy who robbed Harvard and Yale of their best teachers. Paid them a king's ransom."

"That's him. Also, he set up entrance standards for law students that excluded everyone but a certified genius. The law school is regarded as better than Stanford, maybe even Harvard, and they've only been open a couple of years."

"Waste of money. Both you and I have put some time in universities. Nobody cares about the quality, it's the football team that counts. They should have taken the dough they sunk into the law school and bought a few fast backs and some muscle for the line. If you have a winning football team your school is great, and if you don't, you never get noticed."

"Don't be bitter, Harold. This guy Pentecost might even have made a hell of a coach. He's the kind that plays to win, I'm told. He knows how to run things."

Baker reached into his desk and produced a long, thin cigar.

His first of the day. "Being a good administrator doesn't guarantee he's a good lawyer." He lit the cigar and savored its smoke.

"Maybe, maybe not," Deering replied. "But outside of a few speeches and a law book or two he's written, he has no public record for the committee to shoot at."

"How about O'Malley? He's pretty straight."

"Sure, but you know how that works. The screwballs will come out in flocks to protest various decisions he's written in the past. That's how they nailed Judge Shiller. He wrote one anti-busing decision and by the time the chairman and the committee were through he looked like he had been the head of the Ku Klux Klan."

"I remember."

"Well, I'm directed to start looking into the possibility of both O'Malley and Pentecost. Whoever looks the least objectionable will get the nod to fill Howell's vacancy, if there is one."

Baker emitted a long stream of cigar smoke. His eyes followed the course of the smoke as it curled toward the ceiling. "You remember the old Irish saying, the devil you know is better than the devil you don't know? I'd go with O'Malley, if I were you guys."

"If Howell dies, we'll have to have somebody all set. It might end up O'Malley. Whoever it is, we'll have to be ready to ram through the nomination before that Electoral College thing comes up."

"And you think the Democrats aren't aware of that?"

Deering grinned. "They're too busy getting ready to kill each other in the primaries to unite on anything."

"Don't kid yourself. That selection will mean as much to them as it does the President. They know the score."

Deering sighed. "Nothing is ever simple."

Baker grinned. "You can say that again."

Chapter 2

The smoky bar was populated by bulky men in casual clothes. The customers were all off-duty police officers, most of them fresh from the afternoon shift at the Tenth Precinct as well as a few officers from the neighboring Eighth. The only woman in the place was the elderly barmaid.

A group of men was sitting at a large round table. Most of them were drinking beer. A younger officer came in and sat down at the table.

"Hey, Charlie, where you been?"

"Had to put in some overtime," Garcia said, explaining his late arrival. "Have you guys ever seen that thing the fire department has, that big tool they use to pry metal open?"

One of the men at the table nodded. "Yeah. What do they call that thing? Jaws, or something like that."

Garcia signaled to the barmaid. He ordered bourbon straight up.

"Was it a traffic accident?" the other officer went on. "I

seen them use that gadget to rip a car in two. They were trying to get somebody out, they were dead when we got to them, but I was certainly impressed with that tool."

Garcia nodded his agreement. "You know those new trash compactors, the sanitation trucks with the metal hydraulic scoop on the back that crushes the garbage into the truck?"

"Yeah, most of those independent salvage outfits use 'em."

Garcia nodded. "Yeah. That's why I was late. We had a run to an accident involving one of those trucks. The garbage truck was owned by a small company. It was so small that the owner's son was driving the thing. He had an old black man along as a helper. Anyway, the hydraulic crusher got stuck. A piece of metal got jammed into the hinge that swings the thing. The old black guy climbs back there with a sledge hammer and starts whacking away. He did a good job. Of course, as soon as he knocked the wedge out, the damn thing started working again and it crushed him like a grape. Then the compactor stuck again, and when we got there we couldn't get him out. The fire department came out and took that big scoop apart like butter."

"Guy was killed, right?" one of the men asked.

Garcia grinned. "Only his upper half, just his head and chest. Everything else was just fine. He was one hell of a mess."

"Hey, Shirley," one of the men at the table called. "Officer Garcia here would like a glob of spaghetti, heavy on the tomato sauce."

Everyone laughed.

"The young son-of-a-bitch driving the truck tried to deny that the old black guy worked for them," Garcia said.

"Trying to wiggle out of paying workmen's compensation benefits," one of the men at the table said in disgust.

Garcia nodded. "Yeah. At first he tried to say he didn't even know the guy. I think he was trying to make me think the old man climbed into the back of the truck and committed suicide. But finally he caved in and told the truth."

The waitress brought his bourbon, and he quickly jolted it down. "Another, Shirley," he said, putting a bill on the wooden table.

Garcia felt the liquor burn, but it was more consoling than painful. "Money! You know, that's the only thing some people think about. It turned out the old man had been working for those people for over three years. But they always paid him in cash. That way they didn't have to pay his Social Security or screw around with deducting taxes. He got no benefits, no nothing, just a couple of bucks an hour. I guess everybody is trying to screw somebody. At least it seems that way."

The conversation fell off and for a few moments everyone at the table was silent.

"Heard they had a police shooting over at three," one of the older men said. "The accident car came up on a holdup. One of the blue coats nailed the robber right in the head. One shot."

"Black guy?"

"No, white luckily. Shit, if you run into black bandits you're smarter to just fire over their heads and hope they go away. Goddamn, if that punk had been black, the mayor would have sent down the chief and forty-seven commanders just to hang that white copper's ass. I guess that's what the department calls a 'suspension.'"

Everyone laughed.

Again there was a lull in the conversation.

"Any word on the lawsuit?" Garcia asked as he sipped the second whiskey.

Clark, one of the older officers, shook his head. "If we only had a half-wit for association president we wouldn't be in this fix. A half-wit would do a better job than that fool Mandrake."

"But no word on the lawsuit," Garcia persisted.

Clark shrugged. "Nope. It's all up to the Supreme Court now. But at least we'll be famous. They say that whatever the Court does in our case is supposed to set the precedent for all these reverse discrimination cases. The Court has been picking around the fringe of the question for years, but this time the word is they're really going to decide it once and for all."

"And if we lose?" Garcia asked, knowing the answer.

Clark's expression became somber. "All white officers with under ten years senority will be let go. All the rookie blacks and women they hired and laid off in the last few years will be reinstated. All future hiring will be done on a straight quota system."

"Jesus, that's unfair," Garcia said. The others nodded.

Clark shrugged again. "Hey, I got fifteen years in, so it don't hit me. Anyway, it's just the reverse of what it used to be. Hell, in the old days, if you were black you had to eat shit because the majority of the city's population was white. Now that the blacks control the most votes in the city, it's the whites who get it in the ass. That's the American way, ain't it?"

Garcia felt the whiskey bring a relaxing numbness, and some of the tension began to leave him. "It shouldn't be that way," he said. "It was wrong to crap on a black man when the whites ran the city. It's equally wrong now that things are reversed."

"If you're looking for justice, Garcia, you're in the wrong racket. You should know that by now." Clark grinned. "We're screwed, ye olde fix is in."

"The Supreme Court isn't fixed," Garcia protested.

"Well, just consider the record so far," Clark said. "The police association brings the lawsuit in federal court to stop the mayor from firing white officers, right?"

Garcia nodded.

"They got seventeen judges there, two of whom are black. Who gets the case? One of the blacks. Surprise! And lo and behold he finds against us and in favor of our black mayor. Another surprise!"

Clark sipped his beer, obviously warming to his subject. "And when we appeal that to the high-and-mighty United States Court of Appeals, who comes out as head of the three-judge panel assigned to the case? Nobody else than our old pal, Judge Robert

George, the guy who has made an entire career out of being on the black side of things, right or wrong. And we lose, ain't that another surprise!"

"We always lose in the Court of Appeals. They let Judge George have all the cases dealing with racial matters. Everybody knows that."

Clark grinned. "That ain't in their rule book, but you're right, Garcia. Everybody does know it. And being a federal judge, old George don't run for office so there is no way he can be voted out, and that way he doesn't give a shit about the people. That's just one of the little thorns to be endured; the price of democracy, you might say."

Garcia leaned back and lit a thin cigar. "I just asked about the case, Clark. I didn't want a speech."

The older officer laughed. "I don't mind being associated with prostitutes, pimps, and muggers, but I'll never sink so low as to be accused of being a politician. I make no speeches and I'm not a candidate."

"You sound like a candidate for the nut farm," one of the others grumbled.

Clark ignored him. "I'm just imparting street wisdom, Garcia; the pure sweet logic of the people. I think the fuckin' case is fixed. But to answer your question, the guys down at the association say the legal briefs should be in soon. Then they'll argue the case. After that we'll get the opinion, or opinions, as the case may be." Clark again became serious. "They figure it will be another eight months or so before the Court speaks on the case. So you still got a job, Garcia, at least for that long."

"That's a great comfort."

"Anyway," Clark continued, "maybe you won't get canned. Maybe the Supreme Court will insist they retain a quota of spicks. With a name like Garcia, you could get lucky."

"My mother was Polish," Garcia said, grinning. "So I'd probably be out of luck on that account."

Clark chuckled. "Shit, maybe they'll only fire your Polish

half. You'll only work half shifts, but that's better than nothing."

"Thanks for that wonderful ray of hope," Garcia said as he stood up. He left a tip for the waitress. "I have to go. My old lady thinks I'm out humping the hookers, so I have to go home and demonstrate my fidelity."

"Garcia, don't worry if she's cutting you down," Clark grinned. "Hell, I know some guys she's cut out completely."

It was an old joke, but they all laughed.

Patrolman Charles Garcia drove home carefully. He knew two whiskeys would not impair his ability to drive. Still, he was tired and it always paid to be cautious. The traffic was light but he took his time. He was in no hurry to get home. Lately his home had become a very tense place. He knew the insecurity of his job situation was the main reason for all the tension between himself and his wife. The fights had become more frequent and more heated.

He had nothing laid away. Something always came up to drain his savings. He had invested seven years in the police force, with most non-duty nights spent at the city college earning a degree in law enforcement. And now the whole thing was about to go down the sluice. He was a cop, he had no other marketable skills. All he possessed was a wife, two children, a mortgage, and a car loan.

He noticed that his hands were trembling slightly. He knew he had to control the fear or it would soon control him.

He felt he was no different from any of the other officers on the police force, white or black. None of them had had it easy, at least none that he knew. Now he stood in jeopardy—his future and the future of his family depending on what nine lawyers in Washington would do. There were no policemen on that court. From what he had read, few of the justices had had much of a struggle in life. The aristocratic yards of Yale and Harvard were hardly the proper places to gain a feel for the pressures an ordinary man endured.

As he pulled into his driveway he thought of the old black

man who had been crushed in the machinery of the garbage truck. Maybe that was how it always worked out. You were fated to be crushed by unthinking, unfeeling machinery; reduced from the dignity of being a man to nothing more than castaway garbage.

He felt sick. Garcia decided it must have been the whiskey. He shouldn't have taken it on an empty stomach.

*   *   *

It was a strange place for a meeting. He felt a bit conspicuous just standing in front of the Smithsonian Air and Space building. Everyone else was moving about; school classes on field trips, weary parents dragging protesting small children, and squadrons of tour groups. It was the most popular exhibit hall of all the Smithsonian buildings and always busy.

A group of well-dressed, athletic-looking tourists marched behind an authoritative blonde woman who carried aloft a small triangular flag tied to a long thin stick. The flag served as a visual guide for the group. No matter how chaotic the press of the crowd, her flag was always there to be seen. Decked out with the usual tourist cameras and equipment, the group moved at a determined pace. As they passed, he caught some snatches of spoken German. Mentally he conjured up a picture of steel helmets. These Teutonic tourists would look most formidable in battle dress.

Tour and charter buses were parked, one behind the other, for blocks. It was autumn and although the huge throngs of summer had dwindled, there was still no shortage of people. They were enjoying the gentle weather of late October. The trees of the Mall had decorated the ground with their splendid colored leaves, which swirled about in the soft breeze.

He glanced up at the Capitol. Like a white fortress it rose above the Mall's trees. He remembered the view from there, looking down the long green Mall with the Washington Monument at the other end pointing into the sky like a giant's finger.

They called the small rise of ground Capitol Hill. Although small, it was truly more powerful than a volcano. He sometimes missed being away from the power.

The fresh air was crisp and invigorating and he was genuinely glad to be away from the pressures of the law office. He knew he was mentally tired and stale after the long case before the Federal Trade Commission. What should have been easy had turned into a titanic struggle that lasted many weeks. It was over but the end seemed anticlimactic. It would be months before a decision was announced. But that decision would be crucial, not only to the client and the firm, but to himself. He had been taken into the firm for his political connections, no bones had been made about that. He was a full partner but there was a buy-out clause in the partnership agreement. It had seemed a great deal of money at the time, but now it only amounted to a few month's income. If the FTC case was lost, their largest client would be lost. And he had been on shaky ground with the other partners going in. There had been just too many losses lately and he knew they were looking for someone to punish. His connections weren't quite as good as they used to be and he sensed a nonspecific coolness toward him.

He impatiently searched the Mall, looking for Amos Deering. He saw a constantly moving sea of faces, but none of them belonged to Deering. He wondered if he would even recognize Amos Deering after all these years.

He stepped back to escape becoming part of a chattering Japanese tourist group that had suddenly engulfed him. He found himself staring at his own reflection in a polished steel panel, part of a display being moved into the Space exhibit. The panel was set at a slight angle, making his reflection just a bit taller and thinner. He studied himself in the steel: Jerome Green, attorney-at-law, distinguished partner of the prestigious law firm of Harley, Dingell, Spear, and Frank, known to everyone as Harley Dingell. Everyone always used the first two names in a large firm to distinguish it. It was a traditional convenience that everyone seemed to accept as useful.

The Jerome Green he saw in the steel was trim, although a hint of thickness was becoming evident. He at least looked fit although he was able to manage only sporadic episodes of tennis and exercise. His hair, full but gray, seemed suited to his full, mature face. Anyone knowing clothes would instantly recognize that he was expensively dressed. Dark suit, black shoes polished to a high gloss, and a quiet tie; it was almost a uniform. Very good clothing, but conservative and without flair; it was the firm's unofficial dress code. Heaven help any young associate who decided to come to work in anything less. Harley Dingell was no place for jeans or jogging shoes. Even a good tweed jacket was unofficially forbidden.

He glanced about. No one seemed to notice, so he once again looked at his reflection. He was Harley Dingell, no doubt about it. He at least fit in with the look of the firm, if not the people. He had no illusions about his situation. Most of the other partners had come from money, and most were WASPs with degrees from Yale. Harley Dingell was regarded as a "Yale" firm, although several of the partners had law degrees conferred by other Ivy League universities. He was the only one with a law degree from a midwestern school, the University of Michigan. He was also the only Jewish partner, although the firm did employ several young Jewish associates. He never thought of himself as Jewish, having long ago abandoned even lip service to the religion and customs, but he knew the others did.

He often thought that if there were any signs of prejudice at the office it wasn't because of any ethnic differences. Yale was a religion to most of his colleagues, and he was, therefore, of the wrong religion. But they were tolerant.

He knew they always referred to him as the "political" partner, even though he carried an enormous burden of trial work. If anyone in the firm had need of a phone call or a contact, they came to see him. Usually, he could conjure up someone from the past who would be of service. If the firm hadn't been so blue-blooded, with so many important clients, he would have been known as the "fixer." But such a term was unknown in the hushed and dignified offices of Harley Dingell.

Jerome Green's face in the steel panel showed no hint of his origin or his educational beginnings. Like every other important Washington lawyer, he looked trim, knowing, and bland. His was the regulation expression: no emotion, no passion, no humor, just the hint of a smile as if concealing the steel beneath. They all looked alike, dressed alike, and talked alike. It was as if the senior Washington lawyers—the big money men—were all produced by some magic machine, all clones, stamped out from some master mold.

Green glanced at his watch. He hated being late and had found himself growing more intolerant of others who failed to keep appointments on time.

"Hey, Jerry!" The voice was familiar, but the face, concealed behind a huge graying yellowish beard, was barely recognizable.

Green grasped the outstretched hand. Amos Deering's palm was warm and moist although his grip was firm. He was short and stout, and the beard made him look like an evil elf.

"Goddamn all tourists, I couldn't find a place to park." Deering stepped back and appraised Green. "You look pretty good, for an old turkey. Gray as my grandma, but outside of that you've weathered well."

Green smiled. "I didn't recognize you with the beard. When did you grow that thing?"

"A couple of years ago. I was teaching out at a college in Utah. At the time it was the only thing to do. Hell, if you didn't have a beard you weren't allowed into the faculty teas. Now everyone out there is clean shaven, but screw 'em, I don't have to worry anymore." Deering took Green's arm and directed him toward the other side of the Mall. "I know you're accustomed to finer things now, but how about having lunch in the cafeteria in the National Gallery of Art?"

"That's all right, but why there?"

"The cafeteria's strictly for the convenience of the tourists. We won't run into any government people there, and we don't have to worry about being seen together."

Green had no trouble matching Deering's determined stride as they crossed the Mall. "Why should I worry in the first place?" Green said. "I'm an innocent man. Of course, Amos, I was never too sure about you."

"I'm still innocent," Deering replied, but with no answering smile. "We're all still innocent, right? Just a couple of old Nixon alumni getting together."

Green frowned. "You make us sound like 'plumbers.' As I recall, we were both rather minor functionaries in that administration."

"You became an Assistant Secretary of Health, Education, and Welfare."

Green nodded, and a slow, almost sad smile played across his features. "But only for a few months, Amos. And it took me six years to work my way up to that."

"Ford kept you on."

"I was too far down the line for him to even care. Anyway, as you remember, I quit to go with Harley Dingell. I had a good offer and I took it."

Deering guided him up the steps into the magnificent art gallery. Only a few people occupied the vaulted interior and their footsteps seemed to echo in the silence.

"Com'on, it's down these stairs," Deering spoke in a hushed voice.

They entered the bustle of the basement cafeteria, selected their food, and took their trays to a far table. The large restaurant was only about a quarter full.

"Not so bad, eh?" Deering said, as he set down his tray. "And this place has the best pecan pie in all Washington. I think that's what I missed the most when I was away from Washington, pecan pie. I really didn't miss the politics, the excitement, or the intrigue as much as I missed pecan pie. You can't find this delicacy in Utah, believe me. Those Mormons don't really enjoy the finer things in life except maybe procreation."

"Amos, now that you're back in the seat of power, do you really enjoy it?"

Deering swallowed a bite of sandwich and grinned. A bit of mustard remained on his beard near the corner of his mouth. "Are you asking me whether being Press Officer at the White House beats being an associate professor of journalism in the beautiful golden West?"

"Something like that."

Deering shook his head. "Listen, it was like being an exile out there. God knows there were plenty of politicians and politics on that campus. All professors have to be real hustlers just to survive. And you had to keep your eye on everything and everybody, just like here. But it was strictly the minor leagues. So what if you made full professor or became department head, that's about as exciting as lettuce. I missed real politics so I handled the state of Utah for the man when he was running in the primaries. He lost, but by that time I had wormed my way into the inner circle." He grinned. "I'm good at that, if you remember."

"I remember."

Deering took a forkful of pie and savored it for a moment before continuing. "Anyway, I came aboard his staff when he was nominated for vice president. And I stayed on after the election. When the president died, I took over and handled all the publicity concerning the transition for the man. I have the title "assistant" but that's only until Harold Baker finds a job. I'm the real press officer, Jerry. So I'm back, and at the top of the heap. Not bad, eh?"

"If that's what you wanted, I'm delighted."

Amos Deering wiped his stained beard with a paper napkin. "The President asked me to talk to you." The statement was made in a conversational tone, although Deering dropped his voice to a near-whisper.

"About what?"

"He remembers you from before. He was impressed by your ability to get facts quickly."

"So?"

"We need a little job done. It shouldn't take more than a week or two. How about it?"

"I have a heavy case load at Harley Dingell, I. . . ."

Deering held up his hand. "Com'on, Jerry, I'm not asking you to quit your firm or anything like that. We know we can't afford you. We just need a special job done."

"Isn't that how the whole Watergate thing started—somebody needed a special job done?"

"Don't get cute, Jerry, this is important."

"I can't take off for two weeks, at least not right now."

Deering frowned. "Look, this is the President's personal request."

Green toyed with his salad. "You make it sound like a royal command. Did I miss something in this morning's *Post* or are we still a democracy?"

Deering sat back. "What's so damned important that you can't give it up for two weeks?"

Jerry Green instinctively obeyed the first rule of Washington's game of negotiation: never tell the truth, at least not the complete truth. It would serve no purpose to tell Amos Deering that he was in trouble with the firm, that he had lost important litigation, and that if things turned out badly at the FTC he would be ushered out politely. Deering would only use the information against him. Candor could be misinterpreted and, therefore, had no place in the game.

"I handle a lot of the governmental regulatory work for the firm. We both know why. As a former assistant cabinet member, I'm supposed to have clout. I've been away from government a long time and I'm not so sure that's true anymore, but that remains my assignment. Believe me, it's more than full time, Amos."

Deering nodded, and extracted a thin cigar from inside his

coat. "We can't afford to pay your regular fees, Jerry." He kept his eyes on Green as he lit the cigar. "I understand you're one of those five-hundred-dollar-an-hour guys now, right?"

Green shrugged.

Deering blew a ball of smoke toward the ceiling. "But we aren't coming empty-handed either."

"What do you have in mind?"

Deering twirled the cigar slowly in his fingers. "You'll be appointed as Special Counsel to the President for those two weeks, Jerry. Actually, we'd like it to be for a couple of months, in name if not in fact, it looks better that way."

"Two weeks, two months, so what. As I told you, Amos, I'm busy."

The bearded man didn't smile. His eyes no longer twinkled with good humor. "We're both professionals, Jerry, so I won't beat around the bush. You said your firm thought you had clout. Maybe you do, and maybe you don't. But as a former special counsel to the incumbent president, no one in this town could possibly deny your political muscle. If you see what I mean?"

"Amos, I'm surprised at you. You always played things straight before. Surely you aren't saying that I can expect special preference?"

"You know this town as well as I do. Hell, we don't have to do a thing for you. The title will take care of that, Jerry. If you count only the politicians, this is a small town, and everybody loves to gossip. With that title everyone will just assume that you have a passkey to the White House. You won't, but you'll never get anybody to believe that."

Green nodded. It was true enough, and perhaps it was just the thing to restore his flagging reputation within the firm. "And if I took your bait, what do I have to do?"

"We need a man investigated."

Green frowned. "You have the FBI, what the hell do you need me for?"

"Justice Howell has had a stroke."

"Is that what happened? The papers didn't disclose the illness, they just reported he was in intensive care."

Deering nodded. "We're controlling what they get, but it's a stroke."

"Bad?"

"He's in a coma. The doctors aren't sure. He may die."

"That's too bad," Green said.

"You bet your ass, that's too bad. Howell was the Court's swing man. That bitch who was appointed was supposed to be a conservative, but she switched to the liberals as soon as she was sworn in. So the Court went back to four against four, plus Howell. You know, you just can't trust a woman. Anyway, the Court's evenly divided and Howell was flopping back and forth as it suited him."

"I'm in the law business. I know what was happening."

"Right. Of course, Howell hadn't been our first choice. You remember the chop job the Senate committee did on our first two nominees?"

"The whole country remembers."

Deery exhaled a long stream of smoke. "Okay, here's the picture. We have to come up with another nominee, just in case. We have to be ready. There are several big cases coming up for decision and the President wants a man he knows he can count on. You understand? If anything happens to Howell, we'll have to move fast. Congress will adjourn shortly and the Democrats will do everything they can to block any appointment, so we have to make sure we can come up with someone good."

"Go on," Green said.

"We wouldn't be meeting here, you and I, unless we had some people in mind, right? You might even be in the running, Jerry, except you're a Nixon graduate. They'd shoot your ass off in the committee on that basis alone."

"I can live with the disappointment."

Deering laughed. "Yeah. We have two men set up for

consideration. We were ready to go with them last time, in case the committee cut up Howell. Now we have to take another look and decide which man stands the best chance of getting through those long knives up on Capitol Hill. And we have to know we aren't getting a lemon."

"Who are they?"

"You know one, at least by reputation: O'Malley of the Second Circuit Court of Appeals."

Green nodded. "A sound lawyer and a good judge, at least from all I've heard."

"Yeah. But he's a Catholic. That damn broad is a Catholic. It wouldn't look good, at least under these circumstances, to appoint two Catholics in a row. The right-wingers would think the Pope had seized the government. Besides, O'Malley has handled some hot cases over the years. And you can be sure all the losers will troop into the Senate hearings to raise a howl. That's the problem with nominating a sitting judge, he's got a record, and unless the guy's a wire walker he's probably made some controversial decisions. Of course, O'Malley's personal life is clean. He's been in public life for a long time, so at least everything in that area is known, or so we hope."

"Who's the other candidate?"

Deering drew deeply on his cigar, then flicked the ash into his dish. "Ah, that's where the mystery comes in. He's dean of a law school. He worked for the President when he was trying for the nomination. The President likes him. And those are pretty good cards for openers."

"What's the problem then?"

"In a way there isn't any problem. He hasn't decided any cases, so nobody is sore at him. He hasn't taken any controversial public stands. He wrote a book on constitutional law, but it's harmless; just a recap of a high school civics course, only in fancier language." Deering sighed. "We had the FBI do the usual check. But you know how they do those things. They talk to a few co-workers, a neighbor or two, run his fingerprints, and that's that.

They don't really dig down. The report says he's great, but for all we know the guy might be a pervert or a spy. We really know very little about the real man."

"What do you want from me?"

Deering again grew very serious. "Jerry, we want to know what makes this guy tick. We don't want any surprises like that damn woman. The President wants to know what he can expect. And he thinks you're the man who can do it. Anyway, it'll give you a chance to go home again. You know, renew old acquaintances and all that."

Green was startled.

"The guy's name is Roy Pentecost. He started the law school at Michigan State University. Isn't that where you come from, Lansing, Michigan?"

Green nodded slowly, experiencing a rush of conflicting and discomforting emotions. "Yes. The university is in East Lansing, but it's all part of. . . ."

"And it's also the state capital, right?"

"Yes."

"When can you leave?" Deering asked. "Time is of the essence."

Green didn't reply at once. He felt a sense of panic. It was not unlike the sensation aboard a roller coaster as it chugged to a towering summit; that breathless moment when the car is about to scream down the plunging track. It was fear. But the advantages of the White House offer outweighed any reservations about returning home, no matter how strong. "I'll have to check with the other partners. I have to get their approval. I'll call you this afternoon."

Deering looked at his watch. "Oh, Christ, I have to run. Listen, Jerry, here's my card. Call as soon as possible, okay? The President is really anxious about this."

Green looked at the card. "And if I pass this guy?"

Deering grinned as he stood up. "He'll probably end up on the Supreme Court."

"And his vote will probably decide the law, at least in many cases," Green said, almost to himself.

"Ah, just think of the power, Jerry. You're going to be like the recording angel. It will be up to you whether this guy gets into heaven or not."

"And what kind of man he is will determine what kind of heaven it will be," Green said, looking up.

Deering laughed, then hurried out of the cafeteria. Green didn't follow. He just sat quietly for a moment. He wasn't thinking of the Supreme Court, or of the importance of what he had to do. He was thinking of Lansing. It was home, but he felt a terrible sense of dread.

*　　*　　*

"Hey, Ben, do you have time for a quick cup of coffee?" Floyd Grant stood in the doorway, looking around at the cluttered cubicle. Grant was the Chief Justice's senior clerk. The Court staff always referred to him as "the messenger from God."

Ben Alexander looked up from his work. "I'm up to my armpits, Floyd. With my boss sick, I don't know exactly what to key on, so I'm trying to do it all."

Floyd Grant eased past a stack of open law books and cleared off a chair, carefully preserving the order of the papers he displaced. "Actually, I don't think I could stand another cup of coffee. I've been appointed as a committee of one to talk to you. The coffee was merely a civilized excuse."

Alexander put down his pen and leaned back in his chair. "Shoot."

Grant grinned. "You're new, Ben. You have to learn to horse around before you get to the point. It's expected. We should talk about each other's golf first, or racketball; maybe discuss our future plans. You see, we should talk about our families, old school chums, or anything but the thing in point. Finally, once these tribal preliminaries are over, it's only then that we carefully start to approach the real issue. That's how it's done here in the Supreme Court."

Alexander shrugged. "Okay. I don't have time for golf anymore. Anyway, I was never very good. When I leave here next year I hope to go with a big New York law firm as an associate. As a former Supreme Court clerk, I expect to make partner quickly. If all goes well, I should be a millionaire before I hit forty. I hope to meet and marry a beautiful girl whose father owns a giant conglomerate. If I don't make it in the law business, I expect my father-in-law to take care of me. Does that sufficiently meet the qualifications for small talk?"

"Any of it true?"

"No. Except the golf. I'm a lousy golfer."

Grant nodded wisely. "As long as you avoid the truth, you'll do very well here, Ben. You'll fit into the big picture, as the Chief likes to say."

"Good. Now what's up?" Alexander asked.

"Racketball is my game," Grant replied, smiling. "I plan to leave here and accept an associate professorship at Stanford. From there, God willing, I'll end up one day back at Harvard. I will write *Grant on Evidence* and be quoted by every good law journal in the country. Predictably, I will teach thousands how to try a case without ever once stepping into a courtroom myself. And when you are divorced by that beautiful conglomerate heiress, I will marry her, and let her old man take care of me."

"I hope all this satisfies your preliminaries, Floyd. I have work to do."

Grant nodded. "Has to be done. It's all part of the mystique of being a clerk to the greatest legal minds in the land."

"Greatest?"

"Bite your tongue, Alexander. Men have died for even thinking such thoughts."

"Look, Floyd, I really am up to my ass in work. . . ."

"Obviously a Yale man."

"Pardon me?"

"We never say 'ass' at Harvard. Columbia people do it, and obviously Yale, but never Harvard. Unless, of course, we are speaking about the animal so named."

"Look. . . ."

Floyd Grant grinned and held up his hands in surrender. "All right, Ben. If you insist, I'll almost come to the point. What's the word on your justice?"

Alexander instinctively became defensive. "I only know what you already know. He's had a stroke. He's still in a coma. The doctors, at least according to his wife, aren't able to predict what may happen. He could recover completely, he could be a cripple, or he could die. They just don't know at this time."

"The Chief went to see him in the hospital," Grant said. "The Chief reports he looks fine, has good color, and regular breathing, just as if he were sleeping. Only he can't wake up."

Alexander nodded. He too had seen his boss, and the description was accurate.

"He may never come back to the Court," Grant said.

"That's a possibility."

Floyd Grant had lost all hint of playfulness. He had become very businesslike. "And if he does come back, he may be severely impaired."

"That's another possibility."

"Ben, the newest lady member of this Court is complaining that she doesn't have enough staff to handle her work."

"So?"

"She's putting a lot of pressure on the Chief to have Justice Howell's staff, or at least part of it, assigned to her." Grant took out a pipe. "Mind?"

Alexander shook his head.

Grant lit the pipe, sending up clouds of gray smoke. "They say she's very tough to work for."

"I've heard that."

"The Chief doesn't like to bow to pressure, but she does have an argument, seeing as how your boss is out of commission."

Ben Alexander sensed an invisible cord tightening about him. The woman justice was the terror of the Court. Her clerks were treated badly, overworked, and humiliated. She was following in the footsteps of several distinguished previous justices who had established historic reputations as petty tyrants. He did not want to be assigned to her.

"Of course," Grant continued, "the Chief pointed out that Justice Howell's work continued even if he wasn't physically present. But you know women, Ben, logic seldom works. At least it doesn't on this woman."

"So I'm to be assigned to her?"

Grant puffed on his pipe. "Well, you are Howell's leading clerk. Of course, there are others. I'll tell you what's in the Chief's mind, then you can see our quandary."

Alexander knew it was the Chief Justice talking. Grant was only a conduit. The Chief Justice of the United States would never sink so low as to bargain with a mere law clerk. He used other means, quite as effective, if not as direct. And the Chief Justice knew very well when to use the stick and when to use the carrot. Assignment to the woman justice was the stick. Ben Alexander sat back and waited for the carrot.

"As you well know, there are some very hot cases coming up this next term. The Chief has taken an informal poll. He can be very effective, in his own way. The Court will be evenly divided on most of the important issues. If your boss were here he would constitute the swing vote again."

"He has that reputation," Alexander said, carefully choosing his words.

"Yes. Well, if he isn't able to make it back, the lower court decisions will stand. That is, of course, unless someone changes his or her vote. But that isn't likely. The Chief is hoping your boss will be able to make it back, at least physically."

"Physically?"

"Strokes are funny things, Ben. The effects can't be predicted. Remember, Justice Douglas spent many of his last days here in a wheelchair. At that time there was some question about his mental abilities."

"So you want me to influence Justice Howell if he comes back impaired, is that it?"

"How harsh and illegal you make it sound, Ben. I'm surprised. You aren't being invited into any grand conspiracy, if that's what you mean. But the work of the Court must go on. If, God willing, Howell makes a complete recovery, he will have the energy and ability to do the work and make the necessary decisions. However, if he doesn't, he'll need help. That's all I'm saying."

Ben Alexander leaned forward. "That's not what you're saying. You're threatening to reassign me unless I play ball with you. You want me to influence Howell if he does come back and isn't fully capable of making his own decisions. You know, Grant, that really stinks."

Floyd Grant's expression revealed no reaction as he quietly drew upon his pipe. "I'm leaving at the end of this year, Ben. The Chief is on the lookout for a chief clerk. You know what that means. The position is quite a springboard. I wasn't kidding about Stanford and then Harvard for myself. That's almost guaranteed. And only because I have served as the head clerk to the Chief Justice of the United States."

"How nice for you."

"Yes, as a matter of fact, it is. The head clerk position will be open when I leave. The job could be yours, Ben, given the right circumstances."

Floyd Grant was not exaggerating. Alexander knew that people who served as head clerk to the nation's Chief Justice could write their own ticket in the legal world. Alexander said nothing, but waited for Grant to continue.

"Ben, I'm sure you're aware, as I am, that clerks have served as unofficial justices of the court in the past. This isn't the first time that a sitting justice has had such problems."

Alexander nodded. It wasn't well known, but several past

justices had drawn the salary while bright young men had made the ultimate decisions. The situation wasn't unique.

"You know how the Chief works. He's like a congressman hunting votes. He trades off with this one, pairs with another, and promises future decisions to get his way. You know how he works."

Alexander nodded. "Yes. What does he want from me?"

The pipe had gone out, but Grant continued to puff on it, his only display of nervousness. "You put things so bluntly, Ben. Really, it's not good form. Nothing is expected of you. But if the circumstances present themselves, you could be helpful. For instance, the Chief is very interested in the vote on the Electoral College case. Are you familiar with the issue?"

"It's simple enough."

"Exactly. The constitutional amendment received the necessary state votes for ratification, but by the time the last state voted, two others had withdrawn their approval. The question is whether a state can reverse itself, having once voted, or whether the only vote counted is the original. If they can reverse, then the amendment doesn't have enough votes to pass, and the proponents know they can't get anymore. Those who want the Electoral College abolished say the reversals don't count. And those in favor of the Electoral College say the reversals by the state legislatures killed the proposed amendment. The Supreme Court must decide which side is correct. Basically, it boils down to a problem of simple constitutional construction."

"But the decision could change fundamentally the way a president is elected."

"Precisely. A simple issue but with a tremendous effect."

Alexander waited. Grant chewed on the pipe for a moment, as if composing his thoughts. "The Court is divided, if the Chief's poll is accurate. Your man's vote will make the difference. The Chief is voting to keep the Electoral College. He's of the opinion that the withdrawl of the states defeated the proposed amendment. This case is of the greatest importance to him."

"And to the White House," Alexander added softly.

Floyd Grant looked away. "Yes. I understand it is."

"So you're asking that I influence Howell, should he return, to vote to sustain the Electoral College?"

Grant looked at him, his eyes narrowed slightly. "If you choose to put it that way, yes."

"Anything else?"

"Ben, I detect a note of disapproval in your tone. Remember, nothing illegal is being requested."

"What about ethics?"

"Nothing unethical either. You've seen the horse trading that goes on here. My God, man, the Supreme Court is no better than an Arab bazaar when it comes to buying and selling. No money changes hands, of course, but the currency here is the field of interest. For instance, there's a reverse discrimination case coming on."

"The one about the policemen."

"Yes. The Chief obtained one of the votes to keep the Electoral College by bargaining his vote for reverse discrimination, so to speak."

"You mean you would like me to persuade Justice Howell to vote for the affirmative action quota system?"

"Yes. It would help firm up the vote on the Electoral College case. After all, Ben, what great harm does it do? A few white cops lose their jobs. A few blacks are hired to take their place. It's no big deal."

"But it sets up a racial quota system, a change that could eventually fragment our society."

Grant took the pipe from his mouth and grinned. "Come on, Ben. If things get out of hand, the Court will just change them back. Meanwhile, it'll keep the blacks from burning and looting for another summer, although that does seem to be becoming an organized sport."

"And the quota decision will protect the Electoral College."

Grant nodded.

"What else?"

"That newspaper case, the one about the state law providing damages for written negligence. It's a First Amendment issue."

"So?"

"That's really a personal thing with the Chief. You know how he likes to stick it to the media whenever he can."

"Is that decision essential?"

Grant shrugged and tapped out his pipe. "Essential? No, I think not. It would be nice though. It would give those newspaper bastards something to think about. If it can be done, fine. But if not, the Chief won't be greatly disappointed."

"How about the rational suicide case?"

Grant smiled. "The Chief will vote to uphold the nun's conviction. But who cares? He doesn't. People are knocking themselves off right and left, and in rather messy ways. So it might serve a purpose if it were organized. It would be much neater. He feels this one could go either way. As I say, he really doesn't care."

"So I only have to be concerned about the Electoral College and the racial case?"

"Yes."

Ben Alexander thought about how Justice Howell might approach the problems. What was being requested really wasn't that far from Howell's basic thinking. If he didn't agree, Alexander knew he would find himself slaving for a petulant, harassing woman. And if he did go along . . . well, he had been taken to the top of the mountain and shown the wonders of the future.

"If Justice Howell returns, and should he seek my advice, I will be glad to urge the two positions," Alexander said, his voice almost a whisper.

Grant beamed. "It's a complicated world, Ben. Maybe that isn't the way it should be, but we have to take things as we find them, right? I'll convey your position to the Chief. He'll be delighted." Grant stood up and put the pipe in his jacket pocket. "I'll have to take one of your clerks for her ladyship. There's no other way. But if your boss comes back and things turn out predictably, you'll have my job next year."

Alexander merely nodded. "Is this how these things are always done?"

Grant laughed. "Heavens no. Ordinarily, we do an elaborate dance before any agreement is reached. You're new, Ben, but you just demonstrated your ability to learn. You'll do just fine here."

"We'll see what happens."

"Ben, if you run into any problems, just let me know."

"I will."

Grant left and Ben Alexander once again leaned back in his chair. Everything in the court seemed to be a trade-off. This case for that, that legal principle in exchange for this legal precedent. But at least there would be gain in this transaction.

If he became chief clerk to the Chief Justice he wouldn't need to marry any damn conglomerate heiress.

Chapter 3

Judge Joseph Michael O'Malley fidgeted impatiently in his chair as the attorney droned on in his annoying singsong voice. The man should have had the brains to know he had won and should have concluded quickly and gracefully with a few brief remarks. O'Malley and the other two appellate judges asked him no questions. Still, the lawyer plowed on, reciting in his irritating manner the dry, uninspired speech he had apparently memorized.

The oral arguments were only a formality in this case, the law was clear. Even the opposing counsel knew that his cause was lost as he patiently endured the barbed and hostile questions by the judges, questions that consumed most of his allotted time for argument.

O'Malley was anxious to break free from the dull routine of the court. He had much more important things to do. The three-judge panel had spent the morning listening to oral arguments in four cases. The cases were boring. There were no great legal questions presented. And, as if to match the content of their drab legal matters, all the attorneys that morning were bumbling clods.

Win or lose, a snappy presentation was always welcomed by the court. But for some reason, exciting speakers were rare in the appellate court. Dullness seemed to have become a way of life.

O'Malley glanced at his watch. It was almost over.

He rushed through the judges' conference after the hearings. There were no serious disagreements among the three judges on the cases. O'Malley acknowledged the case assigned to him to write, then hurried to his chambers.

It was almost lunch time. It would be difficult contacting people during the lunch hour, but the attempt had to be made. O'Malley knew he had to be careful in his approach; Howell hadn't died, but it was a distinct possibility, and Joseph Michael O'Malley was a realist. The spade work had to be done now and as quickly as possible.

He unlocked his desk and extracted the yellow pad with all the names and telephone numbers. The pad was marked up, with notes showing the results of the call, or how many times a number had been tried. He went through the federal telephone network and dailed the next phone number. It was a Washington call.

"Good morning, Congressman Robinson's office." The girl's voice was cheery, but businesslike.

"This is Judge Joseph O'Malley of the U.S. Second Circuit Court of Appeals. I'd like to speak to the congressman, please."

"I'll see if he's in, Judge O'Malley."

He was put on hold.

He glanced at his watch. He didn't like to wait. But when you wanted a favor, you had to put up with things ordinarily not tolerated.

The line crackled into life. "He's on another line, Judge. He should be through in a minute. Would you care to hold, or shall I have him call you back?"

"I'll hold, thank you."

The line again went dead.

It was wise to make the contact now. There was no telling when Robinson would call back. As a ranking member of the important Ways and Means Committee of the House of Representatives he was powerful and busy, it might be days before O'Malley could expect a call back. It was wiser to wait, even though it would cost him precious time; time he could use making other calls.

"Just a moment for the congressman," the girl's voice popped into his consciousness.

The phone clicked. "Good morning, Your Honor. This is a pleasure." Sid Robinson had the well-practiced enthusiasm of all politicians. He sounded as if he had spent all morning just hoping that Joseph O'Malley would call.

"How are things in the capital, Sid? I haven't been in to see my friends there in quite some time."

"Same old stuff, Joe. We go from one crisis to another. It'll never change." He paused. "What can I do for you?"

O'Malley smiled to himself. He had used this approach so often, it was becoming automatic. "Shame about Brian Howell, isn't it?"

A pause. "Yes. Terrible thing to have happen, especially to a man as young as Howell."

"Sid, I'll be frank. I hate political vultures as much as the next man, but sometimes political realities override normal sensibilities."

"That's true."

"Did you know that the President was thinking of nominating me, if the Senate hadn't confirmed Howell for that seat on the court?"

"I had heard that, yes."

"Sid, I know this may sound a bit ghoulish, but I'm trying to line up as many friends as I can who can urge my nomination to the President, just in case the worst happens with Howell. Normally, I'd sit back and be civilized about the situation, but there are some key cases coming before the Supreme Court, and if anything happens to Howell, the President will have to move very fast to get a name before the committee in order to have that man or woman cleared and on the bench when those cases come up."

"Like the Electoral College amendment."

"Yes, that's one."

There was another pause before the congressman spoke. "Look, Joe, if the worst happens, as you say, I'd be glad to recommend you. We've been friends a long time. You have an excellent record and you're a party man. I'd have no trouble saying a good word."

"I appreciate that, Sid. And your word will carry great weight, I know that. I wonder if I might impose for an additional favor?"

"What's that?"

"Your state's national committeeman, the new man, I don't know him."

"Harvey Taylor?"

"Yes. I knew Eddie Milton, his predecessor, but I never met Taylor. I wonder if you could give him a call and say a good word for me. I think the President might look to the party leaders for a consensus on the appointment, if there is one. I would feel a bit better if someone like you could vouch for me with Taylor. At least that way he would know something about me. You understand?"

The congressman had the annoying habit of never replying at once. He always took a few seconds to consider what he was going to say. He carefully selected his words. "I'd have no trouble with that, Joe. Harvey Taylor is young, but he impresses me as being bright. And you're quite right, if something happened to Howell, the President would indeed have to move fast. Sure, I'll give him a call. Unless he's committed to someone else, I feel sure he would be glad to abide by my counsel. But if there's any problem, I'll call you back."

"It's a great favor, Sid. I won't forget it."

Again the pause. "Just good government in action, Joe. Also,

I do like to see my friends move up in the world. A man is judged by his friends, right?"

"Yes."

"I'll call you back if I run into any trouble. Good luck, Joe."

Judge O'Malley depressed the telephone button, then dialed again. There were many telephone calls to make. The days ahead meant long hours of effort, but he knew he had to keep working. Diligence was the key to success.

*   *   *

"Special Counsel to the President." Haywood Cross seemed to roll the words around majestically as he spoke them. "Imposing title. Very impressive."

Haywood Cross sat behind his immaculate desk. His office always looked as if it had just been staged as an advertisement for quality office furniture. Cross, the firm's managing partner, had a fetish about neatness.

Jerry Green sat opposite the regal desk in a large leather chair. "The President wants me to do a job for him," he said to Cross. "The White House people tell me it'll only take a couple weeks, but they want me to carry the title for a few months. For looks."

"For looks?"

Green smiled. "Public relations. If I'm on and off the payroll in just a few weeks, the press corps might smell something odd, and perhaps connect the short term with my job assignment. But a couple of months won't excite any undue interest."

"It would be very difficult to spare you for several months, Jerry. Although I do rather like the idea of one of our partners being counsel to the President. That sort of thing always impresses the clients."

"Actually, I'd only be gone for the few weeks. After that I can come back and work here. Obviously, I won't be able to appear in court or before an agency during those months, but I can do my normal desk work. If any question comes up, I can always say I was just cleaning up a few things. I plan to donate my federal salary to charity. That should prevent any crackpot raising a conflict of interest issue."

Haywood Cross beamed. "Well, two weeks, that's much better. You're one of our key men around here, Jerry, but two weeks away won't hurt the firm. And, all things considered, I think this arrangement will work out very well all the way around."

"I'll take an official leave of absence from the firm for those months, even though I plan to be here most of the time."

The managing partner nodded. "There should be no problem. Of course, you know as well as I do, Jerry, that petty jealousies exist within this firm. That's true of all large law offices, of course. Still, I don't think anyone can raise any serious objections. It's very much in the firm's interest. If there's any trouble, I'll handle it. As I say, it will be a bit of prestige for us. Also, I daresay, it will open a few doors with the present administration. Of course," he smiled, "that's your field, so I know I'm not suggesting anything you haven't thought of before."

Green was pleased. It was going just as well as he had anticipated. Even if the FTC case went against him, his new position would insulate him against any possible dismissal from the gilded offices of Harley Dingell.

"It certainly won't hurt the firm," Green said, with just the right inflection. He knew Haywood Cross would use his own imagination to make the appointment a hundred times more powerful and influential than it was. Amos Deering had been right about the effect of the title.

"What are your duties to be at the White House?" Cross asked. "That is, if you can say."

He could say, but that would diminish the mystique he had created. "I understand the President has several things in mind. As you know, Haywood, we worked together during the Nixon administration."

"Oh yes, of course." Cross was duly impressed.

"Anyway, I've been assured that my assignment won't take long."

"It's nothing, er, questionable, I trust?" The mention of the Nixon connection had awakened a few memories in Cross's mind.

Green smiled. "Quite respectable in every way."

"Of course." The managing partner smiled. "Of course. You see, I've never had much contact with things political, Jerry, so I suppose all the mysteries of the process go right over my head."

"I'll keep you advised."

"When do you start?"

"I wanted to have this talk with you first, Haywood. I told the President I needed your approval." It was a lie, but he saw the flush of pleasure in Cross's smooth face. "So if it's agreeable with the firm, I'll notify the White House today, and they'll make the announcement tomorrow."

"That quick?"

"If government really wants something, you'd be surprised how fast things can move."

Cross shook his head as he stood up. "As I said, I don't pretend to understand these matters at all. However, Jerry, the very best of luck." He extended his hand. "And we shall be glad when you can return."

Haywood Cross's skin was as dry as old leaves, but his grasp was firm.

"I'll dictate something about the request for leave and have my girl bring it to you, Haywood. I won't be seeing you for a few weeks, but I'll check in by telephone now and then."

"Please do. It all sounds very exciting."

Green walked down the thickly carpeted hall to his own office. It was as large as Haywood Cross's office, all the partners' offices were of equal size, but Green's office was certainly not as neat as the managing partner's. Green felt secure in his office, comfortable and safe. It was very much a refuge. He wished he was an "office" lawyer, as were most of the other senior partners, then he would never have to leave the womblike protection that the place seemed to provide.

He sat back in his high-backed swivel chair and closed his eyes. The thing had worked out exactly as he had hoped. It was a triumph. He would be able to exist in this comfortable cocoon for many years, and just on the strength of a few weeks' work for the President. The title, Special Counsel, would provide the necessary job insurance. But he still wondered about the price he would have to pay.

The universal desire to return home was celebrated in song and story, but he didn't want to go. Lansing. He hadn't been back since the funeral. He wondered at his own acute sense of foreboding.

Green reached across the desk and idly fingered the gold frame holding his wife's picture. It was a typical studio shot, the face lighted and retouched until it was almost unrecognizable. Still, even with the softening magic of the photographer's art, the face reflected the cool hardness of the woman portrayed. She certainly had none of the softness of Regina Kelso.

He drew his hand away from the picture, surprised that he should even remember Regina Kelso. Regina was a part of his youth, part of Lansing, but she was a pleasant part of memory. He tried to recall the name of the writer who said that old loves were always the best. Memory was ever changing, and like an artist, it kept altering the hues and tones until only the desired impression was left. Truth and reality were often discarded by memory as it completed its idealized image.

He pulled out a yellow pad and forced his mind away from recollection and onto the task of composing his leave of absence statement. It would have to be worded just right. He could ill afford to employ language that might allow some envious partner a wedge to eject him permanently from the firm. At the same time, the words had to be definite enough to demonstrate vividly that he was divorced from the firm's business for a while. The White House had to be protected. It was attention to detail that counted. Many an investigation came to nothing because a lawyer had had the foresight to set down just the right words.

But he found it difficult to concentrate. The damn Lansing assignment was like a trip to the dentist, he couldn't stop thinking about it. All kinds of memories came flooding back. He didn't want to, but he thought of his parents and the big house on Okemos Street. He thought of his brother. For a moment he could visualize his brother's eyes when they last met. Then he felt anger.

The thoughts of Regina Kelso, the big house, and the other images fled from his mind. It was the thought of his brother that had done it. He breathed deeply, then expelled the air through clenched teeth. He was now able to concentrate and his pen danced across the lined yellow paper as he wrote.

*   *   *

"Mrs. Howell, this is Dr. Gibson."

"How nice to meet you, doctor. Dr. Kaufman has told me quite a bit about you. All very impressive."

Gibson was a very tall, graying, storklike man. He blinked over his glasses at the small plump woman before him. "Thank you," he said simply.

Dr. Kaufman beamed. "Doctor Gibson is considered the top neurosurgeon in the United States. We have called him in as a consultant. He'll go over our findings and conduct his own examination. Your husband is an important man, Mrs. Howell. He's getting the very best medical care the country can offer."

"I deeply appreciate it."

"Any history of stroke in his family?" Gibson asked abruptly.

She shook her head. "Not that I know of. There have been family members with heart problems, but no strokes, as far as I know."

The tall doctor nodded. "That in itself is a good sign. The more we learn about these matters, the more everything points to the importance of genetic factors."

"Why do you say it's good?" she asked.

Gibson attempted a smile, but failed. His face was not accustomed to the expression. "If it isn't hereditary, perhaps your husband's problem is a comparatively minor mishap involving one of the blood vessels in the brain. We have had some success with surgical repair in many such cases."

"And if it is hereditary?"

Gibson shrugged. "Usually, the stroke signals a breakdown of the whole system. Much like old original auto parts wearing out. When one goes, the others usually do. If we repair, something else will just let go. The people with a family history of stroke usually aren't good candidates for remedial surgery."

"This surgery," she paused, as if carefully selecting her words, "I presume it is, well, dangerous?"

The tall doctor's eyes seemed cold, almost lifeless. "We won't cross any bridges, Mrs. Howell, until we get to them. I will study the CAT scan and the other clinical tests, and then I'll consult with the excellent team of physicians here. If it appears that surgery might be a solution, then we'll discuss it with you fully. The decision, of course, will be yours."

She bit her lip, and her eyes were suddenly filled with tears.

Dr. Kaufman casually put one arm about her and gave her an affectionate hug.

Gibson never changed expression. "I'm a surgeon, not a gambler, Mrs. Howell." The words were spoken sharply.

"Don't worry," Dr. Kaufman said softly.

She nodded. "My children," she began, then stopped for a moment. "My children are grown, and I would want them to, well, help with any decision like that."

Dr. Kaufman gently patted her cheek. "This is a terrible time for you. Let us carry your cross for a while, all right? You quit worrying and let us do it. Just take a break. Go home, have a drink, grab a hot tub, and relax. I promise you that Dr. Gibson and I will worry for you." He laughed. "Is it a deal?"

She looked up at him, blinked and then smiled. "Yes, that does sound good. I think that would make me feel better."

"Fine," Kaufman said. "You go home now and let us take care of things."

"Thank you, doctor."

She left the small waiting lounge.

Kaufman spoke only after they watched her board the elevator. "I know your reputation as a brain surgeon, Gibson, but let me tell you, you have an absolutely lousy bedside manner."

Gibson looked at him coolly. "In my line of work, Kaufman, I end up killing more people than Hitler. I have to maintain a certain detachment just to retain my sanity."

"Maybe so," Kaufman said, frowning. "But if you don't keep the family happy you end up to your ass in malpractice suits. It's not only a kindness, it's a form of self-protection."

"Perhaps. I prefer competency over familiarity, however. And no one has collected off me yet." Gibson's expressionless eyes looked like two stones as they peered over the glasses at Kaufman. "Now let's take a look at sleeping beauty, shall we? I've always entertained a theory that judges really have no brains. Now I shall get an opportunity to actually look."

*   *   *

She knew she wouldn't come, but she was enjoying herself. She used her well-developed stomach muscles to exert pressure. She increased the motion of her body as she straddled him. His hands clutched at her breasts. His eyes were wide, his teeth clenched. She liked the reddening flush of his skin as his facial muscles contorted and turned his handsome face into a grimace. He raised his head, shuddered, then lay back. She experienced a sense of power over him, as if she just had beaten him in a fight. It was pleasant.

He lay exhausted beneath her but she kept methodically gyrating.

"Hey, I'm through," he whispered.

"Good?" she asked.

"Great," he sighed.

She gently slid off and lay beside him. Reaching across his hairy chest, she picked up her watch from the nightstand. It was almost four.

"Does that help relax the tensions of the working day?" she whispered.

He could only nod. It was very much like a victory. She could understand the elation of prizefighters after they had demolished their opponents. She had a sudden urge to shout, to give vent to her triumph, to somehow exult in her physical powers.

"I have to go, love," she said. "I'll grab a quick shower. I want to check in at my office before I go home." She rolled off the bed. She could see her reflection in the bedroom mirror. She was trim, slim-waisted, and athletic. She liked what she saw.

"You're one hell of a woman, Carol."

She smiled at him. He lay like a broken doll, his thick legs akimbo, his muscles lax.

"It depends on the partner, my dear." She knew men always liked to hear that. They always seemed to treasure that image; she was the violin and they were the inspired master player. The opposite was true, but it always pleased them to think otherwise.

She showered and dressed quickly. He still lay on the bed, the sheet pulled up to his waist.

"Carol, I'm crazy about you. When can I see you again?"

She smiled. "I thought we agreed there would be no emotional entanglements."

He sat up. "Jesus, don't tell me Carol Green's nothing but a hit-and-run girl."

"Oh?"

"Like a sailor on leave; just bed them and scram. You don't seem the type."

She laughed. "I've been compared to a number of things, but never to a horny sailor. I think that just may be a compliment."

"I want to see you again." He climbed out of the bed. She admired his nakedness. Most men had beautiful bodies. He was well muscled and had a nice sprinkling of body hair. And she found his dimpled grin infectious.

She smiled in return. "Don't start up with me now, Michael. I just have every hair in its proper place. If you like, you can give me a call. But at the office."

"Of course. Husbands make me nervous."

She picked up her purse and briefcase. "My husband should be the least of your worries."

"He doesn't care?"

"He is too preoccupied to even notice."

"Doesn't take care of the home fires, eh?"

She resented his interest in her private life. She didn't ask questions about his relationship with his wife. "I have my own life," she said coolly. "I have my own business. I do what I choose to do. It's no reflection on him."

He lit a cigarette. "Hey, I wasn't prying. But you have to admit, it's only normal to be curious."

She regarded him for a moment before speaking. "I suppose it is. I sometimes wonder about your wife. Does she know about any of this?"

He almost choked on the smoke. "Whoa, I told you my situation."

She laughed. "Oh yes. The frigid wife, the insensitive woman. Really, I had hoped you would show more imagination than that. Still, it's the accepted explanation in these matters."

"What I told you is the truth."

She looked at him. He seemed entirely unconscious of his

nakedness. "My dear, if that's the truth, I'm the Queen of Sheba. Let's at least be frank with each other. We are a couple of cheaters. Your wife is probably a very nice person. I know my husband is. But you find her dull, as I do my husband. You're looking for sexual adventure, not danger, merely stimulation. It's the same story with me. But at least I'm honest enough to admit it."

He grinned sheepishly. "I suppose you're right, Carol. But we all tend to say things we believe the other person wants to hear."

She checked herself in the mirror. Everything was in proper order. "If you want to get in touch with me, call the office. You can even call home after tomorrow night."

"Oh?"

"My husband is leaving for two weeks. He has some law work in Michigan."

A slow smile spread across his dark features.

"If you're thinking of saving on motel rates, think again. We can have two wonderful weeks, but discretion is something I insist on."

"I'll call you."

"You had better," she said as she left.

*　　*　　*

The phone buzzed. He put aside his papers and picked up the receiver.

"Yes?"

"Dean Pentecost, you have a call from Dr. Mease of the School of Human Medicine. Shall I connect you?"

He was always amused at the name of the school. Michigan State University had a veterinary school and two other medical institutions; one for osteopathic medicine, the other for regular medicine. They always referred to the M.D. school as the School for Human Medicine. He wondered if logic didn't demand that the vet school should have then been named the school for inhuman medicine. However, no one in the medical school seemed to see the humor. Dick Mease was an assistant dean.

"Put him on."

There was a click. "Roy?"

"Yes, Dick. How have you been?"

"Fine, Roy, just fine." He coughed to clear his throat, as if embarrassed. "Say, Roy, I have something of a problem, and I think I just might need a bit of legal advice."

"Go ahead."

"Well, it's really not the sort of thing I think I should discuss over the telephone."

Pentecost glanced at his watch. "I have a seminar in an hour. If you can hurry over, we can talk for a few minutes."

"I'll be right there."

Roy Pentecost replaced the telephone receiver. The medical school was more than a half mile away. On campus most faculty people walked or rode bikes. It was easier than trying to find a parking space. It would be a while before Mease arrived. He returned to the papers before him.

He was gifted with an unusual power of concentration. He forgot everything except what he was reading until the telephone rang again.

"Dr. Mease is here."

"Send him in."

Dick Mease was young. He had gone through medical school, internship, and a long residency without discovering complete satisfaction. He found the academic world much more pleasant and stimulating. Now he served as an instructor and as an administrator. He even looked more like a bland schoolteacher than someone who could menace an entire hospital staff.

"Hi, Roy," he said, carefully closing the door behind him.

Pentecost stood up and shook his hand. "What's the problem? I hate to rush you, Dick, but I do have that seminar in a few minutes."

Mease sat down on a straight-backed chair. "Do you know Dr. George Simons?"

"No, I can't say that I do."

"He's a Lansing ear-nose-and-throat man. And he's one of the adjunct professors, both for us and for the osteopathic school."

"So?"

"He's a young man; thirty-five, give or take. Good credentials."

"That's nice. What's the problem?"

"He's been laying one of the students."

Pentecost sat back. "Female, I presume. You know the old joke about the English lieutenant and the elephant—nothing queer about old Archie?"

"I'm afraid I don't."

"I'll tell it to you sometime. I assume this wouldn't be a problem unless someone complained. The young lady?"

Mease shook his head. "No, the young lady's boyfriend; another medical student. He's mad as hell."

Pentecost sat forward. "Did you talk to the girl?"

"Yes."

"And what does she have to say about all this?"

Mease lifted his hands in a gesture of hopelessness. "Christ, she admits it. This Simons is a good-looking guy. I think she's rather proud of herself."

"Is Simons married?"

"Yes, and he has a couple of kids."

"Is she in any of his classes?"

"She used to be."

Pentecost nodded. "Did he start banging her before or after she was a student of his?"

"After."

"Well, at least that's something. There's an unwritten rule that graduate students are fair game, but only after they are out of the professor's class."

"I didn't know that."

Pentecost smiled. "As I say, it's unwritten. Is she going to cause any trouble?"

"No."

"Just the boyfriend then?"

"Yes."

"And you come to me as the dean of the law school hoping for a magic answer, right?"

"I hoped you wouldn't mind."

Pentecost shook his head. "I don't. The only difficulty is that I really don't have an answer."

"Oh?"

"Dr. Simons has broken no specific university rules, right?"

"Well, there's the Code of Conduct."

"But it doesn't specifically say medical school professors shall not screw their students, right?"

"No."

"All right. Then there's nothing the jealous young man can do against the good doctor, at least through official university channels?"

"Well, I suppose not."

"So the only thing he can do is go to Dr. Simons' wife and make things hot at home, correct?"

"That may happen. He's threatened it."

"Threatened?"

"He came into my office. He was almost hysterical. He made a lot of wild statements."

Pentecost nodded slowly. "That's good."

"Good?"

"You came to this ancient oracle for an answer. Here it is. Have the campus police talk to the young man. Tell the police what he said. They are very professional about these things. Have them make a bit of noise about extortion. But mainly they can drop a hint that if this goes any farther, the young man may see some very low marks. In other words, if he raises a stink, he may be flunked out. Don't have them say that exactly, but I'm sure he'll catch on. As I say, the campus police are very experienced."

"I don't know. . . ."

"And discontinue Dr. Simons' services after this semester. Let the boyfriend know that. It'll help take some of the sting out."

"But suppose Simons raises a howl?"

"Under these circumstances?"

Mease shook his head in admiration and smiled. "You know, I certainly came to the right man. No wonder there's talk of putting you on the Supreme Court. Damn it, Roy, that's a brilliant solution."

"Well, it's a solution, brilliant or not."

"I read about this fellow Howell. From the sounds of it, it's my medical opinion that he won't make it. I hope you get the appointment, Roy. You would do a splendid job."

Pentecost stood up. "I hate to usher out someone who talks so nicely, but I do have to go, Dick. I hope you're wrong about Justice Howell. He's a good man."

"Still, if he. . . ."

"Goodbye, Dick." Pentecost guided him to the door. "If my brilliant solution doesn't work, let me know."

He closed the door and returned to his notes.

It was all a matter of tactics now. He chose not to go after the job, at least not while Howell was alive. But he knew others would be pressing his case. It would look good, this reluctance of his. It would look judicial.

And he damned well did want that job.

Chapter 4

The airplane circled as it approached the landing in Detroit. It was a bright and cloudless day, although the pilot had announced that snow showers were expected later in the Detroit area. Jerry Green looked out the window. The pilot had come in over the western tip of Lake Erie. They passed the shoreline and glided above the almost geometric pattern of the suburbs and farmlands below.

He tried to identify some familiar landmarks. He always did that when he was up in a plane, although he could never really tell one river from another, and all interstates looked alike.

If it wasn't for the stadium he wouldn't have recognized the town. They were passing just south of Ann Arbor. The University of Michigan stadium, a huge bowl with a seating capacity of over one hundred thousand, looked like a child's teacup below them.

The aircraft began its descent and soon they were flying above the roofs of row upon row of suburban tract houses. They all looked alike from the air. Cars moved on the busy streets, completely heedless of the big jet above them. It was as if they were invisible.

He felt the clutch of his usual apprehension as they came down. He knew it was foolish, but it was as if he suspected that the pilot had made a mistake. All he could see was fields and distant houses as they came near to ground level. Only the pilot could see the airfield. Then, just as it seemed to Green that they might crash, the runway came into view and its ritualistic markers streaked past as the big jet touched down. Jerry Green felt his usual sense of relief as the pilot used his engines and wing flaps to slow the airplane.

People began to stir as the jet slowed to taxiing speed. He continued to look out the window. Detroit Metropolitan Airport had nothing to distinguish it from any other major airport. With few exceptions, they all seemed to look alike.

He moved out of the aircraft in the press of his fellow passengers. For once there was no hassle with the luggage. He had made prior arrangements for a rental car, and that too was ready. When things seemed to be going too well, he had to resist a foreboding of impending disaster. A typical Jewish attitude, he reflected as he eased the car out of the airport and into the fast-moving interstate traffic. He always felt it would be a dead heat between the Irish and the Jewish for first place in any superstition sweepstakes. He smiled at the thought. He hadn't been on Michigan's soil for a full half hour and already he was beginning to think ethnically.

He passed a semitrailer then settled back. It was an hour and a half drive to Lansing, and he had no reason to hurry. He turned the car radio dial until he found a classical music station. The lilting strains of Mahler filled the speeding car.

Green looked about at the autumn landscape. Michigan never really changed. The populations shifted a bit, the old core cities decayed, and some of the manufacturing plants moved, but it essentially remained the same. Shaped like a mitten, the bottom half, the southern part of the state, offered miles of flat farmlands broken by clusters of factory-fostered cities. The northern part of the state, including the Upper Peninsula, was sandy, covered by pine and birch, and unsuitable for profitable farming. The north was another country, another lifestyle. Wild and rugged, it moved at nature's own slow pace, while the southern part of the state obeyed the round-the-clock demanding timetable of industrial commerce.

Michigan was home, but Jerry Green found no solace in being back in his home state or in the knowledge that he was moving swiftly toward his native city.

It had been an early autumn and now only a few leaves were left on the trees along the route of the interstate. Despite the sunshine there was a desolate starkness about the stripped trees. The brilliant colors of fall had gone and now only dark browns and grays remained.

They wanted to know about Dean Roy Pentecost and whether he possessed the integrity to honor a commitment.

It was difficult, almost impossible, to find the ultimate truth about anyone. You could know someone for twenty years and still not perceive his true character. Life was an everlasting and changing charade, a dance of many masks.

He swung the car up the ramp into the adjoining interstate and took the quickest route toward Lansing. He hadn't been back since the funeral, and he had planned never to return. Those memories were disturbing, so he forced himself to think again of the task ahead and how to approach it.

People were always reluctant to talk to strangers about neighbors and acquaintances, even if they disliked them. It was a human trait, this suspicion of the curious intruder. So if you came head-on at people, you learned nothing. But with a little tact and patience, the stranger tag could be overcome. And then they opened up with everything, the stories, good and bad, and the gossip. And it was always much easier in a large university town.

Over forty thousand young people thronged into Michigan State University during the school year. And there was a constant turnover as old classes were graduated, and new ones began. Over ten thousand new faces presented themselves every September. In such an environment a stranger was not likely to draw attention, since, in a very real way, most of the population were strangers. Much could be learned in such fertile ground.

And he still might know a few people. He had gone to grade school and high school there. The nucleus of workers who served the giant university would still be there. The sons and daughters of the men and women who used to make the college complex run probably remained, at least some of them, to continue their inherited roles.

He wondered what have become of his old high school chums, although "chum" was really not the precise word to describe the past relationships. Still, it might be interesting. Where are they now? Like one of those newspaper features about faded celebrities, it would be fascinating to know.

Most of the members of his high school class would be forty-six years old, like himself. The realization that Regina Kelso, four years younger, would now be forty-two shocked him a bit. He always pictured her as she had been; young, soft, and with a prettiness that bordered on true beauty. He had held that memory for years, never considering that she would age. It would be crushing if Regina had changed too much.

Green suddenly faced the reality that most probably he would see many of them again. He would be like a ghost returning, a spirit sent to observe their fates. And these would not be the polished people of Washington or New York. They would be men and women quite different from those he customarily encountered in corporation boardrooms or in the marbled halls of federal government.

He was not particularly fond of any of them, with the exception of Regina. That they would have little in common seemed the thought of an intellectual snob. But, he reflected somberly, it was probably true enough.

None of them, he recalled, had ever sat beneath the evening stars and discussed the mysteries of life, at least not with him. There was no reason to think their ability to communicate with him would have been improved by the passage of time. The gulf between them could only have been widened by time and the difference in lifestyles.

To them he would always be Hank Green's younger brother. A pale shadow indeed. Hank Green was strong, breezy, and a local sports star. Jerry Green had been strong enough but lacked the coordination that insured excellence in athletic competition, and he had been painfully shy. The contrast between the two brothers had done nothing to enhance Jerry Green's popularity as a youth.

He sped past the Stadium Exit sign and was unsure whether he should take it. He passed the exit and then saw a big green highway sign proclaiming: Lansing, next 2 exits. He moved into the right-hand lane and prepared to leave the interstate.

The state highway skirted along the western border of the university's lands. He was surprised that most of the experimental farms were gone. Michigan State had been a true agricultural school when his father had been on the faculty. It had offered a program of liberal arts, but the farming courses had been the core of its real function.

Now large multistoried buildings had been built where fields of crops had grown. He experienced no sense of being on a college campus when he looked at those buildings; no ivy covered their walls, no ancient trees shaded their walks. They looked like huge concrete and steel blocks set down in the middle of a flat farm field. And they were essentially just that.

The highway branched off in several directions and the signs were confusing. He made the wrong choice and headed west, away from the university.

He found himself in the city of Lansing. He ended up at

Michigan Avenue. To his immediate right was the bridge over Grand River, the wide, shallow stream that wound through the town. To his left, at a distance, was the state capitol, with its familiar statue of Austin Blair, the Civil War governor, guarding its smooth lawns.

Green turned right and headed back toward East Lansing and the university. Everything was different, and yet nothing had really changed. There was development going on. The old railway station now was a restaurant. Sparrow Hospital still stood but it had been so enlarged and modernized that it was almost unrecognizable. The Church of the Resurrection and its school remained as always. Commerce flourished. The names and the businesses were different now, but they were bright, prosperous, and well maintained. He was at the campus almost before he realized it.

The big sign marked it—Michigan State University, Pioneer Land Grant College.

He tried to look at the familiar buildings, this was the old campus, the places he remembered, but clusters of students lined the roadside, dashing across when they had the chance. He was forced to keep his attention on the driving. The wide boulevard of Michigan Avenue became Grand River. As he approached the student union the students seemed almost suicidal in their urge to cross.

He passed the last grassy island and the boulevard merged into one wide street. He was surprised to find himself caught in a traffic jam.

In the old days, even the idea of traffic congestion at this point of the road would have been considered impossible. He saw the sign ahead and had to squeeze into the left turn lane and inch along with the other cars. Horns blared behind him as he waited for oncoming traffic to clear before swinging left into the driveway of the motel.

It was new, two stories high and rambling along the top of a ridge. Its architecture imitated a Swiss chalet. He registered, drove to his parking space, and unloaded his bags into the room.

The room was attractive and neat, somewhat larger than most hotel rooms. He checked the place over. The television worked. He hung up his suits and unpacked.

He felt tired and sat down on the bed. Somehow things didn't seem complete. He felt he really should call someone and report that he had arrived safely. His wife would be busy at her office in Washington and would only wonder at such an unnecessary call. There was no one else. The White House people would be interested only in results. The fact that he had arrived held no interest for anyone but himself. He had never before realized just how unattached he really was. Jerry Green felt lonely.

The motel had a restaurant. He idly flipped through the room service menu. The desk drawer contained the usual postcards, stationery, and Bible.

He picked up the telephone book and opened it. It was there. He knew it would be.

Green, Henry J. . . . 201 Sunset Lake Lane, followed by the telephone number.

He would have to call his brother sometime. Even if rebuffed, he still felt obligated to make some civilized symbolic gesture. It wouldn't do if he just ran into his brother on the campus, although it was so large and there were so many people that it did seem unlikely. Still, the call was something he felt had to be done.

He took a notepad from his briefcase and jotted down the number and address. He would make the call, but not now. He presumed it would be unpleasant for them both. It could wait. He did not wish to mark the beginning of his task with something distasteful.

Jerry Green loosened his tie and lay back on the bed. He lit a cigarette and watched the smoke waft up toward the stucco ceiling. As always, he wondered what dramas had been played out in this particular motel room. Squalid love affairs, surely. That was an accepted fact. But what of the other human occurrences, the breakup of families, the failed student spending his last night before going home and facing disgrace. He always wondered the same thing in every motel or hotel room he occupied. Despite the discipline of his legal training, he liked to allow his imagination full rein now and then, to abandon the realities of the world and let his thoughts run free, the symptom, he realized, of a hopeless romantic.

The telephone book lay open on the bed. He rolled over and idly flicked through its pages.

There were a number of Kelsos listed. He presumed that Regina was married and wouldn't be listed. Richard Kelso, her father, was no longer listed. There was no Kelso listed as living at the big colonial on Faircrest Drive. Michael J. Kelso was listed. Green didn't recognize the street. It was in the nearby city of Okemos. But it had to be her brother.

He picked through the phone book. Some remembered names were there, although he knew they might not be the same people. Others had disappeared from the pages. He searched through the phone book as if it somehow held the key to the door into the past. Names, long forgotten, floated up through the mists of his memory. He continued the search through the pages, almost frantically.

Suddenly he tired of the phone book. He closed it and lay back. It had been a long trip. The hassle of packing, getting into the National Airport with its inconvenient, ancient facilities, the flight and the long drive from Detroit to Lansing had succeeded in bringing on a feeling of exhaustion. He reached over and ground out his cigarette in an ashtray.

The drapes were already drawn, and the light from outside was fading around the edges. Night was coming on. He closed his eyes. He pictured the face of Regina Kelso. He decided she was indeed beautiful. He remembered her eyes. Soft, sympathetic eyes. He drifted off to sleep.

She knew something was different. She had been escorted down the long hospital hallway to a small private lounge. Dr. Kaufman, the leader of the medical team in charge of her husband's case had walked along with her, guiding her from her husband's room with its bottles, tubes, and machines to this small, comfortable room which was tastefully decorated and, if a bit larger, could easily have served as a nice living room. Apparently it was a staff physicians' hideaway.

"You remember Dr. Gibson, of course," Kaufman said.

Gibson slowly rose from his seat. He did not smile. His only greeting was a quick nod. He peered down at her from over the rim of his glasses.

"Yes, I remember Dr. Gibson," she replied, adding, "the noted neurosurgeon."

She was alone with the two physicians. She saw Kaufman every day and felt comfortable in his presence. A short, stocky man with a perpetual smile, Dr. Kaufman seemed to exude enthusiasm and cheer. But Dr. Gibson was different. There seemed to be an aura of funeral and graveside about him. Martha Howell felt a chill of foreboding as she looked up at the tall somber doctor.

"Please sit down, Mrs. Howell," Dr. Kaufman said, his voice seemed to have lost much of its usual enthusiasm. "Can I get you anything? Coffee? Tea perhaps?"

She sat down and shook her head. Dr. Gibson continued to regard her in silence. There was no expression in his long face. Only his eyes seemed to have any vitality, and they merely seemed to be coldly curious.

Both physicians took seats opposite her. Dr. Gibson hooked one long leg over the other and leaned forward, his elbow resting easily on the top of his knee. Kaufman sat back, his fingertips unconsciously drumming a silent staccato upon the arm rests of his chair.

Kaufman's smile seemed to be flickering out. His eyes looked sad. "Mrs. Howell, I think I know you well enough to know you are a lady who possesses a real strength of character, real courage." He coughed nervously. "And I know you can accept what we must tell you."

"What are you trying to say?" She was suddenly alarmed. She felt confused. She had just left her husband's bedside. He had looked the same as always, as if he were just peacefully sleeping.

"There's been a change in your husband's condition, I'm afraid, Mrs. Howell," Kaufman said. "Dr. Gibson confirms the staff's assessment."

She looked from Kaufman to the tall stranger. He hadn't changed position, his eyes were still fixed on her.

"What kind of change?" She asked. "He looks the same. I saw nothing different."

"There's been a second stroke," Dr. Gibson said, his voice surprisingly deep. "Another blood vessel has burst in your husband's brain. I'll spare you the medical jargon, Mrs. Howell. Basically, this time there has been much greater damage than that resulting from the first cerebrovascular accident."

"But he looks the same."

The tall physician nodded. "Yes, he does. But that's because of the machines. They are maintaining him now."

"But that's always been true."

The tall doctor shook his head. "Not really. All those gadgets you see attached to him just augmented his normal abilities. For instance, he was breathing on his own, the respirator was just helping him along." He paused. "That's not true anymore."

"And now?"

"The machine does the breathing for him."

She looked over at Dr. Kaufman. His round face was solemn.

It seemed to her it was the first time she had ever seen him without a smile. He didn't look natural. Her face was now the same emotionless mask as that of Dr. Gibson's.

"The damage was extensive," Kaufman said very quietly. "What Dr. Gibson says is correct."

"But how do you know?" she protested. She looked again into the cold eyes of Dr. Gibson. He seemed so quietly sure of himself. She felt anger rise within her. "There's been no change. None at all!"

"The monitoring apparatus told us what was happening," Dr. Kaufman said. "We took all available measures to attempt to stem the extent of the injury, as you can imagine. Unfortunately, they didn't work."

"You didn't get me down here just to present an overview of my husband's case. This man," she nodded at Dr. Gibson, "certainly isn't here just for the ride. For God's sake, what are you trying to tell me?"

Gibson leaned back, looking almost relaxed, his hands folded in his lap. "There has been brain death, Mrs. Howell. There's no other way to put it. I'm sorry."

She was surprised at her own reaction. She felt no tears welling, no sorrow, just anger. "That's very nice for you to say, very pat, but I just left my husband, and I could detect no change whatsoever. I don't see how you can possibly say a thing like that!"

Gibson slowly shook his head, his features still expressionless. "I can understand your feelings," he said evenly. "I have no wish to provoke you, Mrs. Howell. These things are devastating to the family of the patient. We know that, of course."

Kaufman again coughed nervously. She looked over at him.

"As we all realize, Mrs. Howell," Kaufman said, "your husband is a very special patient. He is a sitting member of the United States Supreme Court. We are very careful with all our patients, of course, but especially so with your husband. You can be assured that we used every method of treatment known to help your husband. As I say, they weren't successful."

"But how can you be so damned sure!"

Gibson's eyes seemed almost to glitter. "The damage occurred during the late evening," he said. "I was asked to fly to Washington at once. I arrived this morning. I conferred with Dr. Kaufman and the other members of his medical team, then we ran extensive tests. As you know, this facility has the newest and best of all diagnostic equipment. Nothing was spared. Everything that medical science has to offer was used, Mrs. Howell." Gibson's voice dropped slightly as he continued. "Had he not been in a hospital and hooked up the way he is, he would have died a natural death. As it is, our machines took up the slack. They are doing his breathing. They make his heart beat. They provide for continued circulation of blood throughout his body. But there are no electrical impulses coming from the brain. I know it is difficult to face, but your husband is dead."

"He is like hell!" She jumped up, feeling rage at this cold impersonal man. "I just saw him! His color is good. His chest moves up and down. He's alive!"

"Please, Mrs. Howell." Dr. Kaufman stood up and put his arm around her. "Please sit down. I know this is a shock. It always is."

"This happens often?" she asked as Kaufman guided her back to her chair.

"Often enough, I'm afraid. Oh, it can occur because of a number of causes, not just stroke. Our science seems to have outdistanced our medical art. We lack the ability to save such patients. What Dr. Gibson says is true, legal death occurs when the brain dies."

"Who says that? Who the hell says that a machine can pronounce death?" Her anger was subsiding, and the effect of their dreadful news was beginning to weigh upon her.

"Your husband's court, as a matter of fact," Dr. Gibson answered quietly.

"Well, he's not dead. I don't care what your machines say."

Kaufman remained standing. He absently continued to pat her arm.

Gibson spoke. This time there was a hard edge to the tone of his voice. "He is dead, Mrs. Howell. He died last night. What you see as breathing is due only to the devices connected to the body. When the devices stop, everything stops."

"Those machines had better not stop." She had intended the words to be calm and forceful, but her voice rasped into a savage snarl.

Gibson showed no reaction. "In cases such as this, yours is the normal reaction," he said casually. "But usually, after the family discusses it, most people choose the course of shutting down the machines."

"That's murder!"

Gibson shook his head. "No. It is all quite legal, and properly so. Most organized religions recognize the right, as they say, to pull the plug. At least they do, in these circumstances."

Martha Howell knew that her mind was recording this scene, that it would be etched forever in her memory, but it seemed so unreal, like an episode in a horror movie. She wished it was the cold-eyed Dr. Gibson who was lying in a room down the hall, so quietly asleep.

"Unfortunately, Mrs. Howell, those are the facts," Gibson continued. "A decision has to be made. It doesn't have to be made immediately. Sometimes nature itself makes the decision, the kidneys fail, or the heart. Dr. Kaufman says you have grown children. If I were you, I would consult with them, and with your clergyman. They can help you in making your decision."

She hated those hard blue eyes. "I've made my decision. No one touches those machines!"

Dr. Gibson stood up, towering over her. For the first time a hint of emotion seemed to play briefly on his long features. "As I say, your reaction is quite normal. My deepest sympathy, Mrs. Howell." He did not extend his hand, but turned and walked from the room.

"He's a monster," she snapped.

Dr. Kaufman sat down. He looked tired and ill at ease. "No. He sees only the most difficult cases. He has, I think, built up some strong defense mechanisms, not only against feelings he might have for the patients he encounters, but also against the natural reaction of their loved ones."

She shook her head. She felt hot tears as they began to roll down one cheek.

Dr. Kaufman bit his upper lip nervously, then spoke. "Mrs. Howell, I think most people in your circumstances usually consider what decision the patient might have made, if he or she had the power to do so. You know your husband. If he could speak to you, what do you think he would advise?"

She stared at him.

"Com'on," he said, getting up and helping her from her chair. "You come along to my office. You can make calls there, or just lie down for a while."

She shook her head. "No." The tears were unstoppable now. "I just want to go back to Brian. I want to be with my husband."

*   *   *

Amos Deering sat at his cluttered desk, penciling notes on the margins of suggestions typed by his staff.

Ed Huntington, the President's chief of staff, poked his head in the doorway.

"Got a minute, Amos?"

Deering looked up. Usually he was summoned to Huntington's office.

"Sure."

"Let's take a walk. I'd like to get a bit of fresh air," Huntington said.

"It's raining."

"You have a raincoat, use it."

Deering slipped into his loose poplin coat and followed Huntington out into the White House grounds.

The rain had diminished to just a drizzle, but it was cold and Deering could feel his beard and hair getting wet.

Huntington didn't seem to notice.

"I'm glad I got a chance to talk to you," Deering said. "The President has scheduled a press conference for tomorrow to discuss that damn Middle East thing. That will be the second press conference this week. Look, Ed, I can understand his wanting exposure, but it's dangerous, one of these hurry-up press conferences is liable to backfire. He can't go in there half-briefed, not when he's dealing with these Washington news sharks. They allow him to get away with some fuzzy answers now, but as soon as the honeymoon is over, these people will scramble his ass."

"John Kennedy did all right at those things."

Deering grunted. "He didn't hold them at this rate. Besides, I'm told that Kennedy was briefed down to the last molecule. He might have looked casual but he was a programmed talking machine. Ed, without adequate preparation, a press conference can be a disaster."

Huntington nodded to a security officer as they walked past him. "I'll tell the man your concerns, but frankly I don't think he'll change."

"Another thing, Ed. If you hold too many of these things and the press corps gets used to it, then when a time comes when the President doesn't want to go public on something for a while, just the absence of press conference becomes a hell of a story."

"I said I'll tell him," Huntington snapped. "How's your man coming with the dean?"

"You mean Jerry Green?"

"Yes."

"That's right. I forgot you didn't know him," Deering said. "You weren't with us in the old days."

"Some people consider that a plus." For the first time Huntington smiled.

"Look, the Nixon administration wasn't so bad. If it weren't for. . . ."

"Amos, I asked you how Green was coming along with the Pentecost matter?"

"Christ, he just got to Michigan. I told him time was important. He'll do a job, but he isn't a miracle worker." Deering cupped his hands around a cigarette and managed to light it despite the drizzle. "A thing like this takes time, a couple of weeks. That's if you want a good job done. You certainly don't want anybody like her ladyship on the Court."

Huntington nodded. "No. We want to know exactly what we're getting. The President doesn't want any surprises."

"Anyway, what's the hurry? Howell is still unconscious, isn't he?"

Huntington stopped and casually glanced around. They were alone. "According to my reports he's had a second stroke. He's suffered brain death. The machines keep him breathing. If they pull the plug, he dies."

"Where are you getting your information?"

Huntington smiled. "We have a source; one of his treating physicians."

Deering shook his head. "It's beginning to sound a bit like old times around here."

"There's nothing illegal about getting that information. A question of medical ethics exists, perhaps, but nothing criminal. Anyway, the Howell family is trying to decide whether or not to turn off the machines."

"That's a tough decision."

Huntington shrugged. "We have some people, close to them, who I hope can influence them to get this damn thing over with."

Deering inhaled deeply on his cigarette, his eyes on Huntington. "Jesus, it really is just like the old days."

Huntington frowned. "I'd knock that 'old days' crap off, if I were you. You'll last longer. Anyway, get on your man Green and let him know that he really has to move. I expect the plug to be pulled in a couple of days. The President hopes to nominate the new man a few days after the funeral."

"They may not pull the plug."

Huntington shook his head. "I doubt it, but that's my worry, not yours. You just see that Green does his job."

"There's always Judge O'Malley, just in case. At least you know he isn't a double-crosser."

"True. But O'Malley would have a tough time getting through the Senate committee. Besides, ever since Howell had his stroke, O'Malley has been pressuring people to put the heat on the President on his behalf. The man thinks that's poor form. And I don't think he likes O'Malley in the first place."

"Politicians always go for the jugular when there's a job available, or even the possibility. It's a fact of life. O'Malley's no different."

"Maybe, but usually it's done with a bit of tact. O'Malley is carrying on a wide-open campaign for the job, and the man isn't even dead yet. It's the wide-open part that the President finds offensive."

"What about Dean Pentecost? Isn't he trying for the job?"

"We received a couple of calls, but he wasn't responsible for them. I checked. Seems to be strictly upright. The man likes that."

"Then why fart around sending someone to check up on him? Why not just make the decision to put him up if and when there's a vacancy?"

Huntington smiled again. "The man doesn't like him that much. He's still something of an unknown quantity. We need a reliable profile of the real person. You know as well as I do, Amos, that in politics often what you see isn't what you get. Everybody puts on a front. Everybody hides behind a mask. We know what the dean's mask looks like, we just want a peek at the real face."

"Okay, I'll contact Green and tell him to shake a leg."

Huntington nodded. "There's another matter, Amos. You'll be assuming the full title of Press Officer next week."

"I figured, but it's always nice to hear it confirmed."

"That means you'll be before the cameras a lot yourself. You'll be handling the daily press briefings and so on."

Deering inhaled and blew out smoke. "You don't have to tell me, Ed. I know my job."

Huntington looked at him. "The President wants you to shave off that damn beard."

"You're kidding."

Huntington shook his head. "It's an image thing. Get rid of the beard and those tweedy professor-type clothes. The President wants you created in his own image and likeness."

"Shit."

"Bad word, Amos. The man would have said 'that's just swell.' Try to clean up your act." Huntington turned and headed back toward the White House.

"Who are you having talk to Howell's family?" Deering called after him.

Huntington didn't even turn his head as he walked away. "That's on a need-to-know basis. You have no need to know."

Deering stopped. He stood motionless for a moment in the drizzle. "Life and death. Pulling plugs." He spoke the words in a whisper. "Need to know." He took a last drag on the soggy cigarette and then flicked it away.

Amos Deering knew why they had come outside in the rain to talk. Huntington wanted to escape being picked up on any electronic recording devices. It seemed absurd, but perhaps the White House bugs had been reinstalled. Or maybe Huntington was just playing it safe.

Deering looked up into the dark gray clouds above the White House. It was beginning to feel as if the Nixon crowd had never left.

*   *   *

His clothing marked him immediately as an outsider. Jerry Green decided that if he intended to fit in on the campus, he would have to stop by a clothing store and buy something more appropriate, something a lot more casual. The world was a moving sea of faces as thousands thronged by him during the change of classes. Jeans seemed to be the only acceptable covering for the legs, for both male and female. Diversity was allowed for the body's upper half, however. Some wore outsized wool plaid shirts, carefully faded and preferably torn and patched, while others were attired in padded ski jackets or Irish knit sweaters. Most were bareheaded, although here and there a bright stocking cap bobbed upon a head or two. Jogging shoes or woodsman's boots adorned all lower extremities. Nothing seemed to distinguish the faculty from the students except, in some cases, age, and also, occasionally, one of the graying men wore a shirt and tie beneath his woodsman attire.

Green's tailored black cashmere coat and polished dress shoes drew several curious stares.

He had found it a fascinating walking tour. Despite the passage of so many years and the change in the student body, both in composition and dress he felt at home. The stately old dormitories and class buildings still remained, although gleaming new structures had been sandwiched in between them. The changes had been profound. A cyclotron and a planetarium stood close by a new Agricultural Engineering Building. Space age technology and atomic science seemed to have become partners with the mysteries of producing a good asparagus crop.

In a way, the change of classes was not unlike midtown Manhattan during rush hour; there just didn't seem to be enough walkway to go around. Platoons of bicycles glided through the moving human tangle, their riders floating like smoke through a forest, silently weaving in and out, but managing to miss anything that might bar their progress.

He could remember other times, pleasant times, years ago,

when he used to go on campus to visit his father. He had the same feeling now. Many of the physical elements had changed but the spirit of the place remained, tangible somehow, more like a ghost than a memory. He thought of his father, and for the first time in years the recollection was neither bitter nor obscure. He could vividly picture his father in his cubicle of an office, wrapped in a mountain of sweaters, a stained and battered pipe grasped between his teeth, his ragged mustache completely concealing his upper lip. And he recalled the glasses, the half glasses perpetually perched upon the end of his father's nose. They were for reading, yet he could never remember his father ever actually looking through the glasses. In his memory he could conjure up his father's dark piercing eyes, always peering just over the top of the frames of those half spectacles.

His father had been an associate professor, teaching courses in political anthropology, plus a graduate seminar in cultural anthropology. He could recall listening to his father's lectures at the dinner table. Green had enjoyed the anecdotes of classroom give-and-take, but not the subject matter of the courses them-selves. As a boy living in East Lansing it mattered little to him what kind of social structure the Tygodas of Central Africa employed to organize their sweating black ranks. But his father's accounts of student antics could be hilarious, especially when he acted them out, taking both parts, the student and the instructor. His mother, who taught art, tolerated the wild stories, but obviously didn't encourage them. Hank, his brother, seemed to ignore the whole thing, at least during those rare times when Green could remember him being home for family dinner. Yet, today Hank was a full professor of anthropology, a descendant not only in blood, but also in the academic discipline of their father.

Suddenly, as if the memory had been jolted loose and thrust up into his consciousness, he could remember word for word his father's discourse on the anthropological significance of his mother's funeral. It was as if his father had been describing the tribal rites connected with the demise of some far-off African woman; he had been completely objective and analytical. He had showed no emotion, at least not in front of his sons. The death of his mother had been a numbing shock. One day she was there, and the next she was gone. Green remembered there had been songs chanted in some kind of chapel. People had crowded around, looking uncomfortable in the issued skull caps. And then that was that. Life went on the next day just as if she had never existed. They already had a full-time housekeeper, so the usual food was ready on time, the laundry done, everything went on just as before. Or almost.

Hank had been at the top of his form then. He had left high school, serving nine months in the Navy at the tag end of World War II, then he returned to become the hard-charging fullback and hero of East Lansing High. Hank had even played second string on State's football team before President Hannah had brought in Biggie Munn to be State's football coach. Munn had recruited, imported, and raided, putting together invincible teams that could match even professionals. His brother had played out the remaining years of his college eligibility, but only as a member of the hamburger squad. He seldom saw action on Saturday. But his early reputation plus hard work kept him on the squad even if he wasn't lightning fast like the running backs who had come from distant places.

Even Regina Kelso had been impressed by Hank Green. But her appraisal had been objective, not like the near-idolatry afforded Hank by his East Lansing peers. But Jerry had impressed Regina too, or so he thought at the time. Hank was the athlete, but he was the brain, at least he believed that's how people saw the two of them then.

But now that his brother had four degrees, including his doctorate in anthropology, Jerry wondered if those appraisals remained the same. He wondered if anyone really cared.

A young woman on a bicycle almost collided with him. She

deftly swung the front wheel and missed him by a hair. "Sorry," she called after him. He turned and found himself staring at the skintight jeans that clung to her working buttocks. Dirty old man, he thought to himself.

Classes had started and the crowds had disappeared, although quite a few pedestrians and cyclists still moved along the walkways.

He saw the lawn sign Anthropology Building and looked up. It was new, a no-nonsense square structure of concrete and glass panels. He stopped and studied the place. It wasn't anything like the old red-brick building that had housed his father's department, among others. But this new monument to higher education was in familiar territory, next to old Linton Hall and across from the equally ancient Agriculture Hall. On an impulse he walked up to the glass doors of the anthropology headquarters and stepped in. A few students lounged about the large open lobby. They were engrossed either in one another or the books they seemed to be committing to memory. The usual notices were posted on a large bulletin board. He glanced at it. Some of the notices were handwritten, others were typed. They ranged from room ads to offers of used books. A glass-enclosed board held the office directory. He looked at that too. It was there. Prof. Henry A. Green, Rm 202.

He experienced an odd feeling, almost like panic, but the board held a strange fascination for him.

"Can I help you?" A young woman in a plaid shirt and corduroy knickers spoke to him. She wore red skiing boots.

"Pardon me?"

"You look lost." She smiled. "I thought I might be able to help."

He grinned at her. "That's very kind. I am many things, but lost isn't one of them. However, I do appreciate your concern."

She laughed. "Are you thinking of coming on the faculty?"

"Why do you ask?"

"I'm a graduate student. We like to know about these things. There's a lot of jockeying for position around here. An outsider is always considered a threat."

"What's your name?"

"Marcia. Marcia Johnson. Does that mean I'm in trouble?"

He liked the girl. She wasn't pretty, but there was an openness about her, a certain perky confidence in her manner and eyes that made her attractive nevertheless.

"What's this Professor Green like? Have you ever had him in class?"

She stopped smiling. "You're a headhunter!"

"Pardon me?"

"Don't try to fool me, mister. I recognize your New York clothes. You're here to try to steal our Hank Green away, aren't you?"

He laughed. "Not necessarily. Obviously you think a lot of Dr. Green."

Her eyes became wary. "I don't know how to answer that. If I say nice things you'll want him. If I say bad, it just wouldn't be true."

"Maybe I'm just a bill collector. Ever think about that?"

"Not likely, dressed like that." She studied him for a moment. "You know, you look like him a bit. A little older maybe. Are you a relative?"

She couldn't have known she had hit a nerve. Older! He was eight years younger than Hank. The rigors of Washington life must be taking a greater toll than he thought, he reflected.

"I'm a friend. Do you think he's up in his office?"

She glanced at her watch. "Probably not. Too early for this time of day. I think he has a class, but I could be wrong. His office is on the second floor, right at the top of the stairs."

He really didn't want to go up the stairs, but she waited expectantly.

"Thanks." Reluctantly he began to climb. This is not the right way to do it, he thought to himself. Because of the trouble between them, a telephone call would have been better. To just drop in unannounced would only risk an ugly scene. He realized it was a juvenile reaction, but he felt intimidated by the girl who waited at the foot of the stairs. So he continued up.

The office door was plastered by a montage of magazine and newspaper cartoons, all aimed at pricking the pomposity of university life.

The metal sign screwed into the door proclaimed Henry A. Green, PhD.

He hesitated. The girl said it was unlikely that Hank was in. Based on that, he went through the motions of tapping gently on the door.

To his surprise, he heard a gruff "Come in."

It was too late to retreat. He felt like a young boy again, hesitantly violating the sacred precincts of his older brother. He opened the door and stepped in.

The man in the chair was thick, very thick, and the bulky turtleneck sweater he wore accentuated his weight. His faded blue jeans had been cut off at the cuffs, leaving a ragged edge. His feet, propped up on top of the desk, were clad in worn leather loafers. A pair of half glasses perched on the tip of his nose. Jerry Green was shocked. He was staring at a heavier, younger version of his own father.

The man looked up from the book propped up on his protruding stomach. His eyes peered up over the rim of his glasses. "Yeah? What can I do for you?"

If the man had held a pipe in his teeth he would have seemed to be more an apparition than real.

"I was in town. I thought I should stop by and say hello."

The man removed his feet from the desk and squinted at him. There was no sign of recognition. "I'm sorry. I'm afraid I don't. . . ." Then his eyes widened. "Jesus, is that you, Jerry?"

Green felt an urge to deny the fact, to admit it was a mistake, and to flee. But he nodded. "Yes, Hank. How have you been?"

His brother said nothing, just stared. They hadn't seen each other since that nightmare scene at the funeral. No communication had passed between them since.

"If I've come at an inconvenient time. . . ."

Hank Green stood up. He was still much taller than his brother, although the thick bulk had destroyed forever the youthful image of a dashing athlete.

"Jesus, it's not inconvenient, it's just a shock."

Jerry felt as uncomfortable as usual in his brother's presence.

"I know we had our differences, Hank. And I'm sorry about that. How's Adele and the children?"

His brother didn't move. "Jesus, is that all you can do? Ask about the family? How long has it been, Jerry? Five years? Six?"

"Six."

His brother moved around the desk. He was at least a hundred pounds overweight and he moved like an old man. He stood in front of Green.

"Jesus. Six years. I'm really sorry about that."

The overwhelming presence of his brother was almost physically intimidating. "So am I."

Hank Green cleared some books from an old swivel chair. "Sit down." He deposited the books on a larger pile near a wall. "This place is a mess."

"It looks like Pop's old office."

Green saw the flash in his brother's eyes, a quick look of resentment. "I'm usually neater than this," he protested. "But between trying to force some knowledge into empty heads, and some private research, I haven't had much time to pretty things up. Can I get you some coffee?"

"No, thanks."

"It's decaffeinated. You wouldn't know it to look at me, Jerry, but I'm on a diet. I drink buckets of coffee. Sometimes I think it's the only pleasure I have left. Anyway, that's all I have to offer. No milk, sugar, or cream."

"I noticed you put on some weight."

A genuine smile creased his brother's features. "Some?

Shit, I'm a tub and you know it. Not much like the old 'Flying Hebe' of high school days, eh?" His brother smirked wryly. "How did I get this way?" He shrugged. "Who knows. I always managed to hold my weight down pretty good, remember? Of course, then I was a hell of a lot more active. Anyway, I suppose I started eating to compensate for the general frustrations of life. Behold before you, then, a living monument to junk food." He thrust out his arms dramatically. "I'm a cookie addict. I have to have my hourly fix or I go berserk." He opened a desk drawer and took out a tin box. "Today I'm featuring chocolate chip, plus some cream-filled little beauties. They're not on the diet. But I'm trying to wean myself off slowly." He offered the box to his brother.

Jerry Green shook his head.

His brother shoved one cookie into his mouth. Two chews and a swallow, and it was gone. "I'm not the only one who's changed. You look like a banker. I didn't even recognize you. When did you turn gray? You used to have jet black hair and glasses. But now you look like an ad for a New York bank, very distinguished."

Jerry Green offered a pack of cigarettes to his brother.

"No." Hank Green shook his head, rather violently, causing the flesh to shake about his face. "I quit those things. That put on a few pounds too."

"You don't mind if I. . . ."

"I'm no reformer. Blow some my way. I could use it."

Green felt uncomfortable under his brother's steady gaze. But the smoke seemed to help.

"My hair turned gray rather quickly," he said. "At first there were only a few white strands. Then it seemed like it happened overnight. You say it's distinguished, I think it just makes me look old."

"What happened to the glasses, kid? You started wearing them in the eighth grade, as I recall."

"The magic of contacts. The rate of my nearsightedness was accelerating, so they prescribed contacts. I don't know if they actually slow the process but I've become accustomed to them, and I think I see better with them, at least I've persuaded myself that I do."

They looked at each other. They were like two diplomats from warring countries, being carefully civil and urbane, making small talk, trying to ignore the reality of their hostile situation.

"So, how's Alice?" Hank Green asked.

"Fine. At least as far as I know. We're divorced."

Hank shrugged. "I'm sorry."

"No reason to be. We were both glad to get out of the marriage. She's married to a dentist in Oregon."

"And David?"

"He lives with his mother. He likes Oregon much better than Washington. The dentist is an outdoors type. He takes David hunting and fishing. He likes that kind of life."

"You see him much?"

Jerry Green inhaled deeply on the cigarette. "I take a week off in January. I take him down to St. Thomas during his semester break. I sit on the beach while he snorkles, sails, and chases all the young girls. Other than that, we seldom get together."

"Must be tough on you."

Green watched the smoke rise toward the ceiling. "David is very much like you used to be, Hank. He's an active kid, into sports, and on the go constantly. You know me, I like the quiet life. I think one week a year is all we can really stand of each other. At least that way we manage to stay friends."

His brother demolished another cookie. "Your kid must be . . . fifteen?"

"Sixteen."

Hank Green nodded. "Yeah, that's right."

Again there was an awkward silence.

"I'm married again," Jerry Green said to end the stalemate. He didn't want to continue to talk about himself but it was the only thing he could think of. "Her name is Carol. She owns her own accounting firm in Washington. Second marriage for both. She has no children." His own words sounded stiff, like the abbreviated language of a resume or an obituary.

"Happy?"

Jerry Green met his brother's eyes. "As happy as anyone, I suppose. How about you, Hank? I asked about Adele and the kids."

"What can I say? Adele is still as crazy as ever. Christ, I dread the time when she goes into menopause. Shit, she's off the wall most of the time now. God help us all when the hormones zap her."

Jerry Green remembered his brother's wife, a tall dark-haired beauty with a lush, yet athletic body. But what Hank said was correct, he could remember that she was a classic neurotic with a long history of treatment.

"You're still in the law racket, I presume?" Hank asked. Green nodded.

"Well, it's a damn shame you didn't go in for writing soap operas. My family could make you rich. All you'd have to do is follow us around and write it all down. You only remember four kids, but we added another. She's four years old, and by God sometimes I think she's the only mature person in the whole damn household. My oldest girl is an exchange student in Europe. She's majoring in marijuana and abortions. At least they seemed to be her specialties here. Remember my son Charley? Well, Charley quit high school and is an oil worker in Houston. And my son Aaron, pride of Israel, is a wild-eyed born-again Christian, believe it or not. You know, there's something basically screwy about a nice Jewish boy jumping around and singing and shouting in some little storefront church. All I ever hear around the house is Bible quotations. New Testament, of course. He says he wants to be a minister. Rachel, who is fourteen and looks twenty-five, is called 'Cha Cha.' She insists on it. I got a bunch of pimply-faced young studs hanging around the house every damned night like a pack of dogs in heat." He munched on some more cookies. "I guess my family and my attitudes about things are a bit different than last time, eh?"

It was his brother's first reference to their last meeting. Green wondered if Hank was approaching a discussion of that incident. He hoped not.

Hank finished the cookies and grinned. "So that's the family history, Jerry. I'm still employed, although much of the romance of college teaching is gone, now that money is tight. I don't get any more trips abroad to study the skulls of extinct tribes, no more watching thrilling sunsets in the Orient. Now all I see is the same shitty old sunsets everybody sees; the old red ball going down behind the dome of the state capitol. Mine is the song of middle age, kiddo; it's a disgusting time of life."

"I'm in that league too, remember."

Hank Green snorted. "Oh yeah? Look at you. That overcoat you're wearing is worth probably half my annual salary. If not, it sure looks like it. You're a big deal Washington lawyer raking in those big bucks. You have a new wife, who is probably a sex fiend. You don't have any children problems. If anything happens with your son, the dentist takes care of it. Hell, Jerry, you have conquered life. Admit it."

Jerry Green looked around the cluttered office for an ashtray.

"Here, use this." His brother handed him the now-empty cookie tin.

He crushed out his cigarette.

"Is your wife here with you?" his brother asked.

Jerry Green shook his head. "No. I'm here on business."

"Suing some poor bastard?"

He shook his head. "No."

"Well, what then? Of course, if it's going to violate your professional ethics or something, keep it to yourself, I'm just curious."

Green studied his brother. Hank seemed more like a friendly

stranger. He looked different, and he talked differently. He was not the grim angry man of six years ago. That was the brother he remembered: brooding, intense, a powerful trim body, and piercing eyes. The fat man seated opposite him lacked all that, except for the piercing eyes.

"It is confidential in a way. I'll tell you about it when I can. It's a political thing."

"Politics?" Hank asked.

"More or less. I've taken a short leave from my law firm. I'm a special counsel for the White House, at least for a couple of weeks."

His brother whistled to show he was properly impressed. "When did this all happen?"

"Just a few days ago. But don't let me mislead you, Hank, it really isn't a big deal. I'm just doing a job any errand boy could do. But they picked me. I think the White House boys are also impressed by the gray hair and the banker's clothes. Anyway, I'm here for a few days."

"You should have let me know you were coming."

They stared at each other. Again there was an awkward silence.

"If things had been reversed, would you have called me?" Jerry Green spoke the words softly.

His brother continued to study him for a moment. Then he half smiled and shrugged. "Yeah, I see what you mean."

"Yes." Green stood up and extended his hand. "I know you have work to do, Hank."

His brother pushed his bulk out of the chair. His grip was firm, but moist. They were both nervous. "Look, Jerry, what can I say? But if you're going to be around here for a while, how about we go out to dinner? I'd invite you over but you know Adele. Jesus, it could cause her to hide in the attic for three days. Even paying the paper boy can be a major trauma for her. And then some days she's okay, you just never know. Needless to say, we don't entertain a hell of a lot. But you and I could go out. And if Adele is having one of her good days she can come along, too. How about it?"

He wondered if the invitation was just a gesture or whether it was his brother's way of extending the olive branch. But if that was it, it was a conditional peace. He was pointedly not invited to the house. He well remembered Adele, and he recalled that although she did have some emotional problems she was never that bad. Perhaps Adele was just a tactful excuse. Tact—for Hank that would be the most significant change of all. And perhaps it was just as well, they both needed time to consider the possibility of any further contact.

"That sounds good to me, Hank. If I can work it in, I'll give you a call. Are you in the book?" He didn't want his brother to know he had gone to the trouble of looking him up.

"What do you think this is, one of your big bad cities? This is a college town. Sure I'm in the book. Hell, outside of this zoo's president, the board of trustees, my fellow faculty members, and my students, I have absolutely no enemies. I'm in the book." Hank walked him to the door. "Hey, if I can give you a hand in any way, let me know. It might be a nice break from looking into a sea of bored faces."

"I'll call you, Hank." He shook his hand again. "It's been good to see you."

Hurrying down the stairs Green knew his brother had stayed at the office door watching him. Green wondered what he was thinking.

"Hey, Jerry!" Hank called.

Green was halfway down the stairs. He turned and looked back.

His brother had that same half grin on his face. "You remember Regina Kelso, your old girlfriend?"

Jerry Green nodded. He was aware that several students in the lobby looked up, listening to the exchange.

"She's teaching here now. Nursing. Her name's Carter. You ought to look her up. She always asks about you."

He felt a rising wave of embarrassment. The students waited to hear what he was going to say. He looked up at Hank. His brother's heavy facial flesh seemed to curl around the contours of his crooked grin.

"I'll do that," Green said. He turned, hurried down the stairs and out the double doors.

It was only after he was out in the crisp autumn air that he noticed that his brother hadn't asked him to take off his overcoat, nor had he thought to do so. Perhaps the oversight was due only to the shock of the unexpected encounter, or it might have been a reflection of their real attitudes. Green knew he had felt trapped and had wished to leave. Perhaps his brother had been equally uncomfortable and wanted him out.

His feelings about his brother seemed confused. He wondered if Hank might be equally unsettled by their unexpected meeting.

Green was again caught up in the moving river of students. They hurried past him, racing to get to their next class. He moved with the tide, drifting aimlessly across that part of the campus. He again was conscious of the distinctive blending of past and present. There was no "old" campus or "new" campus, at least not in the usual sense. The past and present had been brought together. It was not the old school, and yet, at the same time, it was. Both in the physical setting and in his own emotional preceptions, he was finding it difficult to separate the past from the present.

As the rush of students diminished he found himself in front of the Hannah Administration Building. Inside he located an information office. He waited until two very tall and very hairy young men finished talking to a giggling blonde girl.

"Where could I find a map of the campus," he asked, after the two young men departed.

She looked at him, and suddenly she was all business. She obviously recognized an intruder when she saw one.

• 117 •

"Is there somewhere you want to go?"

He hoped his smile disarmed her. "Several places. That's why I need a map. I'm up here visiting one of my children," he lied.

The suspicion vanished. Parents were safe. They could be trusted with a map.

She produced one from beneath a counter and handed it to him. "If I can help you in any way. . . ." She smiled.

He shook his head. "I'll get along, but thanks anyway."

He stepped over into the lobby area near the entrance and opened the map. It was multicolored, attractive, and professional. His eye searched the office index box. The School of Nursing was housed in building 183, which the building index proclaimed to be the Life Sciences Building, located at the far southeastern part of the campus, well over a mile away.

Green considered walking there, perhaps to follow Hank's advice and casually drop by to see Regina Kelso, now Carter. It was a tempting prospect. Then he realized that Regina might have changed as much as had his brother. It would be shattering if she were overweight like Hank, or even if her lovely hair had turned to gray, like his own. He decided that the memory of Regina Kelso should be preserved; so that she would always be young, soft eyed, and beautiful. Besides, he thought to himself, he had had more than enough of impulsive encounters for one day.

He checked the index and located the law school on the map. It had been built on the banks of the Red Cedar River just south of the Auditorium. He folded the map, tucked it away in his coat, and headed across the campus toward the law school.

It was only a short walk. He turned on to Farm Lane and recognized the old Auditorium. Next to it was a building unlike anything else on the campus, old or new. The law school building was shaped like the hull of a giant ship, its peak rising up like the prow of some massive supertanker. Although modern in every sense, the architect had cleverly blended brick and glass so that the structure conveyed the impression that it was reaching heavenward, not unlike the great cathedrals of Europe. Green stopped and admired it. The building seemed to radiate a sense of power, of vitality. It was an architectural triumph.

Green wondered if the structure was the brain child of a gifted architect, or whether it had been designed by the dean himself. There was a distinct touch of genius about the place, and if it was the product of the dean's mind, then he would be a most formidable and interesting man.

He cupped his hands to protect the flame and lit a cigarette. The law school seemed to hold a fascination for him, much like an intricate piece of modern art. Long glass slats revealed students at study in a multilevel library. The interlacing of floors, bricks, and bookstacks made it seem a scene in stained glass. It was a remarkable effect.

He watched two young men come out of the law school. They were arguing heatedly as they passed him. One carried a pile of lawbooks against his side, the force of his arm seeming to defy the pull of gravity. The other student had a canvas bag of books slung over his back. They were debating the implications of the Palsgraph case. The case was old, the granddaddy decision for determining proximate cause of an actionable injury. It had concerned a series of events set off by a man running for a train, but to these space-age young minds the legal reasoning was still vital. To Green it seemed just another interesting blend of past and present.

He inhaled and then expelled the smoke, watching it whipped away by the autumn breeze. He wondered if this business of past and present was unique to his imagination or something that naturally went with homecomings.

He watched an energetic young couple emerge from the arklike law school. She was striking, a tall girl, beautiful, with a model's high cheekbones. Her dark hair was long and loose. The breeze whirled it about her like smoke. She laughed at something the boy said. The boy, with curling yellow hair, was taller than the girl. They bounced along, their arms intertwined and their heads close together. Their delight in each other seemed almost to radiate from them. Green thought again of Regina Kelso.

It was quite a distance back to his motel. He flicked the cigarette away and started walking. It would be a challenging and interesting assignment. He felt something like a hunter stalking his prey. He had seen the den, now he would find out about the habits of the animal who dwelled within. He felt better, much better.

Chapter 5

The sound of shouting had been reported. That was most unusual. Although no clerk or other Court employee was ever allowed into the sacred precinct while the weekly closed-door conference was conducted by the justices, angry voices had been heard, the words too muffled to be understood. Despite the secrecy, within minutes of the conference's end, word of what had transpired began floating through the Court building's corridors like smoke. It was a lonely job, being a justice of the United States Supreme Court. Wives, family, and friends seldom understood or were interested in the legal nuances of the cases, nor in the intellectual infighting necessary to protect or project a point of law. But the justice's clerks understood.

Although not all the justices confided in their clerks, many of them did. And those confidences generally were quickly passed on to those unfortunates who lacked access to such inside knowledge.

Ben Alexander could always count on a discreet word from Justice Howell on what was happening, but that was before the stroke, and now Brian Howell could speak to no one. Alexander felt isolated.

The only thing he knew was the common gossip. The hall porter had been the first to report the shouting. One of the Court's secretaries confirmed his account. Not since the days of Justice Douglas had such a thing occurred.

Alexander found himself consumed with the desire to know the details. He had heard that several of the justices had stalked out of the conference, their faces grim.

Floyd Grant stepped into Alexander's office and closed the door. As chief clerk, Grant enjoyed the confidence of the Chief Justice.

"You did hear about the conference?" Grant asked as he sat down.

Alexander nodded. "Sure, the whole building heard. What happened?"

Grant tamped some tobacco into his pipe. "The dragon lady," he said simply.

Alexander didn't comment. He waited. The other man might hold back if he appeared too interested.

"The Chief thinks she's crazy," Grant said. "If she were a man I believe the Chief was so damn angry that he would have thrown a punch, he was that upset."

"What happened?"

"She insisted that a vote be taken on certain key cases. She wants to pick and choose. She knows which ones will result in a tie vote. If she likes the result below, she knows a tie will uphold the lower court's ruling. So she wants those cases heard, written, and disposed of *now*. Of course, where a tie would work against her interest, she wants those cases put aside."

"I suppose they all feel that way, at least about the matters they really care about."

Grant nodded. "Sure, that's human enough. But if the justices are allowed to pick and choose on that basis it would cause a legal bloodletting around here unlike anything we've ever seen. And the dissents would be legion. The Chief told them the cases would wait until something was decided about Howell."

"Oh?"

"What the hell, that's fair. Nobody gets any special advantage that way. If your man dies. . . ." Grant paused when he saw Alexander's reaction. "Hey, I'm sorry, Ben, but that is a possibility."

Alexander nodded. "Sure. I understand. Go on."

"Well, if death does result, then a replacement will be quickly appointed. That would make the difference, there would be no even splits then. Another possibility the Chief has discussed lately is having a guardian appointed for your man. The guardian could then resign for him. That would create the vacancy."

"That would be pretty hairy legally."

Grant grinned. "You bet. If Justice Howell suddenly recovered, there would be all hell to pay. It could even put all the decisions rendered in his absence into question. However, I don't think it's being seriously considered, it's just one of the possible avenues being explored."

"They say there was shouting at the conference."

Grant puffed on his pipe and nodded. "It started between the Chief and the dragon lady. She demanded a vote on moving the cases. The Chief refused. That's when they got into a screaming match. Eventually everybody got into it." Great clouds of smoke issued from the pipe. "But it's only a matter of time now before she gets her way. She's been lobbying the other justices. The Chief thinks she'd sleep with them if she thought it would help."

"Maybe just the threat would do the trick."

Grant laughed. "I'll tell the Chief what you said. He'll love it. By tomorrow it'll be all over Washington."

"I'll pass on getting credit."

Grant grinned. "Smart. Listen, what I came down to tell you was this. The Chief knows you're a team player, Ben, and he appreciates it. He wanted you to know that whatever happens with Howell, you won't be assigned to the dragon lady. He says that while he can't guarantee it now, he would like to have you on his staff."

"I'd like that, too. Apparently he doesn't anticipate Justice Howell coming back. What's happening, Floyd? I've heard rumors that his condition has become worse, but I don't want to bother his wife to find out."

Grant pulled at the pipe. "I'm not at liberty to say, but it doesn't look good. Whatever's going to happen will probably happen in a few days. Anyway, that's what the Chief says."

"How does he know?"

Grant stood up and knocked the ashes of the pipe into an ashtray. "You know him, he has wires everywhere. I'm not sure what he knows, but I think things will be resolved very shortly. Apparently the dragon lady has heard the same thing and is trying to force action on the cases before a replacement is selected."

Grant walked to the door. "The Chief wanted you to know you have nothing to worry about." He paused. "And all this is confidential, right?"

"Absolutely."

"Well, one way or another, all hell is going to break loose here soon. So keep your head down and stay loose."

Floyd Grant departed. The pungent aroma of his pipe smoke lingered.

Ben Alexander wondered how anyone could know, with any sort of certainty, exactly what was going to happen to Justice Howell; unless they planned to kill him. He laughed at the thought and resolved to stop reading so many detective thrillers.

*   *   *

As he walked back to his motel Jerry Green formulated the basic plan and the tactics he would use to pry behind Dean Pentecost's public mask and obtain a glimpse of the real man. The faculty would be ripe ground. Universities were always hotbeds of gossip and politics. He knew from experience that some would back the Dean, while others would have their long knives out, glistening and sharpened. He could almost predict what they would say. What he wanted most would be observations and opinions from those members of the faculty who were impartial. He would have to do some careful probing to find them; they wouldn't be wearing signs. And he would have to keep a low profile at the same time. There was no need letting the dean know, at this point, that a man from the White House was poking about.

Students' views would also be important, although they would only know the dean from afar. Still, sometimes a student's fresh perception could be the most valid of all. The eyes of youth often had a much clearer view of things.

Green planned to talk to the dean's neighbors, perhaps even store clerks who served the dean on a regular basis. His barber might be an excellent source, they usually were. And if the dean belonged to any clubs, views expressed by the members might be useful. But it would take a very discerning eye to decide what was gossip and what was fact. But he felt he had such an eye.

The long walk in the brisk autumn air had made him pleasantly tired. He seldom walked anymore. He always planned to use his club for exercise, but his good intentions were usually cancelled by pressures of the law practice. So he was never able to follow any regular routine, but he did manage an occasional swim and a rare attempt at jogging. Like so many others, he much more enjoyed thinking about exercise than actually putting in the time and effort.

His legs felt slightly stiff as he entered his room. He hung up his overcoat and suitcoat. The red message light at the side of his telephone was lit. He loosened his tie and collar, dialed 0 and lay back on the bed.

"Yes," an impersonal female voice inquired.

"This is Mr. Green in 117, do you have a message for me?"

"Just a minute."

He was put on hold and listened to recorded dance music. The music clicked off. "Yes, Mr. Green. You were called by a Mr. Amos Deering. He asked that you return his call after seven this evening at this number. Do you have a pencil?"

Green sat up reluctantly and found a scrap of paper. "Go ahead."

"It's a Maryland number," she said, giving the area code and the telephone numerals. "He said after seven," she reminded him.

"Thank you."

He hung up and glanced at his watch. It was just a few minutes after six. He could take a short nap or get some dinner. The walking had made him sleepy but it had also awakened his appetite. He balanced his need to eat against the need for rest. He yawned and lay back.

He was awakened by the insistent ringing of the telephone. The room was dark. He was momentarily disoriented. He snapped on the nightstand light and picked up the telephone.

"Hey, where have you been? I've been sitting here since seven o'clock." Green recognized Amos Deering's voice. He checked his watch through sleep-blurred eyes. It was after nine o'clock.

"I'm sorry, Amos. I got your message, but I fell asleep. What's up?"

"Sleep? Jesus, you're working for the government now. Have you forgotten? We never sleep. You know, just like the Mounties or who the fuck ever invented that bullshit." His words were slightly slurred. He sounded as if he had been drinking. "Com'on, Jerry, give me what you got so far, baby. Things are heating up."

Green forced himself to come fully awake. "Amos, I haven't even been here one full day. About the only thing I've done is look over the law school. It's in the kind of building in which they used to bury kings. I really haven't had much of a chance to do anything else, Amos. If you wanted a miracle, you should have let me know sooner."

He could hear the ice cubes clink at the other end of the line. "Hey, don't think you're the only one with problems. Shit, they made me shave off my beard. Think about that for a minute. What kind of a bootlicker would let himself be pushed around that way?"

"A rotten, ambitious man with absolutely no scruples or principles."

Deering's chuckle echoed over the phone. "Say, you really do know me, don't you. But that's your game, isn't it? That's what the President of these United States says himself: Jerry Green can smell them out. He said that himself. But then what does he know?"

"What's going on, Amos?"

"Remember the old days, the old White House days?"

Jerry Green again lay back on the bed, but he was no longer sleepy. "What do you mean?"

"Remember when everything was tapped? I mean you couldn't take a pee without figuring the sparkling sound was being recorded on somebody's little tape machine, remember that?"

"What the hell are you talking about?"

There was a pause. "Listen, Jerry, for both our sakes, use the old discretion from now on, okay? I'm not sure that the old days have returned, but I now talk like I'm on candid camera, get me? Even when I make love to the old lady, I'm damned careful of what I say. No more words, just grunts."

Green sat up. "You think your phone is tapped?"

"Jerry, I don't know what the hell to think. But discretion is the better part of valor. It pays to be careful, okay?"

Green wondered if it was just the liquor talking. But perhaps it wasn't. "Okay, I understand."

"Good. You can read between the lines, okay? That matter you've been sent down there on is heating up. The vacancy is expected momentarily. The man is anxious for your report. A lot hangs on this, Jerry. I hate to put you on the spot, but things are moving fast. You talked about a miracle, maybe now is the time to pull one off."

"I can hurry things, but it'll end up half-assed. Does the man want that?"

"Half-assed is better than nothing. The pressure is building, and I mean it is about to explode. When it pops the man will have to ramrod someone through in a hurry. He's counting on you, Jerry."

Green slowly shook his head. "Even a half-assed job will take time, Amos. You can pass the word back that I'll break my ass, but I'll still need some time."

There was a pause. "Time is what it's all about. Look, sport, I don't want to say anything more over the phone. All I can tell you is that what looked like weeks has now come down to days."

"How can anybody know that?"

"I can't talk about it. If you can just get something, anything, it will have to do."

"I took this assignment to do a job, Amos. And I'll do it. I'll put the rush on it, but it will be done properly."

He could hear ice cubes clink again.

"Okay, sport. I've passed the message. What you do is your business. Good luck."

Green thought for a moment. He would have to change his entire plan of action.

"Amos, if your people want this done fast, I won't be able to pussyfoot around. I'll have to talk to some people head-on. Do you understand?"

There was another pause. "Frankly, no."

"I'll have to approach some people directly. I'll have to tell them who I am and what I'm doing."

"Do you think that's wise?"

Green fumbled around for a cigarette. "No, I don't think it's wise, but if this has to be done fast, and if it truly is a matter of days, then it has to be done out in the open. At least, with some people."

"So what's your problem?"

"They will want identification and confirmation."

The ice cubes clinked again at the other end. "Shit."

"Look, I'll do everything I can to keep this quiet, but if they want confirmation I'll have to have them call you at the White House."

"Whoa, Jerry, I can't do that. You know how these things can leak. You talk to somebody, then he talks to some newspaper pal of his. As the Press Officer I have to keep out of these things. How the hell can I deny something if I'm the contact man?"

Green lit the cigarette. The smoke tasted terrible in his dry mouth.

"Pick someone else, one of the other White House lawyers, but someone who is in residence there with the man." Green expelled the smoke from his nostrils. "But pick someone with brains. All he has to do is confirm that I'm a special counsel to the President and that I'm out here doing what I'm doing. If any problems come up, he can contact me."

There was no immediate reply. Deering was thinking it over. "Maybe Chris Clovis would be good: young guy, smart. He knows all about this anyway. Would he be okay with you?"

Green tried to recall if he had met anyone named Clovis. He had been introduced to a number of White House people when he was sworn in. But those names and faces were blurred in his memory. "If he's all right with you, then we'll go with him. Fill him in, okay?"

"Jerry, isn't there any other way you could go about this? I mean, if it gets out that the White House is in town asking about the dean they'll know we expect . . . well . . . a vacancy. It wouldn't look good."

"If you want fast action, Amos, that's just a risk you'll have to take."

"Well you may be right. But be careful as hell, eh? This whole thing could blow up on us."

"I'll do my best."

"And don't waste time screwing any old childhood sweet-hearts, eh? You can do that when the job is all done. Remember what Edmund Burke said about government men and situations like this."

"What's that?"

"I don't know. You're the smart lawyer, I thought you'd know. Anyway, it was something like 'get your ass in gear.'"

"I'll get busy, Amos. Don't worry."

"I'm not. It's just that some of the jerks I work for are having anxiety attacks. Oh yeah, and remember what I said, you know, about the old days and caution."

"I understand, and I'll be careful."

Green hung up the telephone. He was now conscious of hunger. And although he didn't often use alcohol, suddenly he felt the need for a good stiff drink.

* * *

It wasn't the usual stark, ill-equipped six-bed infirmary ward found in other institutions. The order was a nursing order. They were trained professionals and their medical facility reflected that fact. Their infirmary resembled a mini-edition of the most advanced hospital, complete with a two-bed critical care unit. Armed with the best and most modern medical machines, they were ready for everything except actual surgical operations. When one of the sisters needed surgery, she was transported to a city hospital. However, within hours of the operation, if feasible, she was returned to the mother house where gentle and expert care awaited, administered with the finest tools offered by medical science.

Mother General had issued orders that Sister Agatha Murphy was not to be allowed in, or even near, the infirmary. Considering her past history, it could be the occasion of temptation for her, and far worse for the patients. It was the mother house, the place where elderly nuns retired. Most of the population consisted of older or infirm sisters who no longer had the stamina to perform the order's work among the sick. So like the legend of the African elephants, this was their burial ground, and they returned to the mother house to die.

God treated nuns with the same equal hand applied to the rest of the world's population. They expired of heart disease, stroke, and cancer in the same ratio as American women of their age anywhere.

The infirmary beds, because of the nature of the mother house and its retirement feature, almost always held a few nuns who were terminally ill. For the sisters the infirmary had become something like a way station to the afterlife; sort of a spiritual bus stop where a heavenly van would waft the soul away, to a blessed and earned reward, they hoped.

But despite their religious belief and their own skill as nurses, none of the sisters was really fond of the infirmary. They visited their friends there, but they recognized that it was here where they themselves would most likely die. It was accepted, but not relished.

Sister Agatha Murphy had contracted an upper respiratory infection. Her lungs were congested and she was running a fever. Only a healthy Agatha Murphy was barred from the infirmary. Illness was another matter. Therefore, she was admitted, X-rayed, and examined by the order's doctor.

Not quite pneumonia, but getting there, according to the doctor. Sister Agatha Murphy was made comfortable in the isolation room. She would be kept there until her coughing stopped and it was judged that she was no longer contagious. Then a decision would be made as to whether it would be safe to house her with the other nuns in the regular ward.

Mother General, the head of the order and the head of the mother house, was kept informed of Sister Agatha Murphy's condition. The Mother General, kindly by nature, never wished ill toward anyone. However, as an administrator, she couldn't keep the thought from her mind that if Sister Agatha Murphy passed on it would save the order from a continuing embarrassment. And it would certainly save the Church from having to decide what to do with Sister in case the Supreme Court reversed her conviction. Sister Death, as the press called her, was unrepentent. And she had been judged sane, despite what the order, and the Pope himself, considered mad behavior, at least for a Catholic nun. If she were discharged from the criminal charges against her then it would be up to the Church to take appropriate action. They could punish her, or she could leave. No matter what the outcome it would be damaging to Holy Mother the Church. Mother General dismissed from her mind the thought of how very convenient Agatha Murphy's death would be, at least she honestly tried not to think about it.

Within three days of her confinement in the infirmary the antibiotics did their work and Sister Agatha Murphy was much more comfortable, although she still had a hacking cough. So she stayed in isolation.

Sister Barbara Filmore ran the infirmary. Like Sister Agatha, Sister Barbara had several degrees in nursing science and had served both in hovels and giant hospitals during her many years of service. She walked with a pronounced limp, a souvenir of being beaten and shot during a South American revolution. The revolutionary soldiers had stormed her hospital, shooting doctors and nurses. She had been hurt and left for dead but had survived. She was a practical woman who had seen much of life. She visited Sister Agatha daily. She constituted the one and only social caller for Sister Death.

"Feeling better, according to your chart," Sister Barbara said as she limped into the isolation room. She pulled up the single hard-backed chair and sat down. "Still coughing?"

Agatha Murphy looked at the other woman. They were about the same age and had been novices together. "Yes, there's still a cough, but not as much as before. I should be as good as new in a few days."

"We'll see. These things can be tricky for people our age, as you well know."

Sister Agatha seldom smiled, but now just the hint of that expression played on her thin lips. She studied the other nun through her thick glasses. "You're right, lung problems can be tricky. And it would certainly take a lot of heat off the order if I were called to my heavenly reward. I think that may have been on a few minds ever since I was admitted here."

Sister Barbara grinned. "More than likely. By the way, Agatha, are you so sure that the reward will be so heavenly? Why don't you confess to the chaplain? That way you can at least receive the Sacrament."

"So you'd like to see me gain heaven on a technicality?"

The other nun shifted uncomfortably in the chair, her hip always caused her pain on sitting. "I'm not here to lecture you, as you well know."

Sister Agatha sighed. "And I appreciate it. You're one of the few around here who doesn't give me little sermonettes."

"Allow me to make a simple suggestion. If I were in your situation I would continue to take the position that what I did was not illegal, that I had committed no crime. However, I would go on to say that I recognized that the assistance of suicide is a sin in the eyes of the Church. You know Father Benjamin, he would accept that as repentance. You'd be forgiven, get the Sacrament, and the Church could breathe a bit easier. Perhaps even yourself, eh?"

"But it isn't a sin," Sister Agatha replied. Her voice suddenly became stern and her tone that of a person who expected no disagreement.

Sister Barbara frowned. "I'm not going to debate whether what you did was wrong in the sight of God. That's between God and yourself. But the Church condemns the practice, and that makes it a sin as far as the Church is concerned. Why not admit that much publically? What can it harm?"

"Equivocation! You sound like a Jesuit priest."

Sister Barbara laughed. "I'm not advising you to lie. You would be stating an absolute truth; that what you did what a sin in the eyes of the Church, nothing more."

"Is Sister Marilyn still alive?" The question was asked quickly, Sister Agatha's blue eyes suddenly intense.

"Yes. But she is dying hard."

Sister Agatha nodded. "If it weren't against the law, and it weren't a sin in the eyes of the Church, or your own, honestly, Barbara, just between the two of us, wouldn't you go down to the critical care unit and put an end to that poor woman's suffering?"

Sister Barbara thought for a moment, pursing her lips as she weighed her answer. "If the conditions you proposed were true, I would step down there this minute and give her a shot that would end it."

"Then there is no difference between us."

"But the conditions you set up aren't true, and that's the point. I'm not going to talk about God's will, we've both seen too much suffering in this world to try to try to lay it to some simplistic spiritual reason. But life is sacred, Agatha. We've both been trained to fight to preserve it. Of course I would welcome Sister Marilyn's death. I know the pain, but the time she dies isn't my decision. It isn't hers either. That belongs solely to God."

Sister Agatha's expression never changed. "In her condition she may die tonight, or she may linger for a few more days, and there is no chance of recovery, correct?"

"Basically, that's true."

"Then I tell you it is cruel to make her endure these long hours and days of pain needlessly. If there were any chance that she might recover, I'd agree, but there isn't, and to make her go through all this is evil."

Sister Barbara held up her hands. "I don't wish to argue. I just thought I'd try to suggest a practical way out of your difficulty."

"It wouldn't work. Of course, I do thank you for your concern."

Sister Barbara pushed herself erect. "If you need anything to make you comfortable. . . ."

"I have all I need. Thank you."

The nun limped to the door of the isolation room, then turned. "There are others who are watching your case, people who would take human life and profit from it. I trust you know that?"

Sister Agatha nodded. "I am painfully aware of that possibility."

"If you are found not guilty and rational suicide is declared legal, those people will use your case to justify the taking of lives, and not just the lives of the dying either. Agatha, doesn't that bother you?"

Sister Agatha shook her head. "I think most of that is just foolishness, it comes from the scare tactics used by the prosecutor to frighten the Court. Nothing will change, except a number of dying people will have their last moments eased."

"If you win your case, what do you plan to do? You know the order will never allow you to stay, at least not as a nurse."

"I will leave the order and lecture. I am informed there is a great deal of money in that. I shall raise funds until I have enough to start my own hospice." She paused. "Eventually the Church will come around to my point of view. My conscience is clear."

"And if you lose?"

"I suppose I will be sent to prison and given a job in an infirmary. After some of the stations where I have served, an American prison holds very little terror for me."

"When will you know? About the case?"

Sister Agatha looked up at the ceiling, there was no expression on her placid face. "My lawyer says they will soon argue the matter before the Supreme Court, then a decision will come down later. It will be a number of months. I will welcome the decision, no matter what the outcome, for then I will be able to make some kind of life plan for myself."

"What does your lawyer think?"

"If I shall win or lose?"

"Yes."

She continued gazing at the ceiling. "It will be very close. He says it will be decided by one vote. He seems to know about these things."

Sister Barbara stood at the door. "I honestly cannot pray for you to win, Agatha. I will pray that the outcome shall be the best in the sight of God."

Sister Agatha looked directly at her. "That will be my prayer also."

Sister Barbara hurried away from the isolation room. It seemed so incongruous that such a quiet, mild woman could be called Sister Death. Still, she had assisted in dispatching over a hundred ailing men and women, and had admitted all of it.

Sister Barbara limped to her desk and wrote out an order for the other nuns on infirmary service: under no circumstances was Sister Agatha Murphy to be allowed near the dying Sister Marilyn. She thought of Sister Marilyn. She had been their teacher. A good woman, kind and gentle, and now she was suffering greatly. Sister Barbara studied her own order, and was tempted to erase it. She slowly shook her head. The order would stand. Death was strictly in God's jurisdiction.

*   *   *

A plan began to formulate in Senator Dancer's mind as he guided his compact car along the twisting roadway below the vast Arlington Cemetery. He had received his instructions directly from the President himself. And it was fully understood between them that if successful, Senator Dancer could expect significant reward. When he had left the White House gate he had no idea of what he might say, or even how he could approach the subject. But now he smiled to himself as he looked up at the silent slopes of graves. They inspired the beginning of an idea.

He drove leisurely, moving with the midday traffic. He had used the White House telephone to call Martha Howell and alert her that he planned to drop by. He had been there several times since Brian Howell's stroke, so he knew his visit would seem quite natural, they would suspect nothing beyond the ordinary courtesy call.

Dorothy, the Howell's married daughter, answered the door. She held her one-year-old son perched on one hip. Dorothy had a towel around her neck and a loose strand of hair drifted across one eye. She looked harried and exhausted.

"Did I come at a bad time?" Dancer asked as she ushered him into the Howell's living room.

"Oh no, it's just that young Brian here has just discovered the ability to walk. I spend all day running after him, and I'm just not used to all the exercise." She turned and called. "Mother, Senator Dancer is here!"

She put the baby down and he toddled along at a determined clip, passing his grandmother as she entered the room. Dorothy gave chase.

"I'll try to get him to take his nap," Dorothy called as she disappeared down the hallway. "If you hear screaming, it isn't child abuse."

Hugh Dancer grasped Martha Howell's hands. She had lost weight and looked drawn, almost gaunt.

"Sit down, for heaven's sake, Hugh. You're considered family around here." She managed a smile. "Can I get you coffee, or a drink perhaps?"

"A drink sounds fine, Martha. Scotch with a little soda, if you have it."

"I'll join you." She sounded glad to have an excuse. "I'll be right back."

The room was the same, nothing had been changed. However there was one prominent addition. A large framed color photograph of Brian Howell, complete with judicial robes, had been set on the fireplace mantle. It was an oversized portrait more suitable for a courtroom or display in a public place. It seemed inappropriate in the carefully arranged and tastefully furnished room.

Martha Howell returned with the drinks and two coasters.

She was the kind of woman who insisted on neatness above all else. He accepted the glass and placed the coaster on a table at the side of his chair.

She sat primly. The large glass seemed out of place in her hand. She looked a bit guilty. She came from a background where afternoon drinking was considered sinful. She took a dainty sip of her drink. "I'm drinking more lately, but I suppose that's to be expected."

"Why don't you have your doctor prescribe a mild tranquilizer. It might help."

She nodded. "I did. I tried two kinds. The first one knocked me silly, and the second kind didn't help at all. Don't misunderstand me, Hugh, I'm in no danger of becoming an alcoholic. I have two or three drinks in the course of an entire day, no more. Even the doctor said that much would be good for me, under the circumstances."

"It's a terrible strain. But at least you have Dorothy and the baby here now. That should help keep your mind off things."

She smiled, this time easily. "I'm too old for little children, Hugh. I love my grandchild, but I think I'll be able to bear seeing him go."

He laughed. "I know. I have four. I love them, but I can't stand them."

She again sipped her drink. "It's a bit early for visiting, Hugh. Is there something on your mind?"

"Martha, we've known each other a long time. I was the one who recommended Brian for the Supreme Court." He stopped. He knew instinctively that he was coming on too strong, too quickly. "I suppose what I'm trying to say is that I hope you know that I am your friend, both Brian and yours."

"That certainly goes without saying, Hugh."

He sipped his drink. She had made it strong, but he was grateful for that. He wasn't worried about the effect of the liquor, he was used to drinking. "I'm afraid there's a crisis brewing."

"There always is in Washington."

He leaned back in his chair. "But this time I'm afraid it concerns Brian."

She showed no surprise, only interest.

"I'm sure, Martha, that you recall all the fuss about Justice Douglas and his health problems. There were a number of people who wanted him removed from the Court."

"They tried to impeach him twice," she said quietly, "but not for reasons of health."

"That's right. He had many enemies. He was a rather rough and tough old character." Dancer smiled at the memory, then his features became serious, almost solemn. "Martha, there are several very important cases coming before the Court and there's a movement afoot to remove Brian; they want to create a vacancy so that a deciding vote can be added to the Court."

"They can't remove him. That's unconstitutional."

"There's talk of using the impeachment process."

Her eyes widened. "That's nonsense! Brian's done nothing wrong, he's not guilty of any high crimes. He's only sick."

Senator Dancer sipped his drink. She was close to tears, and tears would solve nothing. He weighed his next step, considering the consequences. Then he decided to meet the issue head on.

"The doctors say Brian is dead, Martha."

There were no tears, instead her eyes narrowed in sudden anger. "Yes, that's what they say, Hugh; they tell me he is completely dependent upon the machines. But doctors are often wrong, you know that as well as I do. Besides that, Hugh, I see him every day. He looks fine." Her voice broke just a bit. "He looks as if he's sleeping."

He nodded. "As I said, a major fight is brewing. The Court is evenly divided on several key legal issues. If there's no ninth vote, then the lower courts' decisions will stand as law. There are many powerful people who don't want that to happen. It may turn into something quite nasty, and, of course, poor Brian's condition would be the center of it all. Martha, if it should come down to that kind of scrap, it won't be dignified. Some politicians can be quite heartless. You've been around Washington for a while, surely you can appreciate what could happen."

She bit her lip and looked away. "It seems that everyone wants me to turn off those damned machines: my clergyman, the doctors, and to some extent, even my own children." When she again returned her gaze to him he could see that her eyes were wet. "But that would be like murder to me, Hugh. And that's something I really don't think anyone truly understands."

He remained silent for a moment. To protest now would only reinforce her determination. "I understand," he said simply.

She sipped her drink then rolled the rim of her glass slowly along her lower lip. "I pray every day," she said quietly. "I honestly ask for a miracle. I pray that one day Brian will open his eyes and everything will be just as it was." She paused for a moment, her shoulders seemed to sag. "I know in my heart that it's foolish, but I can't help it. Brian and I have gone through so much together. Some of it pleasant, some of it terrible. We've made a life for ourselves. I can't bring myself to switch off all of that, as if I were turning out some damned light." Her voice trembled as she spoke.

Dancer got up and walked to the windows. He looked out on a pleasant sweep of lawn. The condominium complex had been artfully landscaped. It looked like a park.

"Martha, I can fully appreciate the agony you must be going through. I come as a friend, and please remember I will stand by you no matter what you decide. However, as a friend, I must tell you the most unpleasant side to all this terrible business."

He turned and looked at her. "Do you want it sugarcoated, or would you prefer the bitter truth?"

She finished her drink, her eyes fixed on the picture on the mantle. "I prefer truth, Hugh."

"If you should decide to turn off the machines and Brian doesn't survive, I have been informed a full state funeral is planned. As you know so well, Brian loved the pomp and ceremony connected with government. He would be given a funeral in keeping with his high office."

"That's hardly comforting."

"I know. But if things continue as they are, a full-blown debate and fight will occur in Congress. A special committee has already been proposed. You know how these things go, Martha; television, the press, all the media have a field day. There are feature stories, speculation pieces; every damn magazine and newspaper in the country will call it a crisis in government. It'll sell a few papers. If it comes down to impeachment, and it might come to that, based on all the medical evidence, Brian may be removed."

A single tear trickled down one cheek. "That would be disgraceful." The words were no more than a whisper.

"I agree." He walked to her and gently patted her shoulder. "But I very much doubt that Brian Howell would like to go down in the history books as the first Supreme Court justice to have been removed from office by Congress. As it is, his term, short as it has been, has certainly been illustrious. He has really shaped the law of this country, Martha, and his decisions will be remembered for many years to come."

She looked up at him. Both cheeks were now wet although she gave no other indication of emotion, only silent tears.

"Life is full of hard choices," he said gently.

She stared up at the photograph. He returned to his chair and finished his drink.

"I think it would be in Brian's best interest if those machines were turned off," he said quietly. "A man's name and reputation are often more important to him than his life."

She said nothing.

"If the doctors are wrong and Brian can handle things on his own, then turning off the machines will make no difference. In fact, it would even provide some hope. I'm afraid there really isn't much hope in the present situation, Martha."

She did not reply at once but continued to stare at the photo on the mantle. Then she turned and looked at Dancer. "And if the doctors are right?"

"Then it's foolish to keep on with the machines, isn't it?"

"You make it sound . . . so simple." She dabbed at her eyes with a tissue.

"When you get right down to it, Martha, it is simple."

She studied her empty glass as if she had just seen it. "Did you come here to get an answer from me?"

"Do you mean, did somebody send me?"

"As you say, I'm beginning to understand how Washington functions."

He shook his head. "No, no one sent me. I'm a friend. I'm here on my own, Martha."

She looked up. "I'm sorry, Hugh, that was unkind. It's just that I've been under such a terrible strain."

"I know."

She again looked up at the photograph. "I want whatever is best for him," she said. They sat quietly in silence, an uncomfortable silence, then she continued in a firmer voice. "I'll have to allow myself some time to get ready."

"It's something that should be done quickly, Martha. It will just prolong the agony if you put it off."

She nodded slowly, her eyes seemed almost dead. "Buddy, my son, will have to be notified," she spoke just above a whisper. "He'll have to fly in from New York." She took a deep breath. "I'll call him today. If he can come tonight, then we can all go down to the hospital and see Brian tomorrow. Then I'll give the instructions. . . ." She started to cry.

Senator Dancer went to her and knelt down. He held her in his arms. She trembled but made no sounds, then gently she pushed him away.

"Thank you, Hugh. You are a good friend."

"Would you like me to be there tomorrow?"

"No. I think just Dorothy, Buddy, and myself."

He stood up and patted her shoulder. "It's for the best. And if the doctors should be right, Martha, it will be an honorable end for an honorable man."

She nodded as she covered her eyes with the wet tissue.

*   *   *

Senator Dancer waited until he got home before making the telephone call.

"It will probably be tomorrow," he said simply. "She wants her son there. By the way, I promised a state funeral, the full works. I think that's what swung the deal. I was sure you wouldn't mind, at least, not under these circumstances."

"No, that can be easily arranged."

"With this advanced warning, your people can start cranking up whatever has to be done," Dancer said.

"Yes. I certainly appreciate your splendid efforts, Senator. A very painful episode for you, I'm sure."

"It was."

"I won't forget this, Senator."

Dancer chuckled. "Trust me to make quite sure of that."

"Good night."

"Good night, Mr. President."

Chapter 6

"It was good of you to see me on such short notice."
Jerry Green took the extended hand.

"Please sit down, Mr. Green. It isn't every day that we are honored by visits from White House officials."

Green studied the man without appearing to do so, just a quick appraising glance. Martin Naham wasn't new to the duties of a university president, although he was brand new at Michigan State. President Martin Naham had served in that capacity at three small colleges before taking the Michigan State position.

Young, only forty-two, Naham was small of stature, but he had a trim, athletic build. He looked like the sort of man who was fond of competition; the kind who was without mercy on the racketball court. There was something about his eyes; a certain controlled fierceness.

Naham sat down behind his desk. "I certainly hope you aren't the bearer of bad news."

Green smiled. "No, not in the least."

The university president leaned back in his leather chair.

Every hair was in place. His shirt was perfect, his tie perfect, there were no wrinkles in his suit. There was nothing about him to suggest a pipe-smoking intellectual; no baggy sweaters or mismatched socks. The man across the desk was a hard-eyed executive who would be more at home in a conglomerate boardroom than at a faculty tea.

"All institutions of higher learning are experiencing hard times." Naham's voice was low and resonant, with the smooth delivery of a radio announcer. "It seems that every time an official drops by, we lose another grant. I hope your visit doesn't foretell any misfortune like that?"

"Not at all. However, in a way, I may be here to take away something valuable."

"Oh?" The hard eyes flashed as if challenged.

"I trust you checked on me?"

Naham didn't smile, just nodded. "Yes. You are a special counsel to the President. You told my secretary who you were when you made the appointment, but I'm sure you understand that we would check on anyone who said he was here representing the White House."

"That's only wise."

Naham half smiled. "We had a man in here last month who claimed to be a professor of history from Calcutta. He wanted to discuss a proposed student exchange. He turned out to be a short order cook from Detroit. The man had no intent to commit a crime or defraud anyone, he just liked the delusion of being a professor. The police questioned him. They say when he isn't grilling hamburgers he spends his time putting on his professor act."

"Convincing?"

"Incredible. Somehow he managed to acquire all the magic inside words, all the academic shop talk. He fooled me completely. It was only after we contacted the college in Calcutta that we discovered he was an imposter. It's lucky he wasn't applying for a job. On first blush, I'm sure he would be accepted by any academic selection committee, at least until they checked his credentials."

"I'll come right to the point," Green said. "I'm here to look into the background of Dean Roy Pentecost. He's in line for a possible federal appointment."

"The Supreme Court?"

"That's a possibility, obviously."

"We would hate to lose Roy. He founded the law school here."

"So I understand."

"That school has brought tremendous prestige to this campus. I'm sure, as a lawyer, you know the number of illustrious people he has attracted to his faculty."

"Yale and Harvard, I understand, are almost vacant."

Naham laughed. "Not quite, but close. In any event, our school of law is a national school and has become their equal, at least in my opinion."

"How long have you known the dean?"

"Not long, and unfortunately, not well. As you may know, I'm the new boy here. I started in August. Of course, I have talked to Dean Pentecost, as I have with all the deans of the respective colleges that make up this university. But I really am not familiar with him in any personal sense."

Green knew just how to handle the man. "You said something about government grants. I hope the federals haven't been giving you too much trouble."

"No trouble, just not enough money."

"Perhaps I can help in that area," Green said, and then quickly continued before Naham could comment. "I need to know if there are any skeletons in Dean Pentecost's closet, or any controversy about him, his family, or his job. I need to know all of this rather quickly."

"I presume the FBI has made one of its famous investigations, isn't that sufficient? After all, just as the rest of us citizens, the dean is entitled to his privacy."

"I couldn't agree more. However, this is something of a special situation. The job proposed carries such heavy responsibility that I'm sure the dean himself would want everything known."

"Have you asked him?"

"Eventually I will."

"Don't you think you should do that first? I suppose it could be done like one of those medical waiver things; where you authorize your doctor in writing to hand over information about you. That would seem to be a good first step."

"Cooperation, as we both appreciate, has to be a two-way street. I am not here to prepare a prosecution of the dean. This is strictly fact finding. I'm sure that when you were hired here they didn't rely entirely on your resume?"

The president laughed, but without humor. "No. It was a long process and several contenders were considered. When the selection committee was through I'm sure they even knew the color of my shorts. However, I wanted the job and I made it clear that everything about me was fair game; family, health, everything."

Green wanted a cigarette but he noticed there were no ashtrays around. "I'm afraid this is a much trickier business. I'll be candid. The job is on the Supreme Court. It is expected that Justice Howell will very probably die. That may be putting it bluntly, but it's true. The President cannot at this time indicate officially that he is actively sorting through possible successors. It would offend a number of people, yet it has to be done. Politically, we can't afford to have any press leaks about this business. If I were to go to the dean and ask him for this waiver you propose, it would all become very formal and very out in the open. Then if a newspaper happened to ask him about the job he would be placed in the position where he would have to lie. And that waiver would be floating around. So he would have to lie and risk being caught in it by his own waiver. That would be a no-win game. If he denied the situation now, the waiver might be produced later. That would reflect badly on him and the President."

"That makes some sense, although I don't entirely agree with it."

"Suppose you wanted to find out what made Roy Pentecost tick? Where would you begin? Who would you see? I know you actively screen many academics for jobs. This sort of thing must be old hat for you."

Naham's eyes narrowed. "I trust, Mr. Green, that if I am of assistance to you, I can expect some help if things get a bit sticky with the federal government and its grants?"

"One hand washes the other. That's true of government, and I know that's true of universities."

"You have an academic background?"

"My father was a professor here. My brother is presently a full professor."

"Oh?"

"Anthropology. My brother is Henry Green. He's on the faculty here. But what I know of university politics comes from my father."

"Including the saying that one hand washes the other?"

"Especially. He often said that a college's inner politics rivaled the worst of the Chicago ward wars."

This time there was genuine amusement in Naham's smile. "That's true. Unfortunate, but true. Now what can I do for you?"

The battle had been won. The price was on the table and clearly understood. President Naham was about to present him with the dean much as an ancient priest might present an offering for sacrifice. The god to be appeased was that distant giver of federal educational funds. Naham was a practical man.

"All right then, as far as the dean is concerned, has there been any trouble, or even rumors of trouble?"

Naham shrugged. "As I say, I'm a short termer here. I'm really not much of a source, but I know of nothing detrimental."

"Who would?"

"Malcolm Whittle is the assistant for faculty administration. He has a small office down the hall. Malcolm's job is simple; he rides herd on the faculty. It's his task to head off trouble. He's the one who supplies the lawyers, or the doctors, when needed. He's the resident fixer, as it were. There's always a Malcolm Whittle on every campus. Very valuable. If there was trouble, Malcolm would know."

Green wrote down the name.

"However, Malcolm is as tight-lipped as the Sphinx. You can imagine how many secrets he must know."

"Will he open up to me, if you order it?"

Naham hesitated. "I'm not entirely sure. He should. He's not tenured, so he can be fired. He knows nothing bad about me, so I have nothing to fear should I have to take that step. Yes, I think I could persuade him to help you, considering the circumstances."

"Good. Anyone else?"

"State Senator Lloyd Rock. He's a legislator from Detroit. He serves on several committees to which we must look for state funds. He's become Michigan State's self-appointed guardian angel. He keeps his beady eye fixed on everything here and he loves gossip, or so I've been told. He might help. Of course, you might hesitate to contact him. He's a politician and you might just get your press leak immediately."

Green wrote down the name. "That's very possible. Still, he might be useful later. Anyone else?"

"If I had been here a bit longer I'm sure I could have come up with a raft of names, but I'm afraid those are the only two who I can think of who might be of use. You could talk to some of the law students. Perhaps some of the members of the faculty. No matter how well a man runs things, he always has enemies. But I'm sure you had plans for that already."

"Yes. When could I talk to this Malcolm Whittle?"

Naham shrugged. "There's no time like the present." He

reached forward and depressed the intercom button. "Marie, please see if Mr. Whittle is free. I'd like to see him. As soon as possible, please."

The command was acknowledged.

"I'm not sure what kind of information you may be able to glean from our Mr. Whittle, but I think you'll find him most interesting. He is somewhere between a devil and a saint. It really depends on what you need at the moment." He smiled. "I shall ask Malcolm's cooperation. If a problem develops, please let me know."

"I shall."

"If the university needs help, I shall be quite free about consulting you, Mr. Green. Nothing is quite free, is it? So knowing that, you can feel quite free to take full advantage of everything offered now."

Jerry Green nodded. The polished dapper man seated across from him might not look like a devious, conniving ward heeler, but in spirit, Green sensed, there was little difference. For all his fine talk, Naham would cheerfully sell his mother if it appeared to be the expedient thing to do.

* * *

Patrolman Charles Garcia's regular partner was ill, so Garcia had been assigned Arthur Jefferson as his scout car partner. Jefferson was approximately his own age, and they had graduated in the same police academy class. Jefferson was black.

Although they had known each other since that time and had worked together before, there was a tension between them. The relationships between white and black officers in the precinct had become strained. The easy banter and racial jokes were gone, replaced by cold formality. The court case was the root cause. If the city won, Jefferson would continue working, but Garcia, and all the other white officers with his seniority, would be laid off. Also, it was understood that no white officer could aspire to promotion. A few would make it, but only as tokens. Otherwise, only the black candidates would be promoted. The city operated under a formula, approved by the courts, which gave special preference to black officers.

Garcia glanced over at Jackson as they got into the car. Except for the color of their skin they even looked alike. Jefferson, like Garcia, was darkly handsome, a touch under six feet, and athletically built. Jackson would soon become a sergeant. Thereafter he was assured of becoming a lieutenant eventually. From that point on, there would be competition, but only from other senior black officers.

Garcia always scored well on the sergeant examinations, but not high enough to earn selection as one of the tokens. So even if he were able to hold unto his job, Garcia knew there was no chance he could ever rise above the rank of patrolman.

He felt no major resentment at being foreclosed from promotion, but facing the actual loss of his job, solely because of his race, had embittered him.

"Quiet night," Jackson said as they turned into Romick Avenue.

"Yeah." Garcia made no additional effort at conversation.

They cruised slowly past a nearly deserted business section. It was late, only light traffic moved on the street.

"You ever have the mumps?" Jackson asked.

Garcia looked over at him. "Yeah, I think so. Why?"

"My boy's got 'em. Poor kid is swollen up like a frog."

"Did you ever have them?" Garcia asked.

Jackson who was driving, just shrugged. "I really don't know. My momma is dead, and nobody in the family can remember. The doctor suggested I get out of the house for a while, just in case. He says mumps can really do harm to an adult. I'm staying over at my sister's, at least for a few days."

"What about your daughter, has she had them?"

Jackson shook his head. "The way I look at it, it's best for the kids to get all those things when they're young. The doctor gave her a shot to ward it off or something, but I'd just as soon she got 'em and then we wouldn't have to worry anymore, at least not about mumps." Jackson laughed. "Of course, her momma don't quite agree. But then that's natural since she's the one who'd have to take care of her."

"Both of mine had chicken pox last year," Garcia said. "It wasn't much. They were sick for a day or two, then they were okay."

"Yeah. Kids have a lot of resiliency."

A dim night light glimmered in the rear of a closed clothing store. As they rolled by, Garcia studied the shadows in the store but detected no movement. He wondered what Jackson thought of the case, and their situation. He was tempted to ask. But perhaps Jackson felt a sense of exultation; he didn't have to worry about his job, or even promotion. He wondered if the black man felt pride or pity when he thought about brother officers like Garcia.

Garcia decided not to ask Jackson. It might lead to a useless argument. He wished the damned Supreme Court would do something soon. It was sheer hell to wait, to be suspended in time, unable to make any plans or even think about the future.

"Look up there," Jackson said sharply.

Two young men emerged from an all-night drug store. One carried a paper bag. They glanced at the scout car approaching, then quickly slipped into a walkway between buildings, disappearing from view.

"Let's check it out," Garcia said. As usual, he felt a rush of adrenalin at the promise of action. He was instantly alert.

As they roared up to the store, the night druggist came running out, holding a bloody handkerchief to his lip, his eyes wide with shock and fear.

"They robbed us," he shouted as Jackson rolled down the car window. "They came in and beat the shit out of me and the night clerk. They got all our cash!"

"Those two we just saw come out?" Jackson asked.

"Yeah, one has a gun."

"I'll follow them," Garcia jumped from the car. "Call for assistance, then swing up behind them on Halstead Street," he said to Jackson.

Garcia pulled his .357 Magnum and flicked on his flashlight. His mouth was dry with excitement as he ran between the buildings, trying to detect any sounds or movement, fully aware that they could be waiting for him. But he was experienced, and he figured they were probably running hard. If they were smart, they would split up when they hit Halstead Street.

Garcia jumped a rickety fence and ran through a rock-strewn yard. He caught sight of one of the robbers as he burst out into the lights of Halstead.

The man was fifty feet ahead of him, trying to run, but limping badly.

"Hold it!" Garcia shouted. "Police!"

The man's thin body seemed to sag as he stopped.

"Turn around," Garcia commanded, bringing the hammer back on his revolver.

The man turned. He held a small snub-nosed revolver in one hand. His hands were raised. He was a very young black man.

Garcia sighted on the middle button of the robber's jacket. "Drop the gun!"

The young man was frightened, his eyes wide and his mouth open. Garcia looked at the black skin. Almost involunarily he felt his finger tighten on the trigger. He wanted to kill.

"You heard the man! Drop the fuckin' gun!" Jackson shouted from somewhere behind Garcia. He had brought the car around as a backup.

The young man just kept raising his hands until his scarecrow-like arms were almost painfully straight up in the air. The pistol dangled from one extended finger.

"He's scared shitless," Jackson said. "Don't shoot."

"Why, because he's black?" Garcia's words sounded flat and foreign as he spoke them, as if the question had come from someone else.

The youth's gun tumbled from his shaking hand and fell clattering to the pavement.

The only sound on the street was the intertwining of distant sirens.

"Not because he's black, man." Jackson's voice was angry. "Because he wasn't goin' to use the fuckin' gun."

Garcia ignored him. He approached the youth, kicked away the gun, and then roughly handcuffed him. Garcia turned and glared at Jackson.

Both officers stood staring at each other. Whatever friendship they had ever known was gone forever.

*   *   *

Jerry Green had made arrangements to meet Malcolm Whittle later for dinner. Whittle, the assistant for faculty administration, promised to be a gold mine of information. Green stopped by his motel to freshen up and pick up his messages. He had three.

His brother Hank had called. Haywood Cross, the managing partner of his law firm, had also phoned. And there was a message from Chris Clovis, the young White House lawyer.

Green called his brother first and was surprised to receive an invitation to dinner, this time at the house. He explained about Whittle and agreed to come the following night.

Clovis, the White House aide, wanted to alert him that the university had been checking his credentials. It was old news, but at least it showed that Clovis was on his toes.

Green dialed the law office in Washington and worked his way through the network of secretaries until he got to Haywood Cross.

"Jerry, how good of you to call. How's the old hometown? Everything changed, I suppose?" Cross was being much too friendly, which was not his style at all.

"There's been some changes," Green replied, guardedly.

"There always is. What's that old wheeze—you can't go back again. Nothing ever remains the same, does it? Pity really."

"Sometimes. What's up, Haywood?"

"Jerry, the firm has been retained to prosecute the Marchall Company appeal in the Supreme Court. Are you familiar with the case?"

"I've read about it in the law journals and the news magazines. Big case. If the government prevails, they plan to go after General Motors. Antitrust suit, right?"

"Yes. The implications are enormous, both to American business, and to our firm. Obviously, if we can pull Marchall's chestnuts out of the fire we will not only make a very fine fee, but more importantly, we'll attract a whole new vista of important clients to us. It's probably the most important case Harley Dingell has had in twenty years."

"They're coming to us a bit late, aren't they? I understand that case is up for briefs."

"Well, yes, it is late. But we'll be working with Laritz Loring of Chicago, Marchall's usual counsel. They've done most of the work. They'll do the brief. The oral argument before the Supreme Court will be up to us."

"So? Do you want me to handle it? I thought Fred Casey was our Supreme Court man?"

A chuckle greeted his question. "Oh, he is. Fred will handle it. The justices are quite used to him and he knows them. As a matter of fact, it was Fred who suggested that I call you."

"Why?"

"Jerry, we know generally the reason why you're down there. Washington loves gossip, as you well know. This is no place to keep a secret. The conjecture is that you're there to check on that law school dean, what's his name, as a candidate for Howell's vacancy, should it occur."

"You understand, of course, that I really can't divulge what I'm doing."

"Certainly," Haywood Cross said quickly. "The President is

your client, and he is entitled to the protection of the lawyer-client privilege the same as anyone else."

"Why did Fred ask you to call?"

"Well, this Marchall case is a tough one, all sorts of political complications as well as legal. Fred believes the court will split again, four to four. If Howell gets well and can sit, his vote will make the difference. But if something should happen to Howell, then it is his successor's vote that will decide the issue. Fred feels it's that close."

"So?"

"Jerry, I've never been one to mix in political matters, so I really don't know how these things are done. But Fred seems to think you might be able to sound out the dean on how he might hold in the Marchall case. That is, if he is selected."

"And if he's opposed to Marchall's side I should block his recommendation, or push it if he's for our new client, is that it?" Jerry Green spoke openly despite Deering's warning about tapped phones. The possibility of bugged telephones was something Haywood Cross just wouldn't understand.

"Well, that's very blunt, Jerry. I'm sure Fred didn't have anything quite that blunt in mind. Naturally, we don't wish to misuse your position, but Fred thought the knowledge might be helpful."

"Haywood, I am Special Counsel to the President of the United States. I can't be part of any scheme to put someone on the Supreme Court just to win a case. It's a question of ethics and also possible criminality."

"Well, of course, but this isn't anything like that at all, Jerry. It's just that Fred thought the information might prove useful. . . ."

Jerry Green understood perfectly. A win in the Marchall case would bring in law business by the millions. And anyone in the firm who was reluctant to assist in that worthy endeavor wouldn't be with the firm very long, no matter what other course ethics might dictate.

Green wondered if all this was being piped into some spinning tape recorder. He had to admit to himself that such suspicions might be merely echoes of the past. In any event, Haywood Cross, in his bumbling way, was putting it on the line. Green's future with the firm would very much depend on how he handled this matter.

He began delicately. "Haywood, within the limits of ethical considerations, I may be able to do something. I obviously can't ask the man how he might vote. He isn't familiar with the Marchall case. But I'm sure the President also would be interested in the man's attitude toward suits involving big business. I can follow it up from that aspect."

There was a pause. "This is important, Jerry. I don't know if you fully realize just how important. . . ."

"Listen," Green said. "Let me say this just once, Haywood. In the event this conversation is being recorded, don't you think you should exercise just a bit more circumspection?"

"You can't mean that this is. . . ."

"I see you can appreciate the possibilities." He paused to allow his words to have the desired dramatic effect. "You can be assured, Haywood, that I will carry out my ethical duties. All my duties. I trust you understand exactly what I mean?"

Cross coughed, it was an embarrassed sound. "I hope I haven't compromised you."

"I don't think so. However, I should be back in Washington soon. We can talk then. Is that agreeable?"

Another pause. "Certainly. I'll look forward to it."

"Anything else on your mind, Haywood?"

"No."

"I'll see you shortly then." Green hung up the telephone.

He lay back on the bed and considered his position. It was illegal to tap a telephone without a warrant. To get a warrant, reasonable cause had to be shown. There would be no way such a recording could be used against him in a legal proceeding. No judge could possibly find cause to tap his telephone. But he knew that phones were tapped often, illegally, just for informational purposes. So there was a possibility that somewhere this short conversation had been preserved. And that could prove dangerous for a number of reasons, and to a number of people.

Taped or not, he fully understood Haywood Cross's message. He was regarded as the "political" partner, the outsider who had valuable connections. It was simple enough. Harley Dingell, although a silk-stocking law firm, obviously followed the old Irish adage that it is better to know the judge than to know the law. They merely wanted him to put in the "fix" with the prospective new member of the Supreme Court. It was simple indeed. The Chicago firm must have gotten wind of his assignment for the President. Green felt demeaned. Not only did his own partners think he would approach Pentecost on a pending case, but unknown lawyers from Chicago obviously thought the same thing. It didn't say much for his reputation.

The Marchall case, it was every bit as important as Cross said. He knew he would be expected to come through, ethics or not. There would be no room in the firm for a "political" partner who couldn't deliver when it counted. They weren't interested in abstracts like courage or honor. He remembered his father's story about the fierce courage of Mattathias whose actions in ancient Jerusalem had inspired a national revolt against oppression. No, Harley Dingell defintely had no interest in that sort of thing.

It seemed that his own future had suddenly become entwined with Dean Roy Pentecost's prospects.

All his feelings of security had vanished. This time the title wasn't going to be everything. This time only the results would count.

*   *   *

Malcolm Whittle had arrived at Gim Ling's before Green. He sat alone in a far corner at a table well removed from the others. An immense man, Whittle was vastly overweight. A crown of reddish hair, like a gamecock's plume, ran across his head from ear to ear. The front of his head was bald. His fleshy jowls seemed permanently flushed. His suit was wrinkled and his tie askew, but he had daintily tucked a linen napkin into the top of his vest. He waved as Jerry Green entered the restaurant.

"Sit down, Mr. Green," he said without getting up. "I hope you don't mind, I was famished so I started without you. They create fiendishly good egg rolls here and I am an absolute addict to them."

Green pulled up a chair.

"Have a drink. This is all on me, by the way," Whittle said, sending forth a spray of rice.

"Well, I think I would rather pick up the. . . ."

"Nonsense." Whittle habitually spoke with his teeth clamped together, giving his words a sharp, clipped sound. "I was instrumental in bringing over the owner's family from China. I put the arm on a congressman who owed me. And I am responsible for obtaining the liquor license here. So, as you can imagine, none of this is coming out of my pocket. I could eat here free forever, if I chose to do so. However, I make it a point never to abuse gratitude."

A young Chinese girl hurried to the table. Her lithe form was revealed by a clinging silk dress with a provocative slit up the side. She put a glass of water before Green and handed him a menu.

"He'll have a drink, Ah Sue. And tell Sam to make it a good one. This guy could mean a lot of money to the university."

She giggled. "What you want?"

Green smiled up at her. "Scotch and soda."

The girl made a little bow, her almond eyes fixed inquisitively on Green's. She turned and walked away with animal-like grace.

"That little broad would still be making radios back in Hong Kong if it wasn't for me." Whittle slurped his tea noisily, spilling some on his bib. "Nice little thing, but she has a hell of a time with the English language. Her uncle is the cook here. They try to keep him sober. But drunk or sober, he's the best damned cook to come out of Canton in fifty years. I got him in here, too."

"You make it sound as if these people are your slaves."

Whittle chuckled and put the teacup down. "It's nothing like that at all. I like 'em, and I like their food. I do them favors, they do me favors. I know you are a blue-blooded Washington lawyer, but believe me that's how the rest of the world works, my friend—it's favor for favor."

Green glanced at the menu. It was standard Chinese fare. "That's exactly what makes Washington work, too, only it's done on a truly grand scale there."

"It's done all over. The trick is to get a bigger favor in exchange for the one you're doing." Whittle's bushy eyebrows overshadowed small eyes, deeply set. His face seemed to have an almost sinister appearance. "You want to know all the dirt about Roy Pentecost, right?"

"That's putting it a bit strongly, but that's the general idea."

Whittle signaled and their tea pot was instantly replaced with a fresh one. "Allow me a small demonstration of my awesome powers." There was no smile, his shaded eyes seemed fixed on Green's. "You are Jerome Green. You're a University of Michigan man, a graduate of their law school, with honors. Your old man was an associate professor of anthropology here. You're Jewish, although I must say you don't look it. And I suppose you've heard that old wheeze before, eh? You grew up here. You've been divorced and have a teenage son by your first marriage. You remarried, this time to a lady accountant. You're a senior partner in Harley Dingell, a silk-stocking firm in Washington, D.C. And for some damn reason you just took on the job as a special counsel to the White House. I suppose it was to check out our boy, Pentecost. And it's my guess that as soon as you've done that, you'll hotfoot it back to the big firm and the big bucks." Whittle smiled, exhibiting large tobacco-stained teeth. "How'm I doing so far?"

Green kept from showing surprise. He calmly lit a cigarette. "Who did you talk to?"

Whittle grinned. "A few people here and there. Believe me, nobody can keep secrets from steely-eyed old Malcolm Whittle."

"So it seems."

Whittle swirled a forkful of egg roll around in a saucer of mustard sauce. He brought the dripping concoction up to his mouth and slurped it in, quickly washing it down with tea. "Some people prefer the plum sauce, sweet you know. But I like the hot stuff, clears the sinuses." He licked away a trace of mustard from his lower lip. "Actually, finding out about you was no trick at all. I already knew a bit. I merely called a Washington newspaperman and a political type and asked about you. Then I talked to your brother. See, just simple stuff."

The girl returned and served Green's drink. He took a sip before continuing. "You sound rather experienced at this sort of thing."

"I am. I damn well have to be." Whittle snorted. "It's my job to look after the faculty. Oh, other people take care of their pension plans, their little administrative problems, and the spats that develop between teacher and management. I have an entirely different assignment. What I do is to keep the sons-of-bitches out of trouble. It's just as simple as that. And it's a big job. We have over forty thousand students up here. That's a lot of ignorance on the hoof. We need over two thousand teachers to pound some knowledge into the little darlings."

Whittle demolished another egg roll. "I suppose you could consider me the resident 'fixer.' They call me that, but not to my face. If one of our wonderful professors gets caught flashing at Girl Scouts, or if one of our department heads get a snootful and starts shooting out car headlights, I'm the one the cops call. That's my job. I know every judge, I know every cop. Hell, I know every drunk treatment center and every drug abuse clinic in this state. I have to. God knows, I certainly send them plenty of customers."

"I presume that keeps you busy."

His main course was served and Whittle dished out a steaming mound of rice, then covered it with a thick orange sauce. "Ah Sue," he said to the waitress, "bring this gentleman some of that good sweet-and-sour beef." He grinned at Green. "You'll love it, that's the specialty of the house."

Green shrugged and the waitress hurried away.

Whittle went to work on his food, again with gusto and noise. He continued to talk, spraying small particles about, delicately picking at them with the edge of his napkin-bib. "Most of these academic types are quiet people; deep thinkers who take themselves and the world very seriously. Outside of an occasional suicide I seldom have any trouble there. But we got a few very wild folks up here too. All kinds. Listen, we got some sexual things going on up here that would make an old Roman throw up. But what the hell, that's their business. I don't care so long as the university doesn't get splashed in the mud. But if it looks like trouble's brewing, or that there might be some adverse publicity, then I go to work."

"What do you mean?"

"I've been doing this job for almost twenty years, and I've found most crap can be prevented if you get to it quickly. So you have to keep your eyes and ears open and keep a good line of communication going with a lot of people."

"You mean like a detective with informers?"

Whittle shrugged. "Yes, in a way. I'll give you an example. Let's say some menopausal woman professor starts giving head to our young leaders of the future, you know, she starts making a spectacle of herself. Now if I can find out about it in time, then I can usually do something before the shit hits the fan. I use her clergyman, family, medical people, whatever it takes. Usually I can put out the fire.

"Same thing with drunks. If we start picking up beefs from the students that some young assistant professor is missing his classes, we check with his pals, or even his enemies in the department. If it turns out that he's hitting the sauce, I go to see him. Most of them bitch like hell, but I usually have enough on them to force them into a drunk hospital for the cure, if they're really bad. It depends."

"And if they don't do what you ask, what then?"

Whittle gulped down a mouthful of food and patted his lips with his bib. "Like I said, I usually have quite a bit on them to begin with. But if that doesn't work, then I try a little peer pressure. I have their pals reason with 'em. And, finally, if that doesn't work then I usually frame their ass and force 'em to resign."

"Pardon me?"

"Does that shock you? Look, take the example of the old lady who is going down on half the campus. I use the clergy, family, whatever. It's done to help her at that point. But if she doesn't have the brains to jump at the chance I give her, then I have to protect the school. I set it up with the campus cops. They catch her on her knees. The student gets the shit scared out of him, and the woman, caught in the act, quietly resigns. I don't deal in abstracts, Green, I deal in results." He jammed some more food in his mouth. "And I deal in facts. Hell, I know more about the private lives of the people on this campus than the recording angel. And that knowledge is both my armor and my weapon."

"Armor?"

"You bet your ass. I don't have any tenure here, my job isn't protected. I can be fired anytime. And in a job like this you make enemies, believe me." He laughed. "Every new guy who comes in here as university president does the same thing. As soon as he finds out about me, he makes me number one on his 'to be removed' list. But within a couple of months he knows he can't do his job without my help. He needs me, or someone like me. Besides, by that time I usually know a few things about him that he would prefer to keep quiet. It's a rough world, Green."

"What do you know about Dean Pentecost?" Green asked.

Whittle wiped his mouth with the tip of his napkin and leaned back in his chair. His small, deeply set eyes seemed to glitter with something akin to malevolence. "You understand that I wouldn't be talking to you at all except that I have been commanded to do so by our president. He's new."

"And you don't have anything on him as yet."

Whittle laughed heartily, the loud rasping sound caused other diners to look around to find the source of the disturbance. "Blunt, but correct. You see, I use my inside information only for the benefit of the university. The new man should know that, but he doesn't. Not yet. But he will soon. So be it. Because of this accident of timing I am forced to let you see under the rock, as it were. Usually I'm the only one who looks."

The waitress brought Green's food. He waited until she had served the hot covered dishes and departed before he spoke. "Fortune smiles on me then. What do you know about Dean Roy Pentecost?"

Whittle had finished his meal. His bib bore a number of stains to attest to his poor marksmanship. He pulled out a long thin cigar from inside his coat and struck a wooden match. "I presume you people have had him investigated by the FBI, right? Security clearances, that sort of thing?"

"That's correct."

The billowing cigar smoke formed a cloud about the top of Whittle's head. "Then you know his basic background. He is forty-six years old. He is a graduate of Harvard and Harvard's law school. He served as a clerk to a Supreme Court justice after graduation. After that, as you know, he went into the teaching business. He's a miracle worker when it comes to law schools. He did a hell of a good job at two of them before he came here. He started our thing right from scratch. There had been a big political fight, a lot of people didn't want a law school here. When the legislature finally approved it, by one vote, those same folks wanted to see the school fail. And they did everything they could to kill it."

Whittle sipped some tea. "I have to admire Pentecost's guts, he beat the critics and the odds. I know I don't have to go over the details, you must know them already. But he won. And now we have one of the most prestigious law schools in the nation. We have a lineup of genius types trying to break their ass to get admitted here. The dean has written some legal crap, and like most legal crap nobody reads it but everybody says it's wonderful."

"As you said, I know about that part of his life."

"So now you want to know about the dirt?"

Although Whittle's endorsement was correct and the food was delicious, Green was too intent to eat. He merely toyed with his food as he spoke. "If there is any dirt, we would want to know it. A very crucial decision has to be made by the White House."

"Yeah, it wouldn't look good if a Supreme Court justice went around buggering goats."

Green raised his eyebrows.

"For Christ sake, I'm only kidding! You have my word of honor that Pentecost has never had sex with an animal, at least not to my knowledge." Whittle grinned. "Although we did have one guy in the journalism school who used to slip down to the barns and . . . but you're interested in Pentecost, not some old stories."

"That's right."

"Okay, I'll give it to you straight. He's a goddamned workaholic, if that's a vice. He spends every hour of his life concentrating on that law school. He's well organized and has a gift for wrangling large donations from rich folks and large companies. Everything he does is calculated. He really works at it. He uses computers and everything else that modern technology can offer. And he still manages the usual things a dean does; he welcomes the students at the beginning of the semester, holds bullshit meetings when they think they've been screwed, and generally takes care of the school's day-to-day administration."

Whittle slurped in some more tea, then continued. "He kisses the ass of those wise old men he lured away from the Ivy League joints. They're the magnet for the money and for the students, and he knows it. Whatever those old boys want, they get."

"Sounds reasonable."

"I agree. But on the other side of the coin, he treats the younger faculty members like galley slaves. He seems to go out of his way to make their lives miserable. We have quite a turnover of the younger law teachers. With the exception of one, and I'll come to that."

Whittle shrugged. "On the other hand, around the students he's like a politician, always shaking hands, smiling, that kind of crap. You'd think the job was elective. And if a student gets out of hand, Pentecost will bend over backwards before taking any disciplinary action. Actually, he has quite a bunch of solid competent instructors. The students are kept too busy to get into any serious trouble, so he can afford to be lenient."

Green accepted a fortune cookie from the waitress. He broke it open as she left. It predicted he would soon come into money.

"Pentecost doesn't smoke," Whittle continued. "And if he takes a drink he'll nurse the thing all night, so there's no problem there. I doubt very much if he has even smoked a bit of weed, let alone snorted coke. Not the type. He has no vices, as far as I know. He hasn't even made any passes at the secretaries. And I would know if he had. In other words, the son-of-a-bitch is a paragon of virtue."

"You make that sound distasteful."

"Sometimes it can be," Whittle snorted. "And there is another side to the coin. Pentecost is an overly ambitious bastard who wouldn't hesitate to cut your throat if it meant even the slightest advantage to him. He knows no loyalty except to himself. I get the impression he's the type that kisses the bathroom mirror every morning. The man really likes himself."

"What do you mean, no loyalty?"

"My opinion, nothing more. I just know the type, that's all. He has all the compassion of a computer. If something will benefit him, then he's for it. And if not, he's opposed. It's a simple world for people like Pentecost. He will be your friend just so long as you are in a position to do something for him."

Green waved away some of Whittle's cigar smoke. "Aren't we all guilty of that, at least to some degree?"

Whittle's eyes narrowed. "Your old man wasn't. I knew him. For that matter, I knew you too. Does that surprise you?"

"Yes."

"I was new on the job in those days. Your old man had something you don't see much anymore—integrity. You know, integrity's like good art, it's hard to describe, but you know it when you see it."

"And me?"

Whittle laughed. "Hey, if you were a bad kid I didn't know about it. I did know about your brother though."

"Hank?"

"You got any other brothers?"

"No."

Whittle snapped a match and touched the flame to the now-dead cigar. The resulting smoke was almost poisonous. "Your brother was one of the world's greatest studs. When he went to school here I thought he was going to corner the market on causing pregnancy. I often thought the local abortionists should have erected a statue to him. Jesus, he'd just walk by those young coeds and they seemed to get pregnant."

"And you got him out of trouble?"

Whittle nodded. "A half dozen times at least. I never told your old man about it. Your father knew one or two things about honor. It would have really hurt him. I kept it to myself. What the hell, everything turned out all right. Your brother settled down, more or less. Nowadays he's a model husband and father, and that's something I never thought I'd live to see. He's drinking too much, but I suppose that's just middle age crisis catching up."

"I'm surprised about the drinking."

"It happens. So far it's no big deal. He gets plastered quietly at home. I'm keeping my eye out, just in case."

"For his sake, or for the university's?"

Whittle's eyes narrowed. "For the university. As I say, that is my job. I see the dark side of people. And there is a dark side to most. But not with your father. He was a hell of a guy. I hope some of that rubbed off on you. It did on your brother. That's what saved him from being a bum."

Green nodded. "As fascinating as my family might be, I'm here to find out about Dean Pentecost. So far, you haven't exactly opened up the secrets of the universe as far as he's concerned."

Whittle signaled for a fresh pot of tea. "Funny, you can never make tea like this at home, no matter what kind you use." He studied his little porcelain cup before continuing. "There is a problem with Pentecost's old lady."

"His wife?"

Whittle's fleshy face revealed his disgust. "Yes, his wife. She's a perfect ice queen, just the right type for display at faculty teas. She looks like a New York model; nice-looking if you don't like blood and are fond of bones. She is a chilly, indifferent woman. Oh, she does volunteer work and all of the other usual stuff expected of a dean's wife. I told you Pentecost has a high turnover of young teachers at the law school, except for one, right?"

"Yes."

"Well, that guy ain't ever going to leave. Because every time the dean goes out of town on a trip—and he makes a lot of trips to drum up contributions and promote himself—this young stud comes over and gives the ice queen a jump."

"How do you know this?"

"Well, as you can imagine, she doesn't advertise it. And lover boy never comes to the house after the dean is gone. They meet at a Jackson motel, twenty miles south of here."

"I asked how you know?"

Whittle helped himself to some fresh tea that had been brought by Ah Sue. Green declined as Whittle offered to refresh his cup.

He continued in a low voice. "They had a young guy on the

faculty in the English Department. He was an instructor working toward his doctorate. But he wasn't good enough to cut it. They told him he should forget it. He went down to that Jackson motel, got drunk, and damned near killed some bimbo he had picked up."

Malcolm Whittle again slurped in the hot tea. "Like I said, I know all the cops, and the Jackson boys called me as soon as they identified our little hero as belonging to us. He was screaming about how unfair the old university had been to him. I handled it. I took care of the bimbo's hospital costs, plus giving her a little something for her trouble. The kid resigned without a whimper. It was that or go to jail. Anyway, it was then when I found out about the lovely Mrs. Pentecost."

"How?"

"While I was at the motel, the cops were interviewing other guests, getting statements about the screams and so forth. And who do they flush? Why none other than the icy Mrs. Pentecost and her young assistant professor of law. I saw them, but they didn't see me. They gave the cops false names."

"Maybe it was just a one time thing."

Whittle shook his head. "No. I checked. Everytime the dean leaves town she motors on down to that same motel. Not smart, but then we are all creatures of habit, aren't we? I've been keeping an eye on it because that kind of thing can cause trouble. But they are discreet and they keep their noses clean. And I don't anticipate the dean coming in one night and blowing them away."

"Do you think he's capable of that?"

"He'd be pissed that she was screwing one of the younger members of his staff, that's what would make him angry. If she was humping the university president or the chairman of the trustees he'd probably cater in a towel service. No, even if he did find out, he's not the type given to violence. He would just use it against her, as a lever for something he wanted. That's how I figure him."

"You don't paint a very appetizing picture."

"Truth can be ugly, and often is. But what the hell, there are a lot worse than him. I know, I see them."

"You don't like ambitious people, do you?"

"Sure. Some of my best friends are ambitious." Whittle laughed. "But ambition without integrity is nothing. Do you know who said that?"

"No."

"Your father."

Chapter 7

The day had proved frustrating. Although he had learned a bit more about Pentecost, it wasn't enough. But that was not on his mind. Now he felt nothing but a growing sense of apprehension.

Jerry Green drove along the winding streets, following the directions and watching for his brother's address. Although it was already dark most of the expensive homes had carriage lamps outside and their glow made the street scene look like the background for a slick magazine advertisement picturing the ultimate American success: the big house, well kept, surrounded by expanses of clipped lawns.

His brother's house was a two-story colonial with an attached garage. Both a front carriage light and a spotlight over the garage blazed in the night. It seemed as if every room in the house was lit.

He had never been here before. The house was something new. It had been so long ago, that exploding unpleasantness. He could still remember the shouting, the sudden eruption that had severed the bond between them. It was a bitter memory. He presumed it would be equally bitter, if not more so, for Hank, his wife, and perhaps even his children. He hoped the evening wouldn't be too unpleasant.

Green parked on the concrete apron in front of the garage.

He stepped out of the car and breathed deeply, inhaling the crisp night air. There was a feeling of snow. None was predicted, and even though he had been away from Michigan for years, he still retained his native ability to sense weather changes.

The side door opened and Hank held out his hand. His other hand contained a very large glass. Green remembered Whittle's remarks about his brother's drinking.

"Hey, Adele, it's Jerry!" Hank Green gripped his hand and pulled him inside, leading him down a long hallway and into a large living room.

She stood there. Adele was a different woman, much heavier, her dark hair streaked with gray, and she wore glasses. He remembered Adele as she had been, with a spectacular figure and a wild, almost wanton look about her. Now she looked like someone's frumpy grandmother.

She took his hand and lightly kissed his cheek, but there was no attempt at an embrace. She had not forgotten.

"You look wonderful, Adele," he said, drawing back. "Eternally young."

She smiled but her eyes held no sparkle. "You look well, Jerry. You've changed. I really don't think I would have recognized you on the street." She paused, studying him. "You look more like . . . well . . . you look like Hank. There seems to be more of a resemblance now."

"She's trying to say that you've become better looking," Hank said. "How about a drink? What'cha want?"

"What'cha got?" Green answered, mimicking him as he used to do when they were young.

Hank laughed, reminded of that more pleasant time in their

past. "I got more kinds of booze than the best bar in New York. Just name it."

"Scotch."

"Soda?"

"Jesus, we're standing around here like we were at a convention," Hank said. "Give me your coat and sit down."

Green surrendered his overcoat and sat in one of the living room chairs. Two sofas and two matching chairs had been arranged to form a square around the brick wall fireplace. A family picture had been placed at one end of the mantel. A large framed photograph of their father was at the other end. There was nothing else on the long mantel.

Adele perched her ample form on the arm of a sofa.

"Beautiful place, Adele," he said. "When did you move?"

She thought for a moment. "Oh, five or six years ago. This place was just the right size for our family then. But now that the children are moving away it's really too big. I'd like to move into one of those condominiums."

"I live in a condominium in Arlington. I like it."

"Hank says you were divorced. Do you stay in contact with Alice?"

Green felt uncomfortable under her gaze. Women were dangerous. They plowed right ahead without any regard to tact or sensitivity. They all seemed to be controlled by a primal sense of curiosity.

"I haven't seen her in years. I see David once a year for a short visit. When you last saw him he was just a small boy. He's sixteen now and grown. Alice is married to a dentist in Oregon. We correspond when necessary about David. You know, just the usual things, school business, health, trips, that sort of thing."

"Was it bitter?"

"You mean the divorce?"

"Yes."

He shrugged. "No more or no less than the usual, I suppose. We just came to the point where we couldn't stand the sight of each other. Although it wasn't exactly an amicable parting, we did manage to refrain from physical violence. It seems that being three thousand miles apart is just about right. At that distance we can tolerate each other."

"And you're married again, Hank tells me." Her tone hinted at an underlying disapproval, as if somehow he was being unfaithful to his former wife.

"Yes. My wife is an accountant. Second marriage for both." He paused, sensing her next question. "No children."

"She had no children by her first marriage?" Adele's raised eyebrow showed her definite disapproval.

Hank reentered the room carrying a small tray with brimming glasses. "Hey, Adele, let him alone." He grinned as he handed a glass to his brother. "If she was a prosecutor we wouldn't have a crime problem. A real third-degree artist, my wife."

"It's normal," she replied evenly, almost sternly. "When you haven't seen a member of your family for a number of years, it's normal to want to know about his personal life. I'm not being nosy."

Hank handed her a drink, then set the tray on a table, and slouched down in one of the sofas. "Okay, so you're normal."

Green sipped the scotch. His brother had made the drink very strong. Usually, he would have resented it, but there was an unusual tension in him, almost a fear, and he felt that he could use the assistance of a little bottled courage.

"Do you ever see many of the old crowd?" Green hoped to draw the conversation away from himself.

"Yeah. Hell, I see everybody," Hank replied. "Outside of you, I can't think of anyone who ever left here. If you stick around for a while you're bound to run into them. They all work around here. Remember Elmer Jobst?"

"The stork?"

"Yeah. Big and lanky, remember? Looks just like he used to, only now he's bald. He has three boys, all of them as tall as Elmer and all of them just as awkward." Hank Green laughed at a memory. "He lives just down the street. Sells insurance."

"He owns an agency," Adele corrected him.

"Same thing," he growled at his wife. "It's weird, I suppose, to spend your entire life surrounded by the people who went to high school with you. It's like being inbred. Christ, you know everybody and everybody knows you. This might as well be Pitcairn Island. . . ."

"Washington is a city of strangers," Jerry Green said. "You know only the people you work with, maybe a neighbor or two, but that's it. Carol and I lived next to a cabinet member for two years and never even met the man."

"That stranger business can have its advantages," Hank said, smiling. "Hell, if Adele and I get into a shouting fight the next day the whole place knows about it. This isn't a small town anymore, but it doesn't matter. The inner community, the league of the old boys and girls, they know. Same thing if a man or a woman wants to screw around. How the hell you going to keep it quiet if the motel owner is an old school chum?"

"That never seemed to have bothered you." Adele said it lightly, but there was a sting in her words. She sipped her drink, her eyes emotionless.

"Ah!" Hank gestured with his hand is if pushing the whole subject away. He took a long pull at his drink.

"How are the children, Adele?"

It was a happy choice. She seemed to relax as she began a long litany listing the situation and accomplishments of each of her five children. She spoke of her oldest daughter but did not mention any problems with abortions or drugs. He saw his brother wink at him as Adele went on painting a picture of the perfect American family. Green sipped his drink and listened. It was interesting. Adele was correct, it was normal to want to know the intimate details of one's own family. Hank refilled both their glasses while Adele continued on with her family history.

The children were gathered up to meet their uncle. They appeared to be less than enthusiastic. Aaron, tall and pimply, carried a worn Bible in his hand. His long stringy hair had been tied at the back of his head. He mumbled something about Jesus and left. Rachel, "Cha Cha" to her friends, eyed him provocatively. She had developed too fast. They would have trouble with her. She was petulant when she was informed that she was housebound and would serve as babysitter for her four-year-old sister. Jerry Green knew that but for his presence an all-out family war would have exploded. But it was contained, concealed within snapped words and hard looks. The little girl, Emily, was a charmer, but they all were at that age.

The children had eaten their dinner earlier. Aaron had departed and Cha Cha reluctantly lead her charge to the family room and a quiet evening of television.

"Hey, Adele, tell him about our surprise."

Adele had seated herself in one of the chairs. "Your surprise, you mean. I'm not sure it was such a hot idea, Hank."

"Nothing's a great idea to you, Adele." He turned to his brother. "You were asking about the old crowd, right?"

"Yes."

"I figured you'd be interested so I arranged for some folks to drop by for some after-dinner drinks."

"Who?"

"Guess." His brother's face seemed to lose its age in his animation. His features somehow seemed more near the face of the brother Jerry Green remembered.

"Oh, just tell him," Adele said, getting up. She turned to Jerry Green. "He always likes to play games. I have to finish some things in the kitchen." She flounced out. The extra weight was especially evident as she walked. Her once lovely legs were thick, almost masculine.

"Remember Jimmy Whales?"

"Sure."

"He was your best friend, right? All the way through school."

Jerry Green nodded.

"Well, he and his wife . . . I don't think you've ever met her . . . are coming."

Green felt a flush of excitement as memories were unlocked. He conjured up the picture of the red hair and freckled skin.

"Not only did I line up your old best friend, I snagged your old girlfriend, too, how about that?"

Suddenly Green felt close to panic. "Regina?" It was almost a whisper.

"Sweet Regina. None other. Like I told you the other day, she's a widow. She's a nurse and she teaches at the college. Still looks damn good too. She was very excited about seeing you."

Jerry Green finished off the second drink. Like the first it had been strong. He felt his head swimming. "Anybody else?"

"Oh, I contacted a couple of other people. You're still popular. They wanted to come but they just couldn't make it. Hey, how about another one? Adele will kill me, she thinks booze kills the flavor of her food. But between you and me, sometimes that's a good thing."

Green was going to refuse but the shock that he would see Regina again sharpened his anxiety. He didn't want to get drunk, but he felt he just might need one more drink. He held out his empty glass to his grinning brother. Hank left to get the drinks.

As Green sat alone in the living room he reflected on the fact that none of them had even come close to mentioning the last time they were together. The memory of that incident lay like an invisible wall between them. He wondered if they would ever talk about it. He knew he would never bring it up. Some things were better left alone.

*　　*　　*

Physically Jimmy Whales hadn't changed. His hair was still red, although a bit muted. His skin was just as fair and freckled. He looked youthful with the same bright blue eyes and that half smile, so well remembered, still perpetually fixed on his pleasant face. But the old energy, the remembered lust for life had flown. Despite his appearance, Jimmy Whales had become an old man. During the evening Green had tried to recall memories of their youthful adventures, but every time escalating feelings or wonderful recollections were killed by Jimmy Whale's preoccupation with the woes of his business. No matter what the subject, somehow Jimmy always managed to return to the somber, almost desperate world of his car dealership. He had taken over his father's business and it had become the only thing in his life. His wife, a tired-looking woman who had heard all of Jimmy's woes before, tended to drink a bit too much. She said nothing important or revealing, just nodded and tried to be pleasant.

Regina Kelso was different. She was thinner than he remembered, and her attractive legs seemed even longer. Unlike Jimmy Whales, she had aged, but it seemed to have magically improved her appearance. She was a bit thinner in the face and even that accentuated the delicate structure beneath her still-unwrinkled skin. She was lovely. Her long blonde hair was gone, replaced by a short businesslike cut. But the hair itself was just as fine and blonde as in years past. Her large green eyes hadn't changed, except that now they were gently accentuated with sparse but artfully applied makeup. Her eyes were just as intelligent and as full of laughter as he had remembered. During the evening he kept stealing glances at her, vividly recalling the warm relationship they had shared, that soft beauty of youthful love. She was still just as appealing. He found it difficult to concentrate on Jimmy Whale's stories of the do-or-die struggle connected with moving unwanted makes of automobiles.

His brother, Hank, tried valiantly to turn the conversation to other things. But Hank was older than the others and they had no shared experiences except those impersonal community happenings in the past.

Regina said very little. He often found her looking at him. Hank and Jimmy Whale's wife both were drinking two for every one consumed by the others. It was having its effect. Mrs. Whales slipped into extreme quiet, her eyes half closed. But Hank was becoming loud. He started recounting stories about friends his own age, exploits of fellow football players and athletes. Adele began to snap at him as his stories drifted from merely off-color to disgusting.

"Well, this certainly has been a real pleasure." Jimmy Whales looked over at his wife. She had a placid, distant expression on her face. "But I have to get to the office early tomorrow. I'm trying out a new man for service manager. If you get the wrong guy he can ruin your business. It takes a certain type; half-technician, half-con man. And they don't fall off the trees, either." He was about to launch into another tale of car merchandising when Adele stood up.

"Jimmy, it seems we never see each other except at shopping centers anymore." Her tone left no doubt that the Whales were about to leave. "Maybe when your business eases a bit, you and Marie could come for dinner."

Marie Whales just nodded.

"Yes, that would be nice." Jimmy Whales helped his wife up. "Well, it's been a real kick seeing you, Jerry. You look great. I always knew you'd go far."

"It was good seeing you too, Jimmy." Jerry Green shook his old friend's hand. The man he faced was not really the boy he had grown up with. Somewhere a change had taken place. The red hair and the face were the same, but the personality he had known and loved had long ago departed, washed away by the everyday stresses of adult living.

"Hey, Regina," Hank said as she started to get up. "Don't go." She had come with the Whales. "Stick around for a bit. Jerry

will give you a ride home. That's if you think he can be trusted."
He laughed.

"Jerry can always be trusted," she said smiling. "But I do
have an early class. And I should get home and see if my children
left anything still standing."

"I have to go in a few minutes myself, Regina." Jerry Green
felt as if his face was flushing. "If you don't mind, I'd like to drive
you home."

Her eyes seemed to be laughing in quiet amusement. "Like
old times?"

Suddenly he remembered the prolonged kissing at her door. It
had been the only time when she would permit herself an
expression of real sexual passion. Safety was just behind the door
so she could abandon all reserve. The promise of those wild kisses
had always excited him. He knew he was undoubtedly coloring
now. "Desirable," he smiled, "but not probable."

She laughed. He wondered if she remembered those long
goodnights too.

"All right. I'll stay for one more drink," she said, "but then I
really have to go. There's a constant war between my fifteen-
year-old daughter and her twelve-year-old brother. They need
their mother as a referee."

After the Whales left, the atmosphere was even more
strained. Adele clearly disapproved of Jerry taking Regina
anywhere. Adele had a rigid code, and Jerry was a married man.
But she said nothing. Hank didn't seem to notice Adele's dis-
pleasure. He was visibly drunk now and loudly recalling a high
school game when they couldn't see the markers because of the
snow.

Regina seemed relaxed and quite in command of the
situation. If she sensed Adele's disapproval she gave no notice.

Hank mumbled something about refills but stumbled and
almost fell on his way to the kitchen. Adele snarled and Hank
replied in kind.

Jerry Green seized the opportunity to leave. He said he really didn't want another drink, and that he too had to be up early. Adele made polite noises, the expected things, but Jerry knew that she would be just as glad if this was the last time she ever saw him. Hank was far gone, just mumbling something about family. Jerry Green helped Regina put on her coat and was again impressed at the way she had kept—perhaps even improved—her figure.

Snowflakes whirled past the outside garage light. A white dusting already covered the ground. He recalled that snow came early in Michigan. He helped Regina into the car. He unlocked the driver's side and climbed in.

"Did you think someone would steal the car?" There was amusement in her quiet voice.

He laughed. "Not really. It's just a habit. You can always tell us big-city folks, we lock up everything. It's second nature."

"I live in a condo at Lake Wilson. Do you know where that is?"

"No. I don't remember a Lake Wilson."

"It's not far from here. It used to be a farm. If I could recall the name of the farmer you would remember, but I can't. A developer named Wilson bought it and now we have a little city of condos on the shore of a small man-made lake. There's two rows of units in the development. One row is built along the side of the lake, and the other fronts on a nine-hole golf course."

"Sounds nice." He started the car, switching on the wipers to clean the windshield. He backed out carefully, using the side mirror as a guide.

"It is nice. I love it, and so do the children. I'm ten minutes away from the campus. The schools are close. It's all very convenient."

"Hank said you're a widow." He drove slowly, the snow was sticking and making the winding road slippery.

"Technically, that's wrong."

"Oh?"

"I divorced my husband. He died shortly after that."

"You had nothing to do with that, I trust?" He laughed but

instantly regretted it when he saw her solemn features outlined by the dashboard lights. She was looking straight ahead.

"It was a very tragic thing. I can talk about it now, although for years I couldn't bring myself to discuss it. I was carrying a very heavy load of guilt."

He made no reply. He was acutely aware of the snow. It was coming down hard, making it seem as if the rest of the world had disappeared.

"Turn right when you get to the stop sign," Regina said quietly. She paused for a moment and then continued. "My husband was a schoolteacher. He taught English. After about nine or ten years of marriage he began to experience a personality change. It was caused by a brain tumor, but no one discovered that, not me, not his doctors, no one. You know, it was one of those things where you all agree afterward that you should have known but no one did at the time. Frank, my husband, was a quiet, decent man. Suddenly he became extremely abusive. He went into rages and took out everything on the children and me. It was very bad. I left him, went back to work, and filed for divorce.

"Frank became much worse. He lost his teaching job. He even landed in jail for assault. He didn't oppose the divorce and it went through quickly. He had a convulsion about a week after the divorce. They took him to the hospital and he died in the emergency room. They found the tumor when they did the autopsy. The doctors told me that it was positioned so that even surgery wouldn't have helped. They told me there was nothing anyone could have done for him even if the tumor had been discovered. I'm not sure that was correct. At least we could have made his last days more comfortable."

"And so the guilt?"

"I suppose. I'm a nurse. I should have known, and that's what I had to carry around, the conviction that I should have known what was happening."

"Hank says you teach at the school of nursing now."

"Turn left at the blinker ahead. Yes. After high school I went to Providence Hospital's nursing school in Detroit. They had a two-year program to become a registered nurse. I married Frank and I worked for a while until we had the children. It's funny, but despite the tumor and the madness, Frank somehow found the money to keep up his life insurance. I've often wondered if somehow he didn't sense what was happening to him. Anyway, the insurance wasn't a great deal of money but it was enough to allow me to enroll in the university and pick up my nursing degree. And I added a master's degree. I worked at Sparrow Hospital and I did some clinical teaching. They asked me to join the full-time faculty and I jumped at the chance."

"Do you like it?"

"Jerry, I love it. I don't think I really can explain why. It's just something I look forward to doing each and every day. It's fulfilling for me. And I can work my teaching schedule so that I can be home with the children when it counts. You know, I can remember talking to your father about things and he spoke of the pure satisfaction to be found in imparting knowledge to young minds. I didn't fully understand it at the time, but I do now.

"When you come to the traffic light up ahead, don't turn, go straight, but be careful, the road narrows into just two lanes."

"How about your kids? That must have been a terrible thing for them, about their father, I mean?"

"Yes, it was. In one way we were fortunate, the change in Frank was very fast. It was a very bad time but it was short, thank God. However, I watch both of them closely. A terrifying childhood experience can lie dormant and then one day pop up as a roaring neurosis. So far, there doesn't seem to be any harmful residue, but I keep a weather eye on them both."

"How long ago was that, Regina, when your husband died?"

"Six years."

They drove in silence for a moment, then he spoke. "Can I pry a bit?"

She laughed. "Depends. Try it, and if it's off limits I'll just ignore you, okay?"

He knew he should keep his eyes ahead, the driving was difficult, but he glanced over at her. Her look of high amusement seemed to almost taunt him.

"You're a beautiful woman, Regina. How is it that you haven't remarried?"

She didn't respond at once, pausing as if composing an answer. "Well, as you can imagine, the shock of the divorce and the death numbed me for quite a while. I have known other women who reacted in similar circumstances in an entirely different way. But I wanted no personal relationships. Then there was school. I had to work part time, take care of two small children, and go to college full time. It was demanding. Nursing is no longer just popping a thermometer in a patient's mouth, Jerry. It's as difficult as being a physician, sometimes more. We really have to know what we're doing. Anyway, with the years spent in school I had no time for any kind of a personal life. It was on purpose. I had to wrestle with my own problems and hard work was therapy for me." She stopped speaking and looked out at the snow.

He waited but she didn't continue. His headlights glared back at him from the thickening fall of snowflakes.

"Don't leave me hanging, Regina. Go on."

She laughed. It was the same laugh that used to excite him so when they were young, a sound that held a delicious sensuous promise. It was no song from the Lorelei that lured boats to their destruction, he decided. It was a laugh; low, throaty, and full of promise. He could understand risking a ship for a sound like that, a sound like Regina's laughter.

"What you want to know, Jerry, is whether I have any boyfriends."

He was about to deny it, but then mutely nodded.

She giggled. "If you're looking for stimulation, I'm afraid you're on the wrong track. My love life is as exciting as day-old bread. I once had a mad two-month fling with a young resident at Sparrow Hospital. He was younger than me. He left me for a better residency in a hospital in Boston. Unlike most nurses I'm not really too fond of doctors, they all seem to acquire a God complex sooner or later. He was the only doctor I ever dated. I never wanted to get the reputation as the official pin cushion for staff physicians."

"That happens?"

"In hospitals it happens all the time. There seem to be a lot of sexy people there. I knew one anesthesiologist who had been married four times in twelve years. He was the hospital's champion stud. He juggled his time between his latest wife, four nurses he saw regularly, and two society girls who called the hospital night and day trying to reach him. He really needed a trained diplomat for an answering service."

"Jesus, and I picked law."

She laughed. Again the sound sent a pleasurable chill through him. She was truly an exciting woman.

"I date two men now. Usually, it's just for concerts or an occasional dinner. Both are professors. Neither gentleman wishes to become the automatic father of a fifteen-year-old girl and a twelve-year-old boy, so things haven't become very serious."

"You expect me to believe that?"

She giggled again. "My God, don't tell me you haven't changed? Jerry, you can't still be jealous after all these years?"

He tried to laugh, but it didn't sound convincing even to him. "Mad with jealousy," he said. "Do you remember when I punched Raymond Sedmak?"

"Yes." The word was whispered. "I remember. You thought he danced too close with me."

"You didn't speak to me for days after that."

She sighed. "That was just for show. I was so flattered that it's really impossible to describe. I told my daughter just the other night about how you had fought over me. Most of what I tell her doesn't impress her at all, but that really left her wide-eyed."

He chuckled at the memory. "God, I was angry. Poor Sedmak, I belted him before he could even see it coming. He was bigger, and if they hadn't stopped it quickly he probably would have broken every bone in my body. I risked life and limb, and then you got sore."

"It was put on, Jerry. It was expected in those days. If girls didn't react that way, every high school dance would have turned into a bloody carnage, you know that."

He switched on the defoggers. He was having trouble seeing as the snow blew against the windshield and there was no oncoming traffic to clue him as to the path of the roadway.

"It's getting bad," he said.

"It's not too far now. At the next stop sign, turn right. You go about a half mile down the road and my complex is on the right."

The blowers began to defog the window but the snow seemed to be increasing in intensity.

"What about you, Jerry? Hank said you were married, had a son, got divorced, and then remarried. Tell me, without violating the marriage vows, what about your love life?"

Suddenly he felt depressed, almost ashamed. He didn't know why.

"Nothing much to tell. Hank seems to have covered the territory."

"Your wife, your present wife, what's she like?"

"You know, I think there's some built-in compulsion in the female sex, they always want to know everything about other women."

"Probably. But as you lawyers say, you're evading the question. What's she like?"

"My age, a few years older actually. Second marriage for both. But I suppose Hank's told you that already. No children. She's an accountant and has her own firm. Highly successful woman, very intelligent."

"You could say the same thing about a computer. I asked what she was like."

For a moment he was speechless. Regina had meant it only as

a joke, but she was right, Carol was very much like a computer; slick and sleek, like a well-designed piece of machinery, she operated without any demonstrable emotion. It was the lack of typical feminine reaction that had first attracted him. Her reserve was so refreshing in contrast to the violent mood swings of his first wife.

"Like you, she's blonde. She's a pretty woman, very chic. If you're interested, we share a very cool relationship. There's no trouble, we are just two professionals who share space, but not each other's interests."

"You sound unhappy, Jerry."

"And you're thinking maybe I'm saying all this as though I were some on-the-make traveling salesman at a bar—I'm married, honey, but the wife don't understand me—is that it?"

She laughed. "You do that well, it sounds practiced. No, I don't think that. I know you too well. I'm sorry your marriage is like that, Jerry."

The car started to skid. He turned the wheel into the spin and brought it under control. "Well, what marriage is like the movies anyway? We get along, we don't irritate each other too much. I know a lot of couples who would trade places in a minute."

She didn't say anything, but he could feel her eyes on him.

He was surprised at his own thoughts. He really hadn't realized fully just exactly what the relationship between himself and his wife had come to. It was a convenient arrangement, cordial, comfortable, but really without love, or for that matter, even commitment. He had always been too busy to really analyze it before.

"You'll see two stone gateposts coming up on the right," she said. "Just slide in between them. It's a winding street. You have to follow it to almost the end. I'll point out my apartment."

As predicted the posts appeared through the swirls of snow. The car slid as he turned, but he was able to guide it successfully between the two stone sentries.

"Is your wife Jewish?" Regina asked.

The question surprised him.

"No. She's a White Anglo-Saxon Protestant. Why?"

"Oh, I don't know. I suppose just curiosity. You remember that was a big thing with my father."

"My being Jewish. I remember. That was my first experience with the full meaning of the word 'tolerate.'"

She laughed softly. "Oh, those were different times, Jerry. My father took Catholicism very seriously. His ultimate concern was that any grandchildren be baptized and raised Catholic. I really don't think he was anti-Semitic."

The street curved sharply as he slowed to maneuver past rows of snow-covered cars. "Well, whatever his reasons, he put me through hell in those days."

"Yes, I know." Her voice was soft and quiet.

"Well, maybe it really wasn't hell, but he sure made me feel uncomfortable when I came to call for you."

"But that wasn't because of you."

"What?"

She laughed, the sound again was deep, almost pagan, and terribly exciting. "It was because of your brother. My father knew about Hank's reputation. They said he had sex with every girl in his senior class, except Mary Jane Reilly. Mary Jane became a nun. She spoiled his record. Anyway, my father knew all about Hank and he thought you were a carbon copy. That's why the freeze. I always thought you knew."

"No." He shook his head. "Good old Hank. I certainly have a lot to thank him for."

She giggled. "I'm sorry. Do you see that light on the left? That's my place."

He eased the car into an empty parking space. The snow quickly covered the windshield when he stopped. He flicked off the lights but did not turn off the motor.

The light from the porch was like Hollywood backlighting,

causing her shadowed face to have a dramatic, moody quality.

"I've enjoyed tonight, Jerry," she said. "It was such fun to see you again." She paused. "You're a handsome man. I guess I'll just have to chalk you up as the one who got away, won't I?"

Her eyes were hidden in shadow and he couldn't detect if she was being playful or serious.

"Damn it, Regina, you make me feel as if I had never left, or aged. If Sedmak was here I'd punch him out again, just for starters. You seem to weave a special kind of magic."

"You're sweet." She leaned toward him and lightly kissed his cheek.

Without thinking he grabbed her and twisted her around, just as they had done in his father's car. He kissed her fiercely, consumed with an almost raging hunger. He gripped the back of her hair with his hand. To his surprise and delight, she responded with passion, the remembered passion of old. They said nothing, each clasping the other tightly as they continued to kiss.

Suddenly she broke away. He was on fire and reached for her but she held out a restraining hand. "Don't, Jerry," she whispered. "I don't think I'd be able to stop."

"Those were the very words you used to say to me. Oh, Regina, it's like . . . like. . . ."

She opened the car door and stepped out. She turned and smiled at him. "My children may be watching out the window. I would hate for them to see their poor mother raped, wouldn't you?" She was laughing again.

"I have to see you, Regina. I must. Please!"

She hesitated for a moment before answering. "You're a married man, Jerry. I'm really not in the market for one-night stands."

"It's not like that, and you know it. Please. Have dinner with me tomorrow night. I won't touch you, I promise." He felt desperate. "Look, I know you won't believe me, but I just need to talk to you, Regina. I need that very much."

The snow was beginning to cover her hair. "I believe you," she said softly. "All right. Could you pick me up here tomorrow about five, if that's convenient?"

"Yes."

"I'd ask you in, Jerry, but I have to see that my children get to bed." She laughed, but this time more quietly. "Besides, I don't know if I could trust myself. Good night, and be careful driving back."

She turned, walked to her door, and was gone. He sat there for a moment, his heart pounding. It was as if time had been rolled back. He felt the same remembered joy, excitement, and promise.

No other woman in his life had ever aroused him the way Regina Kelso did. The years had changed many things, but not that.

* * *

"Charley, this is a hell of an hour to get up. It's still dark." Abby Simmons climbed into the car, grateful for its warmth.

"This is the only time you can see for yourself what I been telling you. There's a good northwest wind blowing and at this hour there'll be damn few cars on the bridge." Charley Pesta, the man who spoke, was thickly built. His heavy rugged face had the leathery look of a person who spent much time outdoors.

They sped away from Abby Simmon's apartment house and headed toward the bridge.

The old highway veered gently and the roadway became smoother as they moved onto the new paving put in when the bridge was built. They climbed the gently rising incline toward the bridge itself.

The bridge was ten lanes wide with a toll booth for each incoming lane. Only one booth had the green light on. The others had their booms lowered and were dark and unoccupied.

The booth attendant slid his window open just enough to take the money. He handed out the change, then snapped the window shut to conserve the warmth generated by his small electric heater.

The bridge was well lighted but deserted. They drove out on the main span, some two hundred feet above the river.

"Charley, the signs say you can't park here," Abby Simmons remarked as the car rolled to a stop near the edge of the bridge railing.

"We only need to stop for a moment. Besides, there's no traffic anyway. Come on."

The stout man laboriously climbed out of the car. The wind was strong and the cold breeze chilled Simmons as he too stepped out onto the bridge.

"The wind has to be from the right direction and over fifteen miles an hour to make this happen," Charley Pesta said. "Grip the railing, then look through the railing slats, and fix your eye on something on shore, a light for instance, and then watch what happens."

Simmons obeyed the instructions. He chose a place between two rail struts and sighted on a shore light close to the base of the bridge. As he watched, the light seemed to move, shifting from one opening in the rail to the next. He peered over the railing to make sure the light on shore was fixed. It was. He sighted on a different opening. The wind freshened and it happened again.

"The bridge is swaying," Pesta said. "You can't feel it, but you can see it, right?"

Simmons nodded. His companion climbed back into the car and Simmons followed.

Simmons welcomed the cozy heat of the auto. Pesta put the car in gear and began to drive slowly over the rest of the bridge. The wind buffeted their vehicle.

"It's a pretty view from way up here," Pesta said. "You can see the lights of the city over there. They look like a field of diamonds, don't they? And the dawn can be spectacular when you see it from up here." They began their descent the other side. "I used to drive over this bridge every day, going to and from work."

"So the bridge sways in the wind," Abby Simmons said.

"What's the big deal? I understand all bridges are designed to sway in winds."

The other man slowly shook his head. "You're thinking of suspension bridges. A sway factor is built into them, otherwise they'd whip around and snap their cables."

"And you're telling me there's no sway factor in this bridge?"

"Nope, not this kind. It's all steel and concrete. The supports are supposed to hold that thing as steady as a rock."

"I saw it sway."

"Right, and it's getting progressively worse. Eventually that entire main span will break off. I showed you the cracks in the supports before. That's why she's swaying, those damn supports are unstable."

"Do you think they used inferior materials?"

"No. I don't think they allowed for the gross weight on the bridge during rush hours. Every morning and night, for about an hour each way, the cars are jammed up here bumper to bumper. I don't think the architect allowed for all that concentrated weight at one time. She just isn't built for it, and that's what's breaking her up. At least, that's my educated guess."

"You're the city engineer, why don't you do something?" Abby Simmons lit a cigarette. They picked up speed as they left the bridge and moved onto the regular highway.

"I'm not the city engineer, I just work for him. I'm a building inspector."

"But you are an engineer, a qualified engineer?"

"Yep."

"Then why don't you go to the county authorities and tell them about this?"

Pesta shrugged. "I did."

"And?"

"I talked to the head county engineer. But this bridge was his baby in the first place. He listened to me, even went out there with me. He said the cracks were a normal settling process. And that was that."

"There must be someone else you can give your information?"

"Not unless I want to lose my job. Nobody likes a public servant who goes around making waves. That's why I came to you, Mr. Simmons. I thought your paper could bring the whole thing out."

Simmons nodded. "I wrote the story."

"When are they going to run it?"

"They aren't. They have a law in this state that can make newspapers liable for revenues lost through what they term journalistic negligence. My editor didn't think we had enough evidence to take the risk of running the story."

"That's odd."

"It's because the damn thing is a toll bridge. If people stopped using it because of our story, and we couldn't prove in court that it was unsafe, we could be stuck for all the lost tolls. And my editor feel that's too big a risk to take."

"How about the swaying? Maybe he'll do something when you tell him about that."

"I doubt it. There's a case now before the U.S. Supreme Court testing that state law. If the law is struck down, we'll run the story."

"How long will that take?"

"I'm not sure. It still has to be argued up there. Six to eight months probably."

They were driving through the city now. "I sure hope that bridge holds up that long," Pesta said.

"Do you really think it really might go down soon?"

The other man shrugged. "I'm not sure. Somebody would have to do tests, stress tests and things like that to really find out. Somebody would have to be really interested because those tests cost a lot of money. Look, I'll be frank. I don't know when it will fall. It could stand there for twenty years, or it could go down tomorrow. I don't know the 'when,' I just know that eventually it will fall."

Simmons said nothing, just inhaled deeply on the cigarette.

Pesta continued. "If that sucker goes down during rush hour, it will take sixty or seventy cars along with it. It's a long fall to the river. I doubt if many would survive, even if they could get out of the car before it sank."

"God, that many?"

"That's just counting the cars. Counting car pools, couples, and so on, you have to figure a loss of a hundred people. Of course, if she went down during the night, you'd only lose the few who zipped in before it was discovered."

"And you honestly think it can fall?"

"As I said, I used to drive it every day. I take the long way around now. I drove over it just now but that was to show you about the sway. I stay off the damn thing." He paused, then continued. "It's a shame you can't alert the people who use the bridge."

Pesta looked over at him. "I thought you guys could print anything you wanted to."

"Yeah, so did I," Simmons said. He rolled down the window and flicked out the cigarette. "But then I believed in Santa Claus until I was almost sixteen."

*   *   *

The headwaiter escorted Professor Harold Orwell toward Jerry Green's table. Orwell walked with military bearing, spine straight, shoulders back, his chin elevated slightly. He moved very well, displaying none of the usual uncertainty of movement associated with old age, although he was nearing eighty. Tall, lean, and with close-cropped white hair, he sported a British-style white mustache. There was a definite aura of imperial elegance about him. He cooly surveyed the others in the restaurant much as a reviewing general might inspect troops whom he suspected to be less than battle ready.

Green stood up and extended his hand. "Professor Orwell, this is a pleasure."

The man's grip was firm although a bit tremulous. Orwell nodded and took the chair the headwaiter held in readiness.

A waiter appeared almost instantly. "Can I get you something from the bar?"

Green looked across the small table at the tall man who sat as he walked, straight and military.

"I should prefer coffee," he said in a strong, deep voice. Orwell made an effort to smile although it looked as if he was out of practice in that expression. His teeth were too perfect, obviously a plate. False teeth seemed grossly out of place in such a magnificently aristocratic face.

"Scotch and soda," Green said.

The waiter hurried away.

"*Orwell on Torts* was our case book at law school," Green said. "Meeting you is like talking to a historical figure."

The cool blue eyes flickered over Green for a moment. "That's what I am, a historical figure. I worry constantly about being kidnapped by agents of the Smithsonian and put on display like Lindbergh's airplane. After all, I am considerably older than his *Spirit of St. Louis.*" A small smile curled beneath the trim mustache. "What school did you attend, Mr. Green?"

"The University of Michigan."

The professor nodded. "Not Harvard, of course, but respectable. I understand you're with Harley Dingell, on loan to the White House?"

"Yes."

"Well, then, to business. The president of this godforsaken university asked me to meet with you. He said you would be interested in my observations of Dean Roy Pentecost. He asked me to be candid, which is redundant in my case, since I am always candid."

"You don't like Michigan State?"

The white eyebrows raised in mock astonishment. "Have you ever put any time in here? And I mean it just that way, putting in time."

"My father was on this faculty. I was raised here." Green snapped out the words.

There was no change in the old man's stern face. "Obviously, since you are now in Washington, you left this agricultural center as soon as you reached the age of reason and could escape. Please don't protest, your actions speak louder than any words." The icy eyes seemed to sparkle. "Mr. Green, they say the football field here is covered with that false grass carpeting—astro something or other—so that the homecoming queen won't graze during half time."

"That's an old joke, invented by the people at the University of Michigan."

"Perhaps. In any event, in answer to your question, Mr. Green, this is the mid of the midwest. As a cultural center, it leaves something to be desired. In other words, sir, this is not Boston."

Green felt a growing irritation. "If you miss Boston, why not go back?"

This time the smile was a bit wider. "Do you know why I left in the first place?"

"You got a girl in trouble?"

The icy blue eyes grew even colder, and the long face became stern. "You know, Mr. Green, I came here prepared to dislike you. But perhaps we shall get on after all." A short staccato burst of laughter erupted from the thin lips. "I wish to God it had been that. At my age sex has become just a memory, a fond memory, mind you, but no more than that. No, Harvard was about to make me professor emeritus. In other words, I was being given the sack. Oh, the money would be there, and maybe once a year they would trot me out for a lecture, provided I hadn't become too senile. But as far as Mother Harvard was concerned my active teaching life was over."

Their waiter brought Green's drink and then poured the professor's coffee.

"It was just then that your Mr. Pentecost came a-calling." Orwell took a tentative sip at the coffee. "I have a theory, possibly erroneous, but I believe in it. If a man quits, gives up so to speak, then he starts going downhill. I did not wish to become a doddering old man confined to a nursing home to be fed baby food by some illiterate moron. So between my imagined nursing home and Michigan State University I chose the later. I am active. I keep a full schedule, as a matter of fact, much fuller than my old duties at Harvard. I am, therefore, a vital productive human creature, and I plan to keep it that way for as long as possible. However, as I say, this is not Boston. Culturally, it is as distant from Boston as is Hindustan, as far as I am concerned."

"Better than baby food, though."

"Much. But enough about me, although it is my favorite subject. You have some questions, I believe, about the man who rescued me from diapers and bed sores."

"Based on that statement, I take it that you're one of Dean Pentecost's fans."

The old man's thin lips again curved into just a hint of a smile. "The young men and women of this area, and on this campus, are unable to verbally express themselves without employing that ancient Anglo-Saxon word 'shit.' It is a word not unknown in Boston, but it isn't used as the mainstay of one's vocabulary there. Here, on the other hand, it can be used as a verb, noun, and anything else including a heartfelt exclamation of admiration. Since you come from this area, you are, I presume, familiar with the word?"

Green laughed. "And several others."

"Oh yes. Well, to speak as a native of this region might, and in answer to your question, it is my considered opinion that Dean Roy Pentecost is a shit. Not only a shit, sir, but a perfect shit. It is very difficult these days to find perfection, but the dean has attained it." He sipped his coffee again.

"As America's leading expert on torts, I presume you know that you have just commited slander." Green grinned.

The old man cocked his head. "It depends on where the alleged wrong takes place, Mr. Green. Here in Michigan truth is a defense. Therefore, I feel that no dent will be put in my purse because of my words."

"How is it that you feel this way? As you say, the man did rescue you from retirement."

The waiter returned and they ordered.

Professor Orwell returned his menu to the waiter and continued. "In all fairness, I did him more good than he did me. As you say, my name has become rather associated to the word 'tort.' Just like old Wigmore. It was always *Wigmore on Torts* until my book came along. Anyway, my being here attracted other professors and a number of serious students. A sort of a snowball effect occurred. A few well-known professors gave this place credentials. Then more joined because of that prestige. Pentecost, by the way, is a genius at manipulating publicity. As you know, in the nation's press this became the miracle school, a beacon of learning shining out in the dark night of ignorance. Students who ordinarily would have found their way into the Ivy League, or even your old school, soon started beating at the door of this cow palace." He stopped and finished his coffee. "You are, I believe, looking Pentecost over for a possible place on the Supreme Court. Is that correct?"

"Well, that's been suggested."

The blue eyes flashed. "This lunch was your idea. You're the one who wants information. A simple answer with no evasion is a small price to pay, Mr. Green."

Green could well understand the terror felt by generations of law students. The old man hadn't raised his voice, or even changed inflection, but his words seem to cut like a lash.

"Yes, it is the Supreme Court."

"Howell's spot, if he pushes off, I presume?"

Green nodded.

The old man remained ramrod straight as he talked. "If you were considering Pentecost for a cabinet position, or some post in the executive branch, I would give him a glowing recommendation. The man is a gifted administrator, organizer, and, as I say, public relations expert. He could run any federal department very well indeed. Unfortunately, he is a foggy-headed lawyer who has no real feeling for the basic processes of justice. He just doesn't understand it. And you can't teach him. It's an impossibility, like trying to teach a blind man about color. Well then, that is my beloved dean. He is many things, but he is no lawyer."

"What about his book on constitutional law?"

The waiter returned with their food. Green asked for another drink. The professor picked at his plate for a moment, then returned to the subject. "Ah yes, the book. Well, as I say, the man is a gifted organizer. If you read the dedication in that book of his you will find at least forty names listed. They were students of his at the time. And they are the people who actually wrote the book, sir. Pentecost merely served as a sort of senior editor, if that. As I say, he can organize very well."

"What would happen, do you think, if he were appointed to the Supreme Court?"

The faint smile reappeared. "Probably be running the place within a few months, no matter who the chief justice was. He's that kind. But he would make all his decisions based upon considerations other than legal."

"A lot of that happens now."

"Always has. These are men, not angels. The history of the Supreme Court, the real history, is full of self-serving men. But if appointed, Roy Pentecost would end up as number one in that particular hall of fame. He would always do whatever was expedient at the time. He would view each decision in light of what it could do for him personally. Justice, abstract or real, would be the last thing he would consider, if at all. He lacks integrity. Do you understand the full implication of that word, sir?"

"I think so."

"I doubt it. Not many do. The dictionary defines integrity as the adherence to moral and ethical principles. In other words, sir, it means a man must sometimes do the unpopular thing because of morality. Brother Pentecost is quite incapable of that."

"That's rather harsh."

"Is it? He has the classrooms bugged. Did you know that?"

"Pardon me?"

"Oh, not mine. Or Johnson's. Or any of the other recruited professors who drew the faculty and students here. Even he would not dare to do that. But the junior faculty, the younger instructors, all are recorded by listening devices. The law school building was designed by Mr. Pentecost. Like Mr. Nixon, he likes to know exactly what is being said. The whole place is wired."

"Why doesn't someone complain?"

"They have. They took it to the university trustees. Pentecost pointed out that such devices are common in many high schools and other teaching institutions to monitor the instructors. That was the reason he gave, it was done to insure excellence in teaching."

"He may be right. What other motive might he have?"

The old man did smile. The teeth again seemed very out of place. "To discover faculty disloyalty, sir. Just one joke about the dean and that man or woman is out. Big Brother is listening."

"I doubt if he has the time."

"Oh, he doesn't. He uses third-year law students, and only a handful whom he feels he can truly trust. They listen and monitor all that goes on."

"But he doesn't bother you?"

Orwell shook his head. "No, he knows better." His cold eyes seemed to lock on Green's. "Perhaps the bugging is forgivable, or at least understandable. But I have had a number of discussions with Pentecost and he is just not a lawyer. Oh, don't misunderstand, he has a degree with honors, but despite that, he just doesn't think like a lawyer. He's clever. So if you seek a self-serving, clever man on the Court, pick him. However, if you desire a lawyer with basic integrity, look elsewhere."

"You honestly feel that strongly?"

"I am of the opinion that the American people, once in a while, would enjoy a little justice with their law. They won't get it from Pentecost. I wouldn't trust him to decide a traffic ticket. On the other hand, if you're looking for, say, a secretary of defense, he may be just the man for you." Orwell's false teeth, exposed by the wide grin, looked almost mechanical.

Chapter 8

Dr. Kaufman was waiting for them on the floor. His round face was somber.

"You know my son and daughter," Mrs. Howell said to the doctor. "This is Mr. Whitefield. He is our pastor. He was kind enough to come along."

Kaufman shook the clergyman's hand. Both men merely nodded to each other.

The hospital page system called for a Dr. Pringle, repeating the call again and again in a well-modulated but metallic sound. Nurses and doctors bustled about with their usual energy and purpose. The hospital seemed alive with noise, movement, and life. To Martha Howell it all seemed dreadfully inappropriate.

"I'm not sure what we are to do," she began.

Dr. Kaufman looked increasingly uncomfortable. "It's customary for the family to wait in the critical care lounge. They have coffee there. We try to make people as comfortable as we can," he coughed nervously, "under the circumstances."

"I want to be with Brian when the machines are stopped,"

Mrs. Howell said quietly. "I want to be with my husband at that time."

"Mother!" Her daughter's exclamation showed her disapproval.

"I really don't think that's wise, Ma," her son added, his own voice taut with emotion.

"Wise or not, I will be there," she said evenly, "or the machines don't get turned off."

Dr. Kaufman coughed to clear his throat. "I think your children are right, Mrs. Howell. Sometimes it can be quite unsettling."

"Mother, please." Her daughter grabbed Mrs. Howell's arm. The older woman pulled away, her mouth tight, her eyes determined.

"I insist," she said firmly.

"Then we'll all go," her son volunteered.

She looked up at him, almost angrily. "No. He is my husband. We have faced everything else together. We will face this together."

The son looked over at Dr. Kaufman and slowly shook his head.

"All right." Dr. Kaufman looked at Mrs. Howell and spoke quietly, almost inaudibly. "Come with me."

He lead them to the critical care lounge. It was a bright cheery room with modern, comfortable furniture and racks of magazines. A bored middle-aged woman dressed in a blue and red volunteer uniform sat behind a desk idly reading a paperback. She looked up at them. "You can visit for five minutes on the hour, and then only if the staff permits. You must sign the register."

She seemed oblivious of Dr. Kaufman.

"That won't be necessary," he said.

"They have to register, doctor. That's hospital rules." Her tone showed she would stand her ground.

Kaufman's somber expression quickly turned to anger. "Get the hell out of here," he snapped.

"What?"

"Get out of here"—he looked at her name tag—"Mrs. Webster. Report to Mrs. Grant, the volunteer program chairman. I will be down shortly to talk to her."

The woman stood up. "Now look here, doctor. . . ."

"Get the hell out of here or I'll throw you out. Is that clear?!" Kaufman snarled the words. His anxiety was being translated into exploding anger.

The woman's defiance was quickly replaced by fear. She grabbed her purse and book and rushed for the exit.

"I'm dreadfully sorry about that," Dr. Kaufman said, his voice still trembling. "These volunteers can be wonderful, but sometimes we do get some oddballs." He composed himself and sighed. "Are you sure you won't reconsider, Mrs. Howell?"

"I want to be there." It was a simple statement, but there was determination behind the softly spoken words.

"Would you like me to come along?" the clergyman asked.

"No, thank you, Mr. Whitefield."

Mr. Whitefield looked relieved.

"All right then," Dr. Kaufman said. "Please make yourselves comfortable. Come with me, Mrs. Howell."

She nodded meekly. She accompanied the doctor who seemed to be walking much more slowly than his accustomed brisk pace.

They stepped out into the bustle of the hospital corridor with the sound of its tinny page calling yet another doctor.

"As I told you," Kaufman's voice became slightly stern, "your husband has been clinically dead for quite some time. In other words, he is not dying today, that happened quite some time ago. You understand that?"

"I understand what you told me," she answered.

"When the machines are turned off sometimes the body reacts. There can be movement, sometimes even thrashing about. The tissues, the muscles are demanding oxygen. Sometimes, Mrs.

Howell, it can be quite gruesome. I wish you wouldn't expose yourself to this."

"I want to be there," she repeated, her words spoken as if she were mindlessly reciting a memorized litany.

They walked into Justice Brian Howell's room. Two other doctors and a tall, young nurse waited next to the bed.

"This is the hospital's cardiac care team, Mrs. Howell. They are here to assist me."

"Assist you?"

Kaufman nervously bit his lip. "Actually they are witnesses, Mrs. Howell. Your husband is no ordinary patient. It was felt by the hospital administration that there should be witnesses."

She looked at the quiet figure in the bed. The respirator made a slight whooshing sound. "Like at an execution?" Her eyes were on the face of the man in the bed as she spoke.

Dr. Kaufman sighed. "No, Mrs. Howell. Not at all. These are qualified medical people and they are here to observe."

She said nothing but walked to the side of the bed. Tubes ran into the naked arm of her husband. She carefully reached past the intravenous lines and took her husband's hand, locking her fingers into his. She felt the warmth of his flesh, she watched the sheet as the chest showed shallow but regular breathing. She studied the sleeping face for quite some time. There was no conversation. The doctors looked away. The tall nurse's jaw muscles worked silently beneath her smooth skin.

"I love you, Brian," she said gently.

The only reply was the sound of the respirator.

"All right," she said, never taking her eyes from the sleeping face, "I'm ready."

Kaufman stepped past the other doctors. He quickly snapped off several switches. The blue accordionlike respirator came to a stop within its plastic container. The sound of the respirator and the pinging noise of the electrical support systems ceased. The sudden silence in the room seemed accentuated.

Mrs. Howell cried out as her husband's hand tightened on hers. The doctors rushed forward as a great shudder rippled through the body. His eyes opened as the head jerked loose from the respirator intake.

"He's alive! Turn the machines back on," she shrieked. "He's alive!"

The contortion ebbed, then ended.

Mrs. Howell, her hand gripping her husband's, turned to the doctors, her eyes like a maddened animal's. "Turn those machines on! Oh, you bastards, turn them on now!"

She dropped the hand and rushed for the switches. The tall nurse stepped forward and put her arms around her. Mrs. Howell struck at the girl but did no damage.

"He's dead," the nurse said in a kindly whisper. "Please, he's gone. You can see for yourself."

She gently turned Mrs. Howell around. There was no mistaking what had happened. Brian Howell lay with dead eyes, his limbs lifeless.

"He's gone," the nurse said. "I'm sorry."

One of the doctors moved to the body and closed the staring eyes. He only partially succeeded, one eye was still half open.

Mrs. Howell returned to the bed. She picked up the dead hand and softly kissed it.

Dr. Kaufman waited a moment then he took her by the arm. "We must inform your family," he said.

She did not resist as he guided her from the room. She did not cry, there was no expression on her face, just a blank lost look.

"Damn," the nurse said angrily, her voice shaking. "Why the hell do they let the family see these things?"

The younger doctor answered. "They don't usually, as you know. But maybe the lady was right. It was a bit like an execution. He was an important man, a justice of the United States Supreme Court. We turned off the switches and that was the end of him. Not too much different, I suppose, than hitting the switch that puts the zing in the electric chair. Anyway, we were here to record the legality of it all."

"Will there be an autopsy?" the nurse asked.

"Hell, yes. That's to protect Kaufman's ass. The pathologist is waiting down in the basement for His Honor here. He'll find the stroke damage and make a report. It has to be done quickly though. I understand they're preparing a big funeral, lying in state at the Supreme Court Building, gun carriage parade, the works."

"These things always give me the creeps," the nurse said. "It really is like watching an execution."

"Well, this had to be done. I understand the deceased here was holding up a lot of judicial progress."

"Not anymore he isn't," the other doctor said.

The paging system penetrated their consciousness as a code blue was called: a patient was in cardiac arrest. The team rushed out of the room. No longer witnesses, they were back in their element where death was the foe to be fought.

Impersonally and without a trace of emotion the paging system kept repeating the code blue call.

* * *

Jerry Green eased himself into the barber's chair. It was a unisex shop but the feminine decorations and soft pastel colors made it look more like a beauty parlor. Only the barber looked out of place. He was a small thick-set man whose hairy, muscular arms were revealed by the short sleeves of his white tunic. His skin was swarthy, his thinning hair jet black. There was no expression in his hooded dark eyes. He looked half asleep.

"Did Mr. Whittle tell you about me?" Green asked.

The barber nodded. "You want a styling or just a trim?"

"A trim, very light. What did Whittle tell you?"

The barber placed a yellow bib around his shoulders and chest. The bib had a plastic odor.

"He said you wanted to know about Dean Pentecost."

"That's right."

The barber used his hands to cock Green's head to the desired angle, then went to work with the scissors producing a steady machinelike clicking sound. "I don't know what I can tell you. I just cut his hair, that's all. It's not like we were close friends or anything like that."

"He's not in trouble," Green said. "He's being considered for an important job in Washington. We're just doing a background check. It's more or less routine."

"Are you with the FBI?"

"No, but I am with the federal government."

The barber just grunted. He turned Green's head to a new angle.

"What do you want to know?"

"Anything. Everything. What kind of a man is he? What do you hear about him?"

The scissors clicked away. "To me he's a nice guy. He comes in about once a month. He tells me it's important to look well-groomed in his job. I suppose he's right. He has to make public appearances, give speeches, and that sort of thing. He comes in regular. His secretary makes the appointment. He likes to come in the morning when it's not busy. That's about it."

"What does he talk about?"

The barber stood back and thought the question over. "I don't know. He comes in, maybe we make a little small talk about the weather. Like I say, he's always pleasant to me. Maybe we talk about how the college teams are doing, you know, football, basketball, the usual college sports."

"How about women? Does he ever talk about them?"

The barber shook his head as he returned to working on Green's hair. "Naw. You know, some guys will come in here and give me a line about the babe they made it with the night before. Half the stories are pure baloney, but I guess it makes them feel like big men to brag. But the dean never talks like that. He don't even look at them girlie magazines."

The barber laughed. "We get all them magazines here. It helps business. Even the women look at them. Most of the people wouldn't be caught dead lookin' at them things in a drug store, but they'll sit here, patient as hell, going through them page by page and having a ball. But I don't ever remember the dean even taking a peek."

"How about politics? Does he ever talk about that?"

"It's the same as sports. If there's been something big happening we might talk about it. Nothing serious, just small talk. That's mostly all you get in this business, small talk. It's as much a part of the job as the clippers." He laughed. "I like the kind of customer who climbs in the chair and brings a magazine to read. Then my job is easy, I don't have to try to entertain them."

He used a comb to prepare the hair for the scissors. "But most of my customers like the personal contact. That's how the dean is. He just sits there and we chat about little things. He's a heavy tipper and a barber always appreciates that. Nice man, at least to me."

"You've said that several times; that he's a nice man to you. Have you ever seen him be otherwise to anyone else?"

"Just once." The barber's hand smoothed Green's hair.

"What happened?"

"Hey, I don't know if I should even be telling you this. Look, I've been cutting this guy's hair for a couple of years and it's the only time anything happened. He probably just had a bad day."

"Probably, but I like to hear about it anyway."

The barber shrugged. "It was six or eight months ago. We had more business than usual that morning. There were a couple of women getting their hair done and one of the local businessmen was getting a haircut. The dean was sitting in my chair, same as always, when this young guy walks in.

"Well, from what the dean was yelling I got the drift. It

seems that the young guy was a teacher at the law school. Apparently the dean don't let those guys out of the school in the mornings. This young teacher said he had no class to teach and had just ducked over to get a quick haircut. But that didn't cut no ice with the dean. He sort of scared me, the way he was yelling and screaming. He embarrassed the crap out of the young guy."

The barber laughed. "And he frightened the crap out of the other customers. I thought they were all going to run out the door. It looked like a fight was going to start. I suppose they thought the dean was some kind of madman.

"The dean really chews this guy up and down and then ends up by firing him. But when it's over, the dean comes back and sits back in the chair here just like nothin' ever happened. He starts talking, takes up right where he left off. I forget now what we were talking about. He was breathing kind of hard, but outside of that, he was cool as ice."

"And that's the only time anything like that happened?"

"Yeah. Otherwise he's been just as pleasant as can be."

"Do you hear anything about him, good or bad?" Green asked.

The barber shrugged. "Mostly good. He built the law school here, but you probably know that already. The university people who come in here seem kind of proud of that. I never hear them say anything personal about him though. But I'll tell you one thing."

"What that?"

He laughed. "I sure'n'hell would hate to work for that guy if that's the way he usually treats his teachers. But he's good to his barber, and, as far as I'm concerned, that's what's really important in life, right?" The barber grinned, exposing tobacco-stained teeth.

"Makes sense to me," Green agreed.

"You want me to put on some holding spray?"

"No thanks."

"Hey, I'm sorry I wasn't more help." He grinned again. "I

suppose from your point of view it would have been better if I could of told you about his secret love life, or something like that?"

"Win some. Lose some." Green laughed as he climbed out of the chair. He remembered the hint about the tip and was generous. It was well worth the money to see another part of the puzzle.

* * *

Whittle had set up interviews with two of the younger members of the law school faculty. As Green expected, both painted the dean as possessing the hypnotic powers of Rasputin, the mad monk, combined with the utter ruthlessness of the early czars. But despite this, both admitted to a grudging admiration for Pentecost's organizational ability. Although they said that Pentecost rode roughshod over the younger faculty, everything else within the law school ticked along like a well-oiled clock. Green had interviewed them separately. They had nothing to lose by being candid. The man, a Yale graduate with a background as an appellate court clerk, was on his way to a large New York law firm after the school year ended. The woman, who was completely devoid of humor but who possessed a sharp intelligence, had accepted a position with another law school, a promotion in position as well as money.

Green learned that the younger faculty viewed their tours as a "finishing school," a sort of academic boot camp where they endured a rigorous schedule and harsh discipline in order to acquire experience and to hone their skills and enhance their reputations. Therefore, there was never a shortage of teaching applicants, despite the fearsome reputation of the dean.

After the interviews Green returned to his motel. His brother had offered to put him up, but the gesture was merely for the sake of politeness. Adele was chilly. The shadow of their previous problem still hung over all of them. But even without the burden of their strained relationship Green would have preferred the motel and the freedom of movement it allowed. He didn't have to accommodate himself to someone else's schedule, nor did he have to worry about bruised feelings or other possible repercussions.

Jerry Green felt satisfaction, he had accomplished a great deal. He was finally putting together a picture of Dean Pentecost, the real man, not the facade. Soon, he would begin to target the important aspects of the man's character, and it was there that the true answer lay. It was very much like a labyrinth, this search for a man's integrity—each path veered in another direction, each avenue pointed somewhere else. And he seemed to be discovering some things about himself. He found the search strangely compelling.

But he put aside his thoughts about the search. He would have to get ready in order to take Regina to dinner. He hurried into the lobby of the motel. If he had taken a moment to glance at the headlines on the newspapers for sale there he would have been put on notice. But he was in a hurry. He gathered the messages left for him at the desk and retreated to the sanctuary of his room.

His mind was on Regina. He snapped on the television just to have the company of the sound as he looked through the messages. Chris Clovis, the White House counsel, had called twice. All the other messages were from Amos Deering. They began at one o'clock and had been repeated every half hour exactly. The last two messages had the word "urgent" scrawled across them. Green noted the time of the last phone call and glanced at his watch. If the motel clerk's notation was correct, twenty-eight minutes had passed. Green decided to wait and see if Amos would stick to his schedule.

He lay back and looked at the television screen. He recognized an old rerun of an unfunny family sit-com. He supposed the Lansing station had picked it up cheap for use as a filler between the soaps and the high-priced prime time hours. He looked away from the screen and stared out the window. It was almost dark. Dark clouds tumbled past the outstretched grasp of skeleton-like tree limbs.

The telephone rang almost on the predicted minute. He reached across the bed and lifted the receiver.

"Yes?"

"Mr. Jerome Green, please," an impersonal female voice asked.

"This is Mr. Green."

"Just a moment, please, for Mr. Deering."

She put him on hold and the static of empty telephone noise whispered in his ear. He studied the clouds outside. They looked heavy, like snow clouds. Early snow meant an early winter in Michigan.

"Jerry?" Deering's voice was excited.

"Hello, Amos. I just got in. I saw your messages. Since you were calling every half hour I thought it would save time and trouble if I just waited for your next call. You're right on time. You know, you're wasting your talents in the White House. If you ran the nation's railroads, they wouldn't be in so much trouble. What's up?"

"Jesus! Don't you read the Goddamned papers or listen to the news?" Deering was clearly agitated.

"What's happened?"

"Everybody in the country knows except you. Howell's dead." Deering paused. "Hey, are you at that motel in Lansing?"

"Of course. That's where you called me."

"I didn't call you, the girl called you. I merely told her to find you. Give me your number."

Green sat up and looked over at the telephone. He read off the area code and number.

"Just stay there, okay? I'll get back to you in a few minutes."

"How few? I have some things to do."

"This is important, Goddamn it. Give me twenty minutes, maybe thirty."

"Amos, what the hell is going on? Can't you just tell me?"

"Thirty minutes, tops." Deering hung up.

He had been warned to expect it. Yet Howell's death suddenly made everything he had been doing real, as if up until now it had only been some kind of game.

Green got up and closed the drapes. He stripped down and took a shower, leaving the bathroom door open so he could hear the telephone. It rang as he was finishing toweling himself. He padded naked to the bed and sat down. He picked up the phone.

"Jerry?"

The room was warm but he draped the damp towel across his shoulders. "Who did you think it would be, the maid?"

"Look, Jerry, this is serious business. I had to leave the White House and find a phone booth. I wanted a clean phone."

"This may or may not be serious, but it is certainly becoming ridiculous. I suppose you want me to leave here and find a phone booth to call your phone booth?" Green could hear traffic noises at the other end of the line.

"Maybe I am getting silly in my old age, but you never know. Besides, I didn't want to run the risk of being overheard, tap or no tap."

"Go on."

"As I said, Howell's dead. They talked his old lady into pulling the plug and that was that. There's going to be a big funeral—he'll be laid out in the Court, public mourning, military funeral, the works. That was all part of the deal."

"Deal?"

"His wife wouldn't pull the plug until she was assured that we would do right by the remains of dear old Brian. I think she must be the kind who loves a parade, you know?"

"Howell's dead and so now everything is speeded up, right? You didn't have to call, I could have figured that out for myself."

There was more traffic noise and a honking of horns in the background. "I'm calling from one of these outside telephones, can you hear me okay?"

"Yes."

"Here's the picture. Our people are feeding the media a list of names. It's not official, it's being leaked. But everybody understands that it's really an authorized leak. And they know it's really coming from the man. This is a complicated business, Jerry. The *Post* is carrying a speculation article tomorrow on who may fill Howell's shoes. They got most of the information from us. The man said to cooperate, so we did."

"Go on."

"We fed them six names, and one of them is Dean Pentecost. They'll be on him now, and that will complicate things for you."

"You can say that again."

"The man plans to make the decision as quickly as possible. He won't name anyone until after the funeral, but he really wants to move on this." Deering's voice sounded close to panic. "He isn't very impressed with the other candidates, he wants to name your man."

"He's the President, why doesn't he just go ahead and do it?"

"For the same reason that you're down there. He wants to be sure. Look, we have to be sure that whoever gets the nod will vote right on the Electoral College issue. You were sent down to see if the dean was clean, right?"

Green nodded, feeling slightly chilled now. "That's right."

"Well, there's a new twist. The man says the whole thing is up to you. But he wants more than an appraisal. First, he wants a definite commitment from the dean on that specific issue, and then he wants your assessment as to whether the dean has the integrity to carry out the commitment."

Green shook his head. "If he has any integrity at all, he won't take a position on a case he knows nothing about."

"Hey, it's me you're talking to. I didn't say anything about integrity in general. The guy could be a shit for all I care. What we want is a simple commitment on that one case, and your assurance that it will be honored."

"You want it in writing?"

"Jerry, this may be amusing to you, but I'm the guy with his ass up against the fire. You've been in politics as long as I have. Don't give me any crap. The man knows, and so should you, that we need that vote on that case. That's the price tag for the job. The only thing we need is your assessment that the dean will honor the deal. Hell, the guy could agree without ever intending to do it. It's up to you to figure that out. You know people. The man says you do, and so do I. Get the commitment, then give us your assessment. If you give him the green light, he's got it."

The air in the room seemed to have turned cool, but Green knew it was just the effect of evaporation. It was really warm enough, but his drying skin felt chilled. "I'll see him tomorrow. I want to talk to a few others, too. I'll try to get back with you tomorrow, maybe the day after."

"Check in tomorrow, no matter what happens. This is important to the man and he wants to know what's happening. We'll use the same telephone arrangements." There was a pause. "Say, Jerry, when you see Pentecost, try to keep it private. Christ, if the *Post* or the *Times* gets wind that you're down there, they'll figure we've made our pick and blow it out of all proportion. Then if we don't name the guy it will look like we don't know what we're doing."

"I'll take care."

"You couldn't, say, see him tonight, could you?"

Jerry Green resented the request. A man's integrity, even provisional integrity couldn't be checked like body temperature. It was something that just could not be produced on demand. "No. I'd lose the advantage if it looks hurried. That way he would sense that he probably had it in the bag. And if he gets excited about it he's liable to leak it himself if he really thinks the job is his. I'll see him tomorrow. I'll let him dangle a bit. It's better that way." Green wondered if he wasn't just making excuses so that nothing would interfere with his evening with Regina. But excuse or not, it was logical.

"Whatever you think is best," Deering said. Again there was a blaring of car horns in the background. "Look, I'm sorry to put the pressure on you, Jerry, but the stakes are very high in this thing, you know?"

"I know."

"And you'll call me tomorrow?"

"Yes. I have a few calls from Chris Clovis. Is it about the same thing, or should I call him back?"

"It's the same thing." There was another pause again filled with traffic noise. "You know standing out here like this, making a call from a booth to avoid a tap, makes me think of the old days."

"The good old days?"

"I didn't say good, I just said old," Deering replied. "Hey, you get your ass cracking, old buddy, right?"

"Right."

Green hung up and dressed quickly. He went out to the motel lobby and bought a copy of the *Detroit News*. The story about Howell was on the front page. The headline read: "High Court's Swing Man Dead." The article reported death after a brief illness, of complications resulting from a stroke. Nothing was said about plugs being pulled, nor was there anything about deals for funerals. After giving the highlights of Brian Howell's career, the story went on to say that the body of the late justice would lay in state at the Court building, with burial at Arlington Cemetery. Several important cases coming before the Court were mentioned, including the Electoral College issue. The story speculated that the Court would take no action until a successor for Howell had been named, cleared by the Senate, and sworn in.

He returned to the room in time for the beginning of the national network television news. Howell's death was one of the lead stories. They showed a film clip of Howell being sworn in. The network's legal expert spoke over the film footage. As usual, the story ended with the commentator standing in front of the Supreme Court Building, halfway up the steps, microphone in hand. He profoundly voiced lofty sentiments about duty, independence, and the law. It got very little air time, just a few seconds in all, and then there was a move to the next news item.

Green flipped off the set.

Green wished he had never accepted the project in the first place. He resented being made a go-between, the bearer of a questionable offer. The implication of the demands made upon him, not only by his own law firm, but now also by the White House, made him feel ashamed that they thought him without honor. He had looked forward to a carefree, happy evening, and he had been excited. Now he felt depressed. He was under pressure to produce, and it was real.

He wondered if, with Regina's help, he could keep it out of his mind during the evening.

He doubted that he could.

*　　*　　*

They sized him up quickly. Youth seemed blessed with an unerring ability to do that. Later a myriad of experiences and perceptions would cloud the ability to make clear, quick judgments, but until then, the eye of youth made fast, frank, and usually very accurate appraisals.

He could almost read their minds. The boy saw nothing but a middle-aged man. Nothing outstanding. He was an old friend of his mother's, a school friend, and he was from the White House and a lawyer. No big deal. He wasn't a former sports star. He didn't even know any sports stars. The lawyer didn't look like the type who was interested in fast cars, boats, or racing. There was nothing particularly outstanding about him to arouse interest in a twelve-year-old boy. The boy vaguely understood that there was the possibility that one of these visitors might end up marrying his mother. He did not understand the reason, but he accepted the fact. However, if the man from the White House was a candidate, he saw nothing in him that would give him any edge. The boy was polite but dismissed the lawyer from any further thought or interest.

The girl, on the other hand, being fifteen, viewed the male caller from an entirely different viewpoint. She was a romantic, and the man from Washington was a mysterious stranger. He wasn't bad looking, although the gray hair aged him. He wasn't handsome, but he had a nice smile and seemed gentle. The girl considered these qualities very important assets. She observed her mother's reaction carefully. Like her brother, she had heard the explanation about the old friend from high school, but with a woman's nature growing within her she sensed that the relationship at one time had been much more than that.

Her mother had been increasingly nervous since she came home from the college. She seemed irritable and easily upset as she made almost frantic preparations for the evening. A mere invitation to dinner had never produced such reactions before. The girl knew instinctively that this man was special. He did have nice eyes. Not as nice perhaps as Allen Johnson's in English Drama class, but nice nevertheless. Eyes were very important. And his voice was deep, not rumbling, but smooth and reassuring. As did her brother, she also realized that one day such a caller might be the one to marry their mother. She had daydreams about such a man, a dark and dashing man who would capture her mother the way women were captured in the paperbacks she read by the dozens. This one looked promising, but he certainly wasn't anything like a storybook cavalier.

Jerry Green made small talk as he too did some evaluating. The boy was small and looked ungainly. But perhaps he was a late bloomer and would shoot up in height and gain coordination. It all depended upon the genetic gifts of the parents. He knew Regina, of course, but he did not know her dead husband. The framed photograph on the mantle wasn't sufficient to make a judgment. The boy looked quite normal. He was bored although he did his best to conceal it. But it was obvious he was anxious to get on with his own pursuits.

The girl was unlike his memory of the young Regina. The daughter's hair was different, darker, and not as well kept. Even her complexion was different, chalky, possibly reflecting a problem with powder-concealed acne. But the eyes, the set of the chin, and her general attitude reflected the mother. Like Regina she was tall and slender, and now she was quickly blossoming into a woman's full body. But there was the suggestion of a defiant streak in her personality, which promised trouble when she became a bit older. Unlike her brother, she displayed a keen interest in the visitor. Probably assessing his suitability as a possible mate for Regina, Jerry Green thought.

He smiled at the girl and she smiled back.

Regina stood up, signaling the end of the ceremony of introduction. The boy merely nodded and then slouched off toward the rear of the house. Green could hear a television. The girl also stood up. She lacked her mother's easy grace, but perhaps that would come in time.

"Mr. Green and I will be back, probably about eleven. If there's any homework to be done, do it, I don't want any excuses." Regina slid into the coat Green held for her. Her perfume was light but distinctive. He wondered if it was the same haunting brand he remembered from years ago. "And I want those dishes done when I come home."

"Yes, Mother," the girl said.

Regina turned to Jerry. "We have two television sets, one color and one black and white. When I came in the other night the two of them were battling over the color set."

"His program was just a sports thing, color wasn't important. My movie was. . . ."

"No fights," her mother said firmly.

"If there are any problems between you two, just let it be. I'll settle matters when I come home. Is that understood?"

"Yes, Mother." The girl gave Green one more appraising glance as they left. "Have a good time," she called after them.

As a boy in Michigan, Green had accepted the snow as a fact of life. From late October until March or even April it was there, sometimes more, sometimes less, but there. But he had been away a long time, and now he was surprised to see the heavy flakes falling again as they came out. He helped Regina into the car, then brushed off the front and rear windows.

He climbed in and started the motor. "Do they still have Tassies?" he asked, remembering that it was the favorite restaurant after proms and for other special occassions.

"It was torn down to make way for a shopping center," she said. "There's a nice place in Okemos called Monahan's. If you like steak, that's the place to go. They opened up only a few months ago. Their main brag is their meat; they make quite a thing out of it not being frozen but always fresh cut. I keep getting a mental picture of their kitchen, all blood and sawdust. But despite that, I do like their food."

"Then that's the place for us." He turned carefully to avoid skidding on the slick snow, then drove slowly toward the entrance to the condo complex. "You know the territory, so I'll drive this thing and you navigate, okay?"

The restaurant had been designed to suggest a Bavarian ski lodge. Even the waitresses wore little alpine dresses. They were escorted to a table in the rear, near a giant stone fireplace. A waitress ceremoniously lit a candle in a hurricane glass lamp, the table's centerpiece, then took their orders for drinks.

Green looked up at the ceiling, its heavy wooden beams decorated with Teutonic shields. "You would think they'd call this place Old Vienna or The Heidelberg. Monahan's sure doesn't seem to fit."

"I understand the owner, Timothy Monahan, worked for a while as an exchange student in Switzerland." Regina gestured toward the ceiling. "He was impressed, obviously. And I understand he's doing quite well. In a short time this has become the in place to go when you want to impress someone." She smiled, the contours of her face accentuated by the flickering candle-light. "Of course, considering the places you're accustomed to, this isn't very ritzy."

He laughed. "Regina, as far as I'm concerned there isn't one good restaurant in the entire District of Columbia, or even in the vicinity, except maybe along the Chesapeake. Everything in the capital is just fast food, even the fancy places. The emphasis is on speed, not quality. I suspect that's why so many federal officials travel; they don't have to go, but they want a decent meal."

The waitress brought the drinks and menus. Regina studied her brandy, rolling the liquor in the snifter to catch the hues of the candle flame. "And you, Jerry? Do you do a lot of traveling?"

He sipped his Scotch. "Regina, are you asking me whether or not my wife is a good cook?"

Her eyes seemed to dance with silent amusement. "No. But now that you raise the question, is she?"

"My wife is much too busy for any domestic chores. We eat out a great deal. If there's any cooking, it's scrambled eggs and toast, that sort of thing." He took another sip of Scotch. "Don't frown. It's only because of the pace of our lives. I work at least sixty or seventy hours a week. I do quite a bit of trial work, most of it before regulatory commissions. There's usually quite a bit of money at stake and that means plenty of pressure. The other side stays up late preparing, so I have to do likewise."

"But you left all that to go back into government."

He shook his head. "It's just a temporary thing. I'll be back at the old stand soon enough. I'm more comfortable there anyway." He smiled. "And it pays a hell of a lot better."

"And your wife, does she work as hard?"

"Worse. She's the world's worst workaholic. Compared to her, I'm employed part time. She's busy building her accounting firm into a national company. She's doing well at it, but it takes long hours."

"You must not see very much of each other?"

Green thought of the nights when his wife would silently

come home after three or four o'clock. He pretended to be asleep. He could always smell the odor of soap and the just-showered freshness about her. At first he had felt anger, but then he just put it out of his mind. He said nothing because he felt comfortable with their relationship. If she was being unfaithful, that was her business. As long as she didn't cause him embarrassment and no challenges were laid down, he just didn't care. She was discreet and the episodes weren't too frequent. He considered it a trade-off for the emotional steadiness she displayed. If there was no love in the household, at least it was relaxed.

"We seldom see each other," he said. "Sometimes she works late, sometimes I do. I suppose it's the model of a typical modern marriage." He again sipped his drink. "As I told you last night, there isn't any great joy in the arrangement."

"Was there in your first marriage?"

"My, aren't we nosy tonight?"

She laughed without embarrassment. "I believe you are the man who was inquiring into my present love life. You started it, remember. Besides, after all these years, Jerry, it's just normal to want to know about you. But if it's painful or something, well. . . ."

He shook his head. "It's not painful, it's just hardly worth the telling." He looked at her. Her eyes seemed almost magical in the candlelight. They were the eyes that had always haunted him.

"After your father made it quite clear that I was unwelcome, I contemplated joining the Foreign Legion, or at the very least becoming a deckhand on a Pacific-bound freighter."

"He wasn't all that bad, and you know it."

Green grinned. "From your point of view, no. But from mine, I was rather pointedly unwanted."

"It was the religious thing. All you had to do was stop by any Catholic church and get baptized, then my father would have welcomed you with open arms."

"I'm not so sure about that."

She nodded, a wistful sadness played across her features.

"Maybe you're right, Jerry. Those were different times." She paused. "For what it's worth, I was heartbroken when you went off to college and said we should start dating other people."

"I was hoping you were."

She laughed. "Men can be such bastards. I suppose you felt nothing at all?"

He studied her, the soft curve of her cheek, the full lips, the eyes. "I felt like hell. It bothered me for a long time. But after the talk with your father I decided he was right and that we shouldn't see each other any more. Remember, Regina, at that age everything is deadly serious. You do a lot of role playing. I was playing Ronald Colman on his way to the gallows; noble, compassionate, doing the finest thing I had ever done."

"Life is funny, isn't it? Everything turns out so differently from what you plan. My poor father finally got his fine Catholic boy, my husband Frank. Dad put on the big wedding, the High Mass, the Papal blessing, the works. And he became the typical proud grandfather, attending the christenings, and hosting the baptism parties afterward. His Irish Catholic dream. Then poor Frank's tumor took hold and my father started visiting the emergency room after the times I had been beaten up. He lived to see me divorced. God, how he fought against that, even though I was being killed. He had a heart attack several years ago and died. It had all turned sour on him."

"I'm sorry about your father."

"In a way, it would have been much better if he had died right after that damn wedding. It was what he wanted. He could have gone as happy as an angel." She sipped her brandy. "But then we very seldom get what we want in life, do we, Jerry?"

"Depends on what you want."

"Everyone wants the same thing."

Green frowned. "And what's that?"

"Happiness," she answered.

He snorted. "Regina, you really are a romantic. Hell, I know some politicians who lust only for power, that's all they want, not family, friends, money, love, or anything like that, only power. What about them?

"Power is their happiness, it's what they want."

He signaled the waitress for another round of drinks. "In Washington they love to play little parlor games. Let's try one now. Regina, in all honesty, what do you want out of life? What will bring you happiness? It has to be honest."

"You named the game, you should go first." Her eyes narrowed with interest. "Let's hear it, Jerry. Remember, it's your game, your rules, and it has to be honest, right?"

He was about to answer, then stopped. His amusement began to turn into a feeling of panic. What did he want? He was a partner in a prestigious law firm, and he wanted to remain with the firm. It was the only ambition he could think of, the only thing he really wanted. He certainly didn't want to retire, the thought of being in close contact with his wife was repugnant. There was nothing else. Suddenly he was painfully confronted with the realization of just how empty his life really was.

"It's your game, Jerry," she said softly.

"If I answer, I'll sound like such a shit that you'll be ashamed of me."

"I doubt that."

"I just want to hang on in the law firm where I am."

"That's all?"

He felt himself coloring. "It's a stupid game. But that's about it. Not much of an ambition is it? I don't want to be rich or famous, I just want to hold on to my job."

"Why does it mean so much to you? Remember, be honest now."

He nodded solemnly. "When I started out in the law, I started in Washington. I was no more than a super clerk in a federal agency. But I dreamed of being one of the real big shots, one of the partners in the super law firms that seemed to me to control the country." He shrugged. "Well, things happened and I moved along. For a short time I even had a sub-cabinet position under Nixon. I received an offer to go with one of those firms, Harley Dingell, a real WASP outfit—silk-stocking all the way. I was Jewish but I wasn't being taken on as a token, they wanted me for what I could do. To get it that way was very important to me. They wanted me because I was a good lawyer and I had good connections among the bureaucrats." He looked up at her, hoping she would understand. "It was the most important thing that ever happened to me. I don't know why. I've tried to figure it out several times. But that's all I want out of life, just to continue as a partner in Harley Dingell. As I say, not much of an ambition."

She sat quietly for a few moments. Her eyes seemed to have become even softer than before. "No other ambitions, Jerry? No hobbies, no secret dreams?"

He felt ashamed of himself. It had been the confession of a very shallow man and he knew it. He tried to smile as he shook his head.

"Jerry, your father always told me that everyone had a secret dream. Surely you want to sail around the world one day or write a novel? I'm not talking about real expectations, just dreams. Your father told me dreams were the most important thing in life for happiness. Let's have the truth now."

He had heard his father say those exact words himself, the importance of dreams. And he knew the terrible consequence the lack of dreams had held for his father.

"I have no dreams, Regina. What dreams I might have had died a long time ago. I'm a lawyer, I deal with reality."

She looked at him, her eyes interested, her face reflecting her puzzlement.

"Would you folks like to order now?" The waitress stood beside their table.

Regina shook her head.

"Not just now," he said.

The girl smiled pleasantly and left.

He sipped the Scotch. "Now that you have stripped me down to my bare and miserable soul, Regina, it's your turn. What will bring you happiness?"

"I have plans, Jerry. I have dreams. Oh, I'm very happy at the university. I'm proud of my accomplishments and I love the job. I love to teach. And right now my children are the center of my life. Everything revolves around them. I have a full life now. But I have plans and hopes, Jerry. Women are different than men, I suppose. We need love, or at least we like the prospect of it. When my children are grown, and that's not too far distant, I hope to share my life with someone. I would hate going home to an empty house or apartment, to just the cat and the television. That may eventually be my fate, but it's not my dream. I look for love one day."

"Ah, sweet romance."

She looked away. "Not really. Oh, romance is always wonderful, Jerry. It's fun to think about. But I'm talking about love, the sharing of a life. It's hard to explain, I think the only description I can give is that it is the opposite of loneliness. And I'd like to travel. But not alone. They say the greatest poetry in the world is to see beauty with someone you love."

"That sounds like a slogan invented by a travel agency."

She studied him. "I don't believe you've become quite as hard as you'd like me to think. You were always very sensitive, very gentle, Jerry. I rather think that hasn't changed, not basically."

He looked directly into her eyes. "Nothing remains the same, Regina. Everything changes. I'm not the person you remember." Then he smiled suddenly. "But the strange thing is, you are. You haven't changed, not a bit."

"I hope that's a compliment."

"More than that, it's a damn miracle. You know, and I mean this absolutely honestly, you look even better than when we were young. I can't exactly put my finger on it, but it's as if the beauty has deepened."

"God, I pity those poor Washington women. Jerry, who could possibly resist a line like that?"

He smiled at her. "I wish it were just a line, Regina." He started to say something more, then stopped.

Her green eyes were sympathetic, as if somehow she could understand his thoughts without having them spoken.

"Are you really sure you have no dreams, Jerry?" She spoke very softly.

He looked at her. "I'm not as sure as I once was."

The waitress broke the spell. They looked over the menu, then ordered.

The food was excellent, but Jerry Green found he had little appetite. He noticed that Regina also picked at her food. They finished the meal with brandy. For all his allegiance to facts and reality, it seemed to Green as if he had suddenly been transported back in time; the years seemed to have been magically rolled back and he again sat with his first love, and he realized now, his only love. He wondered if perhaps the twist of circumstances might have granted him a second chance.

"We used to go walking along the banks of the Red Cedar on campus, do you remember?" he asked.

She smiled slowly. "Some things are never forgotten, Jerry."

He felt apprehensive. He wanted to ask the question, but was afraid of rejection. But still it seemed terribly important to him that he ask. "Would you, well it may sound silly, but could we go walking there again?"

"Now? In the snow?"

"That never used to bother you."

She nodded, remembering. "No, it never did." She looked across the candle, her eyes catching the dying flame. "It's changed. There are some places where it's considered dangerous. But where there's light it's usually safe."

"You sound like you walk there often."

Her tongue touched the tip of her upper lip before she laughed. "You are jealous, aren't you?"

"No."

"Actually, I'm rather a well-known figure along the banks of the Red Cedar. If it isn't one professor, it's another. It's such a bother keeping all the names straight."

He tried to laugh but was surprised that he could not. "Don't tease me," he said softly, looking away in embarrassment.

She reached across the table. The touch of her hand was almost electric. "I won't tease, Jerry. I'm really very touched."

He paid the check, got their coats and they left the restaurant. There was no wind and only an occasional snowflake drifted down. When he climbed in behind the wheel she slid across the seat and sat next to him as she had when they were young. He kissed her cheek softly. She snuggled against him as he started the car.

It was a short drive to the campus. Only a few people were about. He parked near Jenison Field House, and then they walked, her arm tightly interlocked with his own.

The snow lay untouched, except in the roadways. It was a lovely sight. The campus lights illuminated the tranquil scene. The huge statue of the Spartan warrior, the school's emblem, stood a silent watch. They strolled toward the bridge.

"It's so beautiful tonight, Jerry," she said. "It's as if nothing had ever changed."

"I know."

Below the bridge the dark waters of the Red Cedar River flowed past the whitened banks. They stopped and looked over the bridge's railing, listening to the sound of the whispering water.

A car moved slowly past.

"Want to take a walk down along the bank," he asked.

"Well, I'm afraid that's something that has changed, Jerry. It's best to stay up in the light. It's safer. There have been a few incidents. I suppose with a student body of over forty thousand you're bound to get a few oddballs."

"Okay. How about over there then?" He nodded toward the field house parking area. The lighted reaches of the parking lot followed along the path of the river.

She nodded her agreement and they walked along for a while in silence.

"Regina," he said, surprised at his own thoughts and the need to put them into words. "I'm still in love with you."

She laughed. "You're in love with a memory, Jerry. See, you're a hopeless romantic after all." She stopped laughing when she looked up into his eyes.

He tried to smile but couldn't. "Hell, I suppose I've always been in love with you."

"It's just the night, Jerry. And a memory. It's a magic night. I'll always remember it. But don't say anything you'll feel foolish about later." She squeezed his arm.

"I've never forgotten you, ever. All those years, Regina, I thought about you. I know that sounds contrived, but it's true."

She looked away from him. A snowflake landed on her cheek and for a moment seemed like a white beauty mark. "We were young, Jerry. You never forget your first real love. I'm flattered. And, as a matter of fact, I have often thought about you. But I think that's natural."

"Part of the human condition."

"Most probably."

He stopped suddenly and swung her around so that she faced him. "That's bullshit and you know it. We've been in love since we were kids. It was just a twist of fate or time that kept us apart. Regina, I don't want to let you go, never again."

Her face grew solemn, her eyes questioning. "You're married, Jerry."

He snorted. "Some Goddamn marriage. I'm married to a woman who is more masculine than I am; a tough, domineering female. And you want to know the whole damn truth, Regina, the whole rotten truth? She cheats on me. She screws half her customers." He saw her eyes widen in shock. "And you **know** what's even worse?"

She shook her head.

"I don't give a good Goddamn. That's what's worse. It's a lousy arrangement, loveless and cold. There's no marriage to break up, Regina, if that's what's bothering you." He shook his head and sighed. "It's not even a good business arrangement." He tried to laugh. "I pay all the bills even though she makes more money than I do."

He realized he was gripping her arms, almost shaking her. He let go, then folded his arms around her and held her close.

She circled her arms around him and he felt the comforting pressure of her embrace. "I'm so sorry, Jerry," she whispered.

"I'll get divorced," he said slowly. "There'll be no trouble. Then we'll get married. You'll love Washington. There's an indescribable excitement there. It's the center of the most powerful government on earth. It can be intoxicating, I promise you."

She said nothing, but her embrace increased. He felt a comfort that he could not express.

"And it's just not Washington, it's the whole area. There's Chesapeake Bay, the whole Eastern seaboard. Your kids would love it. And it would be a learning experience for them, a guided tour through America's past."

She began to giggle. "Are you offering marriage or an advanced degree in history?"

He kissed her gently on the lips. "Marriage," he said simply.

She looked up at him, her eyes wet. "I said I had dreams, Jerry. Perhaps you've always been in the background of my mind, I'm not sure. I think you probably have. Maybe you are my dream." She hugged him more tightly. "But I'm no longer a young high school girl. I have responsibilities. I know what my children can expect here. They're with their own kind, Jerry. They're happy and adjusted here. If I were alone, I think I'd jump at the chance, but I can't leave here. Not yet, anyway. Do you understand me?"

He felt closer to her than he had ever felt toward any other person. "No, I don't understand. What I propose is Washington, D.C., not Timbuktu. They have schools in Washington, good schools. They're normal kids, they'll adjust. Hell, they'll grow intellectually."

"And what about the long hours you put in?" She whispered.

"What do you mean?"

"You told me about your job, your work and its importance to you. Do you honestly think that would change, Jerry?"

"I could adjust. It's a rat race, but I could make some changes." Even to his own ear his protestation sounded weak and unconvincing.

"No, you couldn't, and I wouldn't want you to," she said softly. "It wouldn't work, my love. I want someone to hold my hand and watch sunsets. You just wouldn't be there, not if you stayed with your firm."

"What are you suggesting?"

She held him tightly and looked up into his eyes. "Come home, Jerry. You're a lawyer, a good one. There's opportunity here. And we wouldn't need much. It wouldn't matter to me what you did just so that we could be together. You could teach here. It could be a wonderful life, Jerry. There's concerts, plays. You remember. There's a rich cultural life here. It's your home. We could be together."

"Leave Harley Dingell?"

"Among other things, like your wife." She started to laugh. "This is ridiculous, you know that?" She pushed gently away. "You're willing to leave your wife, but not your law firm. How does a woman compete against a law firm, Jerry? I feel ashamed even thinking about you leaving your wife because of me, but the idea that you'd balk because of the firm, well, that brings us back to earth." She brushed at her hair. "Maybe you're right, maybe there are no dreams."

He looked up at the sky. The heavy cloud cover obscured any stars. There was no wind. "If I said that I'd come back here, then you'd marry me?"

She took his hand and lead him slowly along. They could hear the rustle of the river water nearby. "If what you've told me about your marriage, and your life in general is true, I think it would be more like a rescue. I don't mean to sound flip. Marriage is a coming together of two human beings, Jerry. It's really not a romantic thing, it's a pledge, a welding of two souls. Life can be hard, my love, I've found that out. To me, marriage is a total commitment. I'm not in the market to trade my quiet life here for an expensive place near the Potomac with long lonely hours and a meaningless existence." She drew him to her, encircling him with her arms. "In the long run, Jerry, I think I can offer you more comfort and satisfaction than you may reasonably expect from the elegant offices of your Harley Dingell."

He kissed her, gently at first, then forcefully as he was seized by a newly awakened hunger. She resisted for only a moment and then responded. They embraced, unmindful of time, or of anything, except themselves.

"Regina. . . ." he began.

She held her fingertips to his lips. "Not now, Jerry. It's a magic time. No answers tonight. Let's just enjoy it. People are granted very few nights like this in their lives."

He kissed her again.

They kissed when they returned to his car. They passionately kissed again when he had parked in front of her house. Then suddenly she was gone. He saw her front door close behind her. He sat there for a few moments before he even thought about leaving.

He wanted her. And he refused to think about anything except his need for her. Anything else would have broken the spell. And it was indeed a magic night. He was deeply in love.

The snow was beginning to fall again as he began the drive back to the motel.

Chapter 9

As Jerry Green had previously observed, the law school, at a distance, resembled the prow of a giant ship, rising and pointing toward the sky. Closer, the effect of the building was more like that of a cathedral, it seemed to reach beyond the sky, out toward Heaven itself. Green reflected it was an inspired blend of modern simplicity and the majesty of ancient European architectural concepts.

He entered with a group of students. They carried large bags of books, looking more like peddlers than scholars. A small female law student trudged ahead of him, her mukluks kicking off snow as she bore her burden with the determination of a Russian peasant woman.

Green stamped the snow from his feet and looked around. The vaulted interior was just as impressive as the exterior. The large atrium, or lobby, was a pleasant, no-nonsense place, with strategic bulletin boards placed at convenient spots. On one side of the building's prow a multistoried law library was visible through glass panels. A visitor could look down into the basement level and see comfortable study cubicles surrounded by neat rows of book stacks. Each of the floors was visible. It seemed like a montage of books, stacks, and students. A work of art. Green was impressed.

He turned to his right toward the other side of the "prow." He faced a series of doors, each bearing dignified metal signs. He chose the one marked Administration and walked through. He found himself in a reception area, small but comfortably furnished. It reminded him of a doctor's waiting room. A pleasant-looking young blonde woman sat behind a counter. She was typing. Beyond her other typists were busy at their machines. The far wall was filled with pastel file cabinets.

The blonde looked up. "Yes sir, may I help you?"

Green walked over to the counter and smiled down at her. "My name is Green, Jerome Green. I'm an attorney. I'd like to see Dean Pentecost, if possible."

She frowned as if she had somehow committed an error. "Oh, I'm sorry, Mr. Green. The dean hasn't come in. Do you have an appointment? I didn't see your name on the appointment list this morning."

"I'm afraid I didn't have time to make an appointment. I'm from Washington."

"Could you tell me what this is about? Perhaps we can fit you in." She was up now, smiling across the counter as if he were the most important man in the world. She was well trained. She would tactfully weed out the unwanted. She knew her job. The dean would see only the wheat, she would get rid of the chaff. "Of course, his schedule is pretty tight," she added sweetly.

"If I told you I was selling life insurance, do you think that would help hurry up the appointment?"

She coolly appraised him, as if seeing him for the first time. Then her plastic smile was replaced by a real one. "Not for this year, probably not for the next decade."

"Then life insurance is out."

"Unless he found out he had a fatal disease, then I'm sure he would call you."

Green laughed. "The matter involves public business. I'm with the government. Please have the dean contact Mr. Whittle in the Administration Building. He knows the situation. I'll leave a number where I can be reached." Green pulled out a Harley Dingell business card and scrawled the motel number on the back. He handed it to the girl.

She studied the card, then looked up at him. "You did say the government?"

"That's my old employer. I haven't had time to have new cards printed."

She nodded slowly. Her quick intelligence was obvious as she weighed the possibility that a meeting with this stranger from Washington might be important to the dean against the possibility of it being a mere nuisance.

"He has a full schedule for the next few days," she said brightly, "but perhaps we can work you in."

"I'd appreciate that."

She grinned. "And you're sure this isn't really about insurance?"

"Damn it, found out every time."

She laughed, her eyes still appraising. "We'll get back to you." She looked at the card. "Mr. Green."

"Thank you."

He left the reception room and returned to the high-vaulted atrium. He took a minute to inspect it. A tasteful blend of brick and tile, the construction looked haphazard, but Green knew, even with his little knowledge of such things, that it cost a fortune. The university had spared the dean nothing.

A tall young man lounged against a wall as he read a law book. His bag of books lay at his feet, his Arctic parka draped over the bag. The young man was attempting a beard but the resultant tufting made him look unwashed.

"Are you a student here?" Green asked as he walked over.

The young man looked up. He nodded. "Yes." His manner was defensive.

"I'll tell you what my problem is," Green said quietly, almost conspiratorially. "My son is thinking about entering law school. He's been accepted by several places. I'm a businessman, not a lawyer, but I thought I'd look over the schools first. I want him to attend only the very best."

The student became even more wary. "This is a good school," he said as if he hoped that would end the discussion.

"Well, that's understood, isn't it? I mean, everyone recommends this place. But I've bought many recommended products, young man, that haven't been worth a damn. It's always been my practice to inspect the merchandise first."

Green looked around. "Frankly, I'm not impressed. Oh, this is a great place for show, a nice building and all that, but after all it is just a brand new school set down in the middle of a damn cow college, if you see what I mean?"

Suddenly the defensive look was replaced by irritation. "Hey, you're dead wrong about that, mister. Sure, this is a new school, but it has the best legal faculty in the country. It's a national school, the students come here from all over. There's no part-time students here. The work is too demanding. The dean doesn't allow outside employment."

"That doesn't sound American to me. Working your way through is a tradition."

"Yeah, maybe it is, but you can't do it here. The courses are just too damn hard, and they throw so much law at you that you haven't time for anything but study."

Green smirked. "And you like that?"

"Hey, I don't like it, but because of it I know I'll be one hell of a better lawyer when I get out of here. We all will."

Green shrugged. "It's still a cow college."

The young man's eyes narrowed with hostility. "Look, I was accepted at Harvard and Yale. I'm an honors graduate from the University of Chicago, an engineer. That's a tough degree to get, in case you don't know it. Hell, I had no trouble with Harvard or Yale, but I really had to work to get in here."

"You'd have been better off at Harvard."

"Like hell! They have the very best professors here, many of them came from Harvard. The whole purpose of this school is to turn out the absolutely best lawyer produced in America, and it works." His eyes narrowed even more, as if coming in for the kill. "Do you know how many of our graduates passed the bar last time?"

"No."

"Well, the University of Michigan never scores better than an 80 to 90 percent pass ratio. The University of Detroit, a tough Jesuit outfit, gets only 70 percent of its people by, sometimes less."

"So?"

"So this. Our school, the Michigan State School of Law, passed 100 percent! Everybody who took it made it. First damn time in the history of the state bar exam that's ever happened. What do you think about that?"

"It probably means that this school targets everything toward just the bar. I want someplace for my son that provides a complete legal education. Besides, I understand the dean here is something of a screwball."

The young man's face was stiff with suppressed rage. "Dean Pentecost may show no mercy, but, by God, he's fair. And he's not a faculty stooge, he'll listen to the students, and they know it. He may rule this place with an iron hand, but the results are worth it."

"Did you ever talk to him?" Green asked quickly.

The young man seemed flustered by the question. "I've attended many of his talks and lectures."

"But have you ever talked to him, man to man?"

The youth stopped, surprised for a moment. "Well, come to think of it, no. But that's not important. If I wanted to, I could walk right in there," he pointed to the administration office, "and talk to him. He has an open door policy."

"But you haven't ever used it."

"That doesn't mean it's not there."

Green nodded, as if agreeing. "I take it then that you'd

recommend that my son pick this school, say in preference to the University of Michigan?"

The student snorted. "Damn right."

Green shook his hand. "You've been a big help."

The young man, still wary, quickly gathered up his books and jacket, then hurried away.

Green took a moment to survey the place once more. It was truly awesome. Did it reflect the dean? The student firmly believed that the dean was a great man, even if he never actually talked to him. Green presumed the young man was typical. Dean Pentecost had constructed an image for himself; the supreme father figure, the firm but fair god, dwelling just beyond those administration doors—a god seen only at a distance.

Green walked outside and buttoned up his coat against the chill. He turned and looked again at the law school building. This "god" had raised a great cathedral unto himself.

Well, Green reflected as he trudged through the snow, if you were going to be a deity, that was the only way to do it: keep a good distance, create a little fear, and raise an awe-inspiring monument to yourself.

Distance and awe were the keys to success. Gods cannot afford to be human, Green thought ruefully, because someone was always waiting with a cross and nails.

*   *   *

Ben Alexander wanted to get away from the Supreme Court Building for at least a few minutes, so he took a short walk. It had been hectic. He was in charge of packaging up all the papers of his late boss. He had to be careful, he discarded only the obviously unimportant things. He knew the family was discussing giving the justice's papers to several colleges that had expressed interest. Besides the work, there was the anxiety. He had come to feel like a target himself.

He no longer enjoyed the mantle of protection afforded by a

sick but living boss. Now, with the shortage of manpower at the Court, he knew he was being watched by some of the justices with greedy eyes. The damn female justice had even come in to see him, to discuss the differences he would find in her style of approaching a case compared to that of his late boss. The news of Howell's death was only minutes old when she had presented herself. She obviously wasn't a lady of great sentiment. He had felt like really telling her off, to vent some of the genuine sorrow he felt for Howell, but he restrained himself. Voluntarily leaving the Court, as opposed to being fired from it were two decidedly different things. Besides, he had been assured by Floyd Grant, the head clerk for the Chief Justice, that he would not go to the woman. He was given no other assurance, but that was enough.

As he returned to the Court building he saw the people. The line extended halfway down the steps. They seemed to be moving along briskly. He guessed they were more curious than honestly mourning. Howell had become well known during his short tenure, but not beloved. Alexander surmised that most of the people in line were federal workers killing time on their lunch hour, together with the usual tourists.

He started to move toward the other entrance when he saw Floyd Grant signaling to him from the top of the stairs near the line of people. Alexander trotted up the stairs and joined him.

"How would you like to see something, something you can tell your grandchildren about?" Grant was grinning.

"Sure."

"Come on." The senior clerk lead Alexander past the guards. As members of the Court staff, Grant and Alexander were known and did not have to obey the signs or follow the roped-off pathway leading into the Court and toward the bier.

The closed casket was almost engulfed in huge banks of flowers, decorations sent by unions, businesses, and others who figured it was just good business to let the living justices know how much they thought of everybody down at the Court. A silver-framed colored photograph of Justice Howell, in his black robe, was propped up on top of the bronze casket. Lights had been arranged to spotlight the picture and the American flag nearby.

"Take a look at that," Grant whispered.

A stout, florid-faced man stood at the foot of the casket, greeting the mourners as they approached. He had stark white hair and an imposing manner. The mourners mumbled to him as he looked properly solemn and managed just the hint of a sad smile as they passed by.

"Family?" Alexander thought he knew most of the Howell family and this man was a stranger.

"No. Guess again."

"The funeral director?"

Grant shook his head. "Heavens, no. He has too much class to be doing that."

"Then who is it?"

Grant studied the big man shaking hands with the passing line. "That's what you can tell your grandchildren about. There is one of the finest specimens of *Politicus americanus* you'll ever see, and his kind is becoming extinct, thank God."

"A politician?"

Grant nodded. "And not just any politician. That is the Honorable Joseph Michael O'Malley, distinguished judge of the United States Second Circuit Court of Appeals."

"You have to be kidding me."

Grant snorted. "Can you imagine that? He showed up about a half hour ago, went through the building glad-handing everybody from Chief Justice to janitor, and then parked himself right there by the coffin like he was the sole surviving heir of the deceased."

"Why doesn't someone ask him to leave?"

"Very practical reason. He's just liable to be picked by the President to fill your late employer's shoes. In other words, that ward-heeling, glad-handing boob may be the next associate justice of the U.S. Supreme Court."

"Does the Chief Justice know about this?"

"Yep. And he understands the tactics too. He told me that good old Judge O'Malley flew in this morning because he knew the President will be making an appearance here at two o'clock. The Chief says that as soon as O'Malley latches onto the President, shakes his hand, and reminds him that he need look no farther than Judge Joseph Michael O'Malley, then he'll hit back for the National Airport and fly out again. This is just a part of his continuing campaign for the job."

"That's bizarre." Alexander watched O'Malley skillfully shake a dozen hands as a cluster of people passed by him.

Grant chuckled. "Hey, he's a judge of the second highest court in the land, and that's part of the technique that got him there. It may not be dignified, but it apparently works."

"He's a clown!" Alexander turned away in disgust and began walking toward the Court offices. Grant followed along and caught up to him.

"Ben, I thought you would be amused. I'm sorry if that offended you."

Alexander stopped. "Floyd, whoever gets that job will be making decisions that will profoundly affect every American, even our national way of life. Damn it, think of the important issues coming up in just this term alone. If the Court absolves that nun, suicide clinics will spring up all over the country. The police case will set the racial policy for the nation. My God, don't they realize the new man will be the one who will make the key decisions? I just can't believe that the act that clown is putting on back there would help qualify a man to assume such tremendous power."

"You missed a few key cases," Grant laughed. "Freedom of the press, that's a big one this term. The Chief is really interested in that one. And the Marchall Industry case, that could blow General Motors and most of the other giant companies right out of the water." He shook his head. "But what the hell, this term is no different than most. The Court picks only the key cases to hear, the life and death stuff, it's always been that way."

"But with a split Court," Alexander said, "this vacancy becomes crucial. The new man will actually decide most American law, at least until the Court shifts to one side or the other. God, there must be some way to keep creeps like O'Malley from getting in."

Floyd Grant shrugged. "I don't know if you can properly call him a creep. The American Bar Association found him fully qualified, at least they did the last time, when the woman was finally selected."

"Then there's something very wrong with the system of selection, it shouldn't come down to a political pick."

Grant sighed. "Oh, I don't know about that. It would finally work out to be a political choice no matter what system you chose, except maybe a lottery. The Court is part of the political process, and there's usually too much at stake to ignore politics. Besides, the next man will be faced with the most crucial decision in the world, at least from one point of view."

"Oh?"

Grant laughed. "Hell, yes. He will either keep you on or fire you. That's the important decision. You know what I'd do if I were you?"

"What?"

"I'd go back there and get in line. Then when you've worked your way up to O'Malley, buttonhole him and get a commitment from him to keep you on."

Shock registered on Alexander's features, then he slowly smiled. "Floyd, why don't you go take a flying fuck at yourself?"

Grant pretended dismay. "These imitation Grecian walls may tumble down in presence of language like that. Oh well, it was just a suggestion. But I can see from your attitude that you lack the chutzpah to become a Supreme Court justice, or for that matter, even a member of a lower federal court."

Alexander laughed. "I think you're right." He thought about the man at the coffin, grasping at passing hands. "In fact, I know you're right."

*   *   *

Jerry Green had been busy. He interviewed another professor recommended by Whittle. The man was the dean's neighbor. It proved to be a fruitless contact. The professor, an engineer, equated virtue with cut lawns, snow removal, and neat garbage. The dean scored high on all three counts, therefore, the professor counted him as an exceptional man, clearly qualified for anything good the universe had to offer. The neighbor only had contact with the dean at the annual block cocktail parties. He said he was favorably impressed by the dean and his wife, describing them as well bred and dignified.

Green presumed "well bred and dignified" probably meant they were a pair of stuffed shirts. But so long as the lawn was cut and the garbage neat this neighbor would have forgiven anything.

Green called the law school to inquire if arrangements had been made to meet the dean. They had been waiting for him, and this time he received royal treatment. He had a three o'clock appointment, and the dean's secretary almost purred as she suggested that if Mr. Green wished to meet someplace other than the law school, the dean would be quite agreeable. Green had the feeling that the dean might be listening in, at least to her end of the conversation. She was overdoing it a bit, as if playing for an audience. The newspaper stories would have alerted the dean. He would be ready.

Green informed the woman that the law school would be just fine and he would be there at the appointed time. The secretary sounded so absolutely thrilled that Green knew the dean was listening. Pentecost knew the prize and he wasn't about to allow anyone to muck it up for him with a display of the wrong attitude, at least that was Green's speculation.

Green felt he now had a fairly complete composite mental picture of the man he was yet to meet. Both from the FBI check and his own sources he had discovered no hint of possible criminal or erratic behavior. There were no unexplained lapses in the dean's history that might have suggested a period of drying out or a stay in mental hospitals. Judging from all the evidence gathered, there was nothing psychiatrically questionable about Dean Roy Pentecost. Green mentally checked off that part of his general investigation as complete. However, it was still subject to revision when he finally met the man. He had a sense about people, an uncanny gift for sniffing out hidden drunks and broken souls. He supposed that was the real reason he had been selected for this job. But despite all the information he had gathered, much of his appraisal would still depend upon the face-to-face encounter.

The dean's personal life was as clean as a whistle. He lived for his career and it seemed, based upon investigation, that nothing else was of any real importance to him. Certainly not his wife. Green wondered if the dean knew about Mrs. Pentecost and the young professor. He supposed that he did, and if not about that particular man, he probably sensed the unfaithfulness. Green wondered if he might be reading into the dean's supposed attitude a reflection of himself and his own situation. Perhaps he was. In any event, Mrs. Pentecost was discreet and the problem was not the kind to raise alarm bells that might obstruct appointment. Green knew well that politically it was considered a plus if a man had a pleasant little wife, clearly devoted to her husband and children. It was the old *Saturday Evening Post* dream of the American family. Given the sexual revolution, the pressures of everyday life, and the changes of the American social and political structure, that was a dream long dead.

The White House was aware of Pentecost's background. They knew he wasn't a true scholar, despite his teaching credentials. His gift was organizing. And he could handle people. He could be a cloying fingerlicker or a petty tyrant, depending on the need of the moment. But he was effective. His legal writings

demonstrated no great ability, but on the other hand they didn'
espouse any radical theories, nor would they embarrass or trouble
anyone. Pentecost looked good politically, and that was the pri-
mary consideration. Green speculated that the dean would be a
much better candidate for a cabinet post or an executive position
than for the judiciary. His talents were undeniable, but they would
be of little use on the high court. Still, he could obviously handle
the job, although his real talents would be wasted.

The decision would turn on Green's judgment of the man, the
real man. The President wanted to take no risks on this Supreme
Court appointment. He wanted a man who would appear to be a
scholar and above petty politics, but he damn well wanted a man
who would commit himself on one important case and who would
honor that commitment, taking that secret with him to his grave.

Green wondered at how he could delicately put the proposi-
tion, and what kind of answers Pentecost might make. The
exchange would be vital. It would be, he knew, an elaborate dance
between them, each watching the other, each feeling for what
might be expected, probing for weakness—it would be an intellectual fencing match. And it promised to be interesting.

But Green, despite the importance of the task ahead, found
his mind wandering, disturbed by thoughts of his own life problems. And the storm centered around Regina Kelso. It was most unsettling. He had never before questioned what he considered
to be the holy calling as a partner in Harley Dingell. That
partnership had been his own personal Holy Grail, and he had
searched for it and found it. It had never before even occured to
him to question its value. But that was before the snowy nocturnal
walk with Regina. Green realized that he was coming into that age
when men did begin to question their life aims, themselves, and
their desires and dreams. He wondered if his thoughts didn't
merely reflect the expected midlife turmoil, but he knew the
answer wasn't as easy as that.

There was a world beyond the confines of Harley Dingell, a

world full of people, challenge, promise, and even love. In Washington, knowledgeable people might mentally genuflect in the presence of a Harley Dingell partner, but as far as the rest of the country was concerned he was just another lawyer. The firm's power and importance mattered only to a very select circle.

What had seemed so important became less so when considered in the light of a more normal existence. Still, Green thought, a man couldn't just walk away from a life's conquest.

On impulse, he called the School of Nursing. Regina was in her office.

"How about lunch? I have to be at the law school at three, but I'm free until then."

She laughed. "It's after one o'clock. This is the midwest, Jerry. We eat at noon. Besides, I'm in the middle of grading some exam papers. And judging by some of these answers, these nursing students are being financed by the funeral industry."

"How about a cup of coffee? You can watch me eat. It's one of life's more amusing experiences."

She giggled. "Do you remember the lemon pie thing when we were kids?"

It had been a high school pie eating contest that had ended up as a Keystone Kop pie throwing riot. He had emerged that day covered from head to foot with pie filling.

"I still eat the same way, just as dainty as ever. Come on, you can leave the papers of your young butchers for later. One quick cup of coffee?"

She relented. They met at a new cafeteria near the School of Nursing. In the days when Michigan State had its own farms and provided meat and produce for the campus the food was as good as anywhere in the world. However, that had changed, at least in this cafeteria. Green munched on a typical mass-produced sandwich— a hamburger with more cereal than meat—and a salad of wilted lettuce topped with an undersized pear half. He didn't care, he was happy.

The years again seemed to slip away as they both laughed over things triggered by the memory of the pie contest. Some of the students glanced over at them, obviously dismayed by older people making a noisy spectacle of themselves.

"What happens after you talk with the dean?" she asked. He noticed that Regina had carefully avoided prying into his purposes for being on campus. He knew that took control, and he respected her for it.

He pushed the half-eaten pear away. "My business here will be decided on his answers to some questions. I won't know what I'm going to do until after we talk."

She bit her lip, displaying a rare nervousness. "Will you be going back to Washington directly?"

"Maybe." He was going to say more, but stopped when he sensed that she wanted something.

"Needless to say, Jerry, I've thought a great deal about what we discussed, about us, about you and me." She laughed, but there was a hollow, almost forced sound to it. "I've practically thought of nothing else." She looked down, as if ashamed of that fact.

"I meant every word, Regina. I admit it was a lovely, magical night, but I honestly meant everything I said. And don't concern yourself about the divorce. That's been coming for quite some time. I suppose Carol and I could never really find the time to bother about it, that's all. I know that sounds very blasé, but it's also the truth."

She nodded without comment, then looked up at him. "You talked about romance, Jerry. And I told you I have a dream, just like most other single women my age. It would be nice to live a sort of Fred Astaire–Ginger Rogers existence, a wonderfully happy dance, but you and I both know that life just doesn't permit that sort of thing." She slowly shook her head. "Happiness, God, how many definitions that word can have."

"Regina, if I started divorce proceedings now it wouldn't take very long. My wife wouldn't oppose it, that's just not the sort of thing she would do. She really wouldn't care. I'd be free in a matter of months."

"And would you chuck it all, Jerry? Would you kiss your law firm goodbye and come live with me?"

He wanted to answer, but somehow he couldn't seem to form the words. He just stared at her.

"It could be nice, Jerry. Oh, there would be problems, but it could be pleasant, a coming together of two people, a true happiness." She looked down at her coffee cup. "I'm modern, I wouldn't even insist on marriage." She laughed quietly. "Although I'd have a hell of a time explaining that to the children." She looked at him.

He paused, looking away. "Well, I suppose anything is possible. But it's more complicated than it appears, Regina. If you came to Washington to live. . . ."

Her smile was a bit wistful. "I read somewhere, I guess in a women's magazine, that no man on earth would leave a career for the sake of a love affair, and no woman on earth would not. However, I think they really meant only unattached ladies."

"Regina, I can understand how you feel about your children. God, I'm not asking you to leave them. Look, they'd love. . . ."

She held up a hand. "I've heard all about you slick big-city lawyers." She laughed, but there was no humor in it. "I know you have tricks to beat down a poor female's determination."

He felt sudden irritation. "Look, this isn't some Goddamn play."

She looked at him. "No, it certainly isn't, Jerry." Her voice was soft, but firm. "It's real life, and that's what destroys some of the very best dreams. As I see it, my very first love, it's really quite simple. If you want me, I'm yours. But this is my home, and you'll have to come here. I don't mean this to sound melodramatic, Jerry, but it really boils down to whether you want to continue your Washington life, or start a new one here, with me."

"It isn't that simple, Regina. Look, the divorce will take

months. You could bring the kids down for a vacation. I'll show you around. There are fantastic private schools there, I'll take you around to those. You don't have to decide now."

She stood up. There was still a hint of a smile around her lips, but her eyes looked sad. "You're right, I don't," she said, stepping over to his side of the table and gently kissing his forehead. "But you do, Jerry. You're the one who has to make the decision."

She was gone before he could even reply. His first instinct was to rush after her and continue the discussion, to persuade her. It was so damned important, it was his entire future!

He started to go after her but then he stopped. The slow realization began to sink in. She meant it. This was no female posturing, no game. He knew Regina and she just wasn't capable of that, it wasn't part of her nature. She was always honest, always straightforward. So there would be no compromise. She was an intelligent woman and he knew she had carefully thought the matter out. He too had been thinking, but not clearly.

He stood up and slowly put on his coat. This was not the time to consider his own personal problems, or his future. He must now think about his approach to Dean Pentecost. Green realized the importance of his mission. It would not only affect the nation's law, but its destiny for many years to come. He knew it demanded his total concentration. A good lawyer was always capable of pushing his personal problems into the attic of his mind when the occasion demanded.

He was surprised as he trudged along with the moving stream of students that he couldn't just command the thoughts of Regina to be banished from his consciousness.

However, as he sighted the prowlike law school in the distance he began to shift into thoughts about the man who had caused that monument to be built.

Answers, he desperately needed answers. If he couldn't get any for his own problems, perhaps he could extract some from the dean, perhaps then his own thinking would clear to the point where he could solve his own riddle.

The impression that the law school was like a cathedral became stronger as he drew closer.

He wanted to think about Pentecost, but his brain felt numb, and he could muster no intelligent thought except a determination to carry out the task he had been assigned.

Chapter 10

Green was escorted into Dean Pentecost's office. The man behind the desk stood up and Jerry Green suddenly and vividly recalled his own image as he had seen it in the Smithsonian's metal plate. Dean Roy Pentecost could easily pass as his brother, perhaps even his twin. They were both just under six feet tall and slightly stocky. The dean's features matched his own; Pentecost presented a bland, pleasant face contrasted with sharp, intelligent eyes. Even their hair matched. Both men were gray at the temple and favored businesslike haircuts. They were the same age, a fact Green knew from the reports he had seen on the dean. They looked like they had picked out their suits together. Each wore a muted gray pinstripe with a conservative dark tie. The startling physical resemblance was obviously noted by the dean as he came around the desk and extended his hand.

"This is a pleasure, Mr. Green." The dean's handshake was firm but slightly moist, despite his apparent calm. He knew why Green was there.

"I've been looking forward to this, Dean Pentecost."

Green realized that his own smile must be just like the dean's, a pleasant expression, warm but not too open. They were playing each other's game.

"Please call me Roy. When I'm addressed as dean I always feel like an Anglican clergyman." The statement was smooth and practiced. Green presumed that it was the dean's standard opening line, designed to show that he was just one of the boys, a true democrat, small "d."

"It's a pleasure to be back in the informality of the midwest. Please call me Jerry."

The dean's trim eyebrows raised slightly. "You're originally from the midwest?" He said it as if it were some rather unpleasant secret, and best kept that way.

"You come from Connecticut," Green said, his words more of a statement than a question.

"Yes. Please have a seat, Mr. . . . . Jerry. Can I get you some coffee or tea perhaps?"

"I just finished having coffee. But don't let that stop you."

"I'm afloat. This job requires that you wander from one damn meeting to another. They all serve coffee, and if you have no taste for it then your career's at an end." He allowed himself a quick smile, then his face relaxed again. "You said you come from the midwest, where?"

"Here." Green made himself comfortable in a large chair in front of the dean's desk. "As a matter of fact, right here. Michigan State. My father was a professor in the anthropology department. This is where I was raised."

"Then this is a homecoming for you." The smile only flickered now. "Do you have family here?"

"A brother. He's also an anthropology professor."

Pentecost nodded. "I've probably met him. You meet so many, but know so few. As I'm sure you know, academic life can be one round of teas, meetings, and similar get-togethers, all rather impersonal."

"Yes, I remember." Green glanced around the large office.

It was done in a simple federalist style, good quality without show. The large desk was actually more of a long table. There were no personal items around the office; no framed diplomas or awards, no trophies, no personal photographs. The only decoration was a muted landscape done in oils. It was much like Jerry Green's office back at Harley Dingell. Like the dean, he preferred no distractions, no trophies. It was really a bit of reverse ostentation. A visitor would know that a man like the dean, or Green, would have a number of diplomas, admission certificates, and other memorabilia. To hang none at all was to proclaim that there were so many that modesty forbade display. Also, it gave the workplace an austere, no-nonsense appearance. Green did note that the dean's office was neater than his own, however.

"I suppose you find the campus greatly changed?" The dean managed a pleasant half smile.

Green knew that his own expression matched exactly. "Well, with the addition of all the new buildings there has been change, but I find somehow they seem to blend in with the older campus I know. I suppose it's a bit like new neighbors on the block, it's changed in a way, but it still remains the old block. More of a feeling than a fact, I suppose."

"And this building?" The dean's expression never changed. He had an excellent face for poker.

Green leaned back in his chair. "It's magnificent. Who thought up the design? I think it's unique."

"The idea was mine, although I'm afraid it isn't really unique." The dean's voice was smooth, exhibiting no discernible emotion. "I saw a church in Denver that impressed me. Rather than having a spire or two rising from the roof of the building, the structure itself was the spire, rising rather majestically toward the sky. When I saw it I was struck by its beauty, although I must confess that until I investigated I thought it was probably a terrible waste of space. Not a useful design for anything but a church."

The half smile widened just a bit. "When the legislature finally gave the green light for a law school here and I was selected to head it, I sought bids and ideas from a number of architects. That's not to say that I had complete control of the project. I had to have everything approved by a committee." He sighed. "I often wonder how far Western man might have gone if it hadn't been for the invention of the committee. In any event, a young Japanese submitted this design, or close to it anyway. There is, of course, some wasted space, but most of the building, which is constructed a bit like a beehive, is quite efficient.

"The design is unique for a law school," the dean continued, "but not for churches." He smiled a bit wider. "As a lawyer, I know you appreciate that at final exam time there's more fervent prayer offered in this building than in any church, I'm sure."

Green smiled, nodding his agreement. "You certainly have done wonders in such a short time."

The dean shrugged. "I'm not so foolish as to start believing my own publicity, Mr. Green, er, Jerry. I've had a good many lucky breaks. First, the university trustees gave me an open checkbook." He laughed. "If our football coach used my recruiting methods, our team would either be the national champion, or barred from football, depending on whether or not he was caught. There wasn't much art to it, I merely identified the men who were known as the leading authorities in the basic legal fields and—how does it go?—made them an offer they couldn't refuse."

"Still, bringing those people in was quite an accomplishment."

"There was a domino effect. When Bradford of Yale heard that Slocum of Harvard was coming, he signed aboard. My real challenge was getting the first big name, after that it was easy."

"I think you're downgrading what you've done."

The dean shook his head. "Not really. I'm quite proud of what I've been able to accomplish. But I'm a realist. I have carefully dissected the elements that won for me. For instance, publicity. Most educators don't fully realize what worlds can be accomplished with the skillful use of the media. I believe I have a definite knack in that department. Perhaps I should have been a Hollywood public relations man. In any event, we were able to make the move of a professor from one school to another front page news. Again, a sort of domino effect took place. The first story paved the way. After the first story newspapers seemed to accept that such things must be news. They aren't, of course, but we made them into front page items. It was quite an exhilarating time for me."

"I can imagine. A bit tense too, I'll wager."

For the first time Green saw a true glimmer of the real man behind the placid mask. There was a flash of annoyance in the dean's eyes, quickly hidden. "I suppose it should have been tense, but it wasn't. I thoroughly enjoyed the whole thing. I felt no sense of anxiety, if that's what you mean. For me, it was quite a grand adventure."

The man was proud of his accomplishments, and justly so, but he resented any suggestion that he might experience the fears and feelings of normal men. That was pride for pride's sake, and it presented an interesting facet to the man's character. Green made a mental note.

"I called Martin Naham's office. I believe you did tell one of my young ladies that the university president could vouch for you?"

"That's right," Green said. "I presume he told you that I had been checked out with the White House."

"Yes. Although I was a bit mystified by your Harley Dingell card."

"Why is that?"

The dean leaned forward, the same confident half smile fixed upon his features. "You were a partner there?"

"Yes."

"Well, that's what I mean. Usually the road leads the other way. Special counsel to the president and then out to a fancy law firm, not the other way around. Not usually anyway."

Green wondered if the dean was really intimating that Green

couldn't last with a prestigious law firm and had retreated back to government work, or whether it was merely a probe to provoke and test reaction.

"I'm on a leave of absence from the firm," Green responded. "I have some special duties to perform for the White House. When that's done I will return to Harley Dingell." He suddenly realized that his words sounded just as full of pride as had those of the dean.

"Fascinating." Pentecost's eyes were fixed on his own. The score was even, each man having made the other exhibit unseemly pride.

Green was irritated but took special pains not to show it. "I wonder if we could go for a short walk around the campus? The weather isn't too bad. A bit chilly, but not much wind. Good walking weather."

"A walk?" The bland expression altered just a bit.

"Or a drive, if you like. I can get my car."

The dean smiled. "May I ask why this preoccupation with the great outdoors?"

Green paused a moment before replying. It would be interesting to observe the man's reaction to the words. "I understand you've had the building wired so that classes and conversations can be monitored. I presume that is done by taping?"

A flash of anger passed over the dean's face, but only momentarily. He recovered and gave an almost playful shrug. "I can understand your concern," he said. "But let me assure you that it's only the classrooms that have the monitoring equipment. And also be assured that it was installed for no sinister purpose."

"I didn't think that at all."

The dean's smile widened, but his eyes were without humor. "Then why the need for a walk?"

"I think better in the outdoors," Green replied evenly, also smiling, and equally broadly.

The dean nodded. "I do monitor the classrooms, particularly

the new instructors. Just as one minor flaw can render a great jewel almost valueless, an incapable or indifferent teacher can leave a dangerous void in an otherwise complete legal education. My purpose is to insure that the students here are receiving superior instruction. We hire the best-qualified people, but sometimes references don't tell the full story. If I didn't keep close check, this school could develop soft spots that would show up later, far too late for anything to be done to correct the problem. Thus, the monitoring."

"Still, you must admit that it is an unusual practice for a law school."

The dean never changed expression. "Perhaps, but this is an unusual law school, Mr. Green, ah, Jerry. In a matter of only a very few years we have become the equal of such regal institutions as Harvard, Stanford, and the other handful of prestigious national law schools. I have used unusual methods to bring that result about. But monitoring is certainly nothing new in education. In fact, this system is a duplicate of one used in a large Catholic high school in Chicago. The Mother Superior there had the control panel set up right in her office." He laughed. "I saw it. It looked like the cockpit of a commercial airliner, all gauges and dials. Now the good sister was not sinister certainly, nor paranoid. She just wanted to see that the children, whose parents were paying a very high dollar in tuition, were getting full value for their educational money. And that is also my purpose." He seemed to almost stare at Green. "My only purpose."

Pentecost had been stung by the issue of taping, but he had handled himself well, even though Green knew the man was angry. The dean would do well before the inquisitors on the Judiciary Committee.

Green nodded. "I accept your position, of course. Still, I would prefer a walk or a drive."

The dean stood up, an almost mischievous smile playing at the corner of his lips. "A walk. I would prefer a walk. I think your car would be fine, but as I understand from our university president, you were part of the old Nixon crew. As I recall, you fellows had something of a reputation for fooling around with recording equipment too. I think a walk would be fine."

Green carefully hid his anger. "I was a little too far down the line to pick up on any of the fine points of tape recorders," he said evenly, smiling as he did so. "And the car is rented. It has everything except microphones. Still, I too prefer a walk."

Both men donned their coats and walked together out of the law school. To Green, the air seemed to be a bit colder.

"I'm surprised that your president's office didn't mention my origin in these parts," Green said.

"They just mentioned the highlights of your career. They probably were read a press clipping from the White House." He turned and looked at Green. "If I had done the checking, we would have known. I like to be thorough."

They strolled along together. Even their outer clothing was similar. Students and faculty hurried by dressed in ski jackets or parkas, rough clothing suited to the environment. But both Green and Pentecost were outfitted in expensive cashmere overcoats and fashionable hats. They both favored slip-on rubber boots over their expensive shoes.

"Shall we walk toward the stadium?" the dean suggested. "It's not quite as busy and it will be a bit more private."

"Fine."

They walked along for a while in silence. "I presume there's some purpose in all this?" The dean tried to make the question sound light, as if he didn't really care, but Green knew he had won their little waiting game.

"I think you know the purpose."

The dean kicked at a rough piece of snow on the plowed path. "I believe I do," he said. "But let's say, for argument's sake, that I'm wrong. I should prefer you to state what was on your mind, that way I won't look like a fool if I'm incorrect." He looked directly at Green. "Let's get down to business, shall we?"

"Yes, of course." Green noted that the dean was an impatient man. "You have been recommended as a possible choice to fill the vacancy on the Supreme Court left by the death of Justice Howell. But I presume you already knew that."

"Yes. Nothing official, of course. The newspapers have begun calling, and some of my friends. But I asked my friends not to do anything on my behalf. Some of them had wanted to move even while Howell was ill. I wouldn't allow it, and I won't allow any activities of that sort until after the funeral."

"Do you really think that was wise?" Green again hoped to provoke the dean into revealing a bit more of himself.

"Under the circumstances, it was the only decent thing to do. It would have been churlish to start campaigning for the job while poor Howell was in the hospital. Also, I think it's indecent to start the drums rolling before the body grows cold."

Green gave no indication of his thoughts on the matter. "Very honorable, I'm sure. However, there are other candidates, and none of them seemed to think it unseemly to try early on for the appointment."

"To each his own," the dean replied.

"It may have even cost you the job," Green said, intimating some secret knowledge.

Pentecost looked at him and chuckled. "I doubt it. Let's not examine it from any honorable viewpoint, just tactically. Our new president is a product of his environment. A go-getter by all means, but a gentleman. I think he's the type who would resent such greedy and unseemly conduct."

"And so that's why you didn't make any moves for the job?"

The dean's face again assumed the defensive placid mask. "Not at all. I too would resent anything like that, no matter what the circumstances."

Green reflected on the man. The dean had restrained his supporters as a smart tactical ploy. Pentecost had read the chief executive very well. And like a master chess player he had resisted charging into the easy and expected move. Green wondered if honor had had anything at all to do with it. It was one of the questions about the dean's character that had to be answered.

"Honor is all well and good," Green said, "but I think it may have cost you the match."

"Do you?" The dean's smile spread slowly over his face. "Then I suppose that's why the White House sent you down here to talk to me? To tell me I can't have a job I haven't sought? Unlikely, Mr. Green, er, Jerry. No, I rather think the President appreciated my conduct. Do you see my point?"

Green didn't reply at once, he allowed his silence to work on the other man. Finally he spoke. "Why do you think I'm here? It's in connection with the Supreme Court vacancy, of course, but what do you think my function is?"

The dean seemed to assume an air of indifference, grasping his gloved hands behind his back as they strolled along. "I have several thoughts on the matter," he said. "First, as I'm sure you know, I was being considered as a nominee the last time. I was waiting in the wings, with others, I'm told, in case that lady couldn't make it through the Senate. At that time I was checked out by the FBI, and I know several key government people carefully reviewed my record. The American Bar Association and other lawyer groups cleared me and certified my competence for appointment. Therefore, I presume your arrival here, and your very short, ah, investigation, is some sort of final step as to whether or not my name will be put forward this time." He smiled at Green. "Am I close?"

Green realized that the dean was also trying to provoke feelings and attitudes in him. So far, it had been mostly an even contest.

"How badly do you want the job?" Green asked quietly.

The dean made no immediate reply, but walked on for a while before answering. He seemed to be weighing his reply carefully. "I'm very happy here," he said. "The law school has been the greatest achievement of my life. In a very real way, it has been my life. To stay here isn't the worst thing in the world. However, the school is built, it is completely established. In other words, I wouldn't mind a new challenge, a new mountain to climb, as it were."

"And the Supreme Court would be that new mountain?"

The dean shrugged. "Not a bad ending to a career in the law, eh?"

"Have you consulted your wife?"

For only an instant there was fear in the dean's eyes, but the bland mask covered it instantly. "There's no problem there. Actually, I think my wife finds the midwest somewhat confining. You know women. I rather think she would love the excitement, the parties, and so forth."

Green had noted the alarm. "But have you asked her?"

Pentecost's mouth drew into a tight line. "We haven't discussed it since the last time I was proposed for the job. At that time she was most agreeable. I know of nothing that would have changed her mind." He looked away from Green.

The dean obviously knew about his wife, just as Green did about his own. Perhaps Pentecost thought a change of environment might make matters better between them. Or maybe he didn't really care. Maybe it was merely a convenient arrangement, and not a real marriage at all. Green wondered if the dean and he shared that in common, in addition to their taste in clothes.

"The reason I asked," Green said evenly, "is sometimes family considerations can change a man's plans."

"In that area, I have no worries," Pentecost answered briskly.

He knows all right, Green thought to himself. It would serve no useful purpose to prod him further in that area.

"Philosophically, what would you think your role might be on the Court, if appointed?" Green asked.

The dean stopped dead and turned toward him. "Look, let's stop horsing around, shall we? They didn't send you down here to sound out my philosophical views. You wouldn't have been so worried about a tape recorder in my office if that were true. You want something. This is a big bad world, Mr. Green, and although I may not approve of it at times, I damn well do understand it. Now why don't we quit this game? I presume certain assurances are desired before my name is put forward."

Green didn't reply. He merely studied the dean's face, a tactic to unnerve him, to make him believe he had committed a blunder. It was a useful approach in a trial or at a deposition.

The dean smiled. "In order to build that school back there I have had to deal with some of the most reprehensible politicians, both public and academic, since man's first relative crawled out of the slime. I have promised, traded, and wheedled with all manner of men. So you can give me all the reproachful blank looks you wish, my friend, it won't work. I know how this game is played. If you don't choose to tell me now what is expected of me, you will before we finish our little walk." The dean's speech had been completely without any emotional display. He turned and resumed walking. Green followed and caught up with him.

"The late Justice Howell set things up so that he became the Supreme Court," Green said as they walked. "He became the swing man. The Court was, and is, evenly divided between so-called liberals and conservatives on most issues. Howell used his vote to control the general direction of American law."

"That's well known," the dean replied.

"If appointed, would you do the same?"

The dean again walked with his hands clasped behind him. "It's possible, I suppose. I don't think I could be classified as a liberal or a conservative. I try to look at most issues independently. On that basis, I could very easily become the swing man, so called. Of course, I don't have to tell you that the Supreme Court is like the sands of the desert; it shifts endlessly, blown about by the political winds of the moment. But most presidents get one or two appointments to the Court during their term of office. Given the advanced ages of the present justices, I expect the Court will change greatly in the near future. Therefore, I really couldn't look forward to a very long career as swing man, even if I wanted that role, could I?"

"Howell sometimes traded votes."

The dean shrugged. "You come from one of the most powerful law firms in Washington, surely vote swapping comes as no news to you? It's done in every appellate court in the land. Some more than others."

"You approve the practice?"

"It doesn't matter if I approve of the sun, Mr. Green, it will come up anyway. No, as a matter of fact, I don't approve of trading votes, but if it has to be done, I shall do it, albeit reluctantly."

"The Judiciary Committee will be a rugged gauntlet to run. They'll be waiting to take a whack at anyone the President puts up. The conservatives don't want a liberal, and the liberals will be gunning for any conservative. Do you think you would be able to handle them?"

"I'm ready. If nominated, I shall prepare definitively. I've had to testify before committees, even hostile committees. I'll have no trouble. Fortunately, there are no skeletons in my closet, by the way."

"Are you sure?"

The dean looked at him, a slight smirk playing at his lips. "Absolutely. Now shall we get to business? What is it that the President wants in exchange for the appointment?"

"That's blunt."

Pentecost laughed. "That's honest. Well, what is it?"

The dean seemed somehow to have gotten the upper hand, for it was Green who now felt slightly uncomfortable. The dean was as experienced at handling people as he had said.

"There are several important matters coming before the Court," Green began.

"Such as the Electoral College question?" The dean glanced

over at Green, the knowing half smile again set upon his bland features.

"That's one of the matters," Green replied.

"Yes. An interesting case. Oddly enough, I've made quite a study of it. Constitutional law is my main card, as you probably know."

"So I'm told."

Pentecost smiled, this time broadly. "If the Electoral College system is defeated, that is, if the Court holds that the states have legally ratified the proposed amendment, then the President stands in jeopardy of losing the next election. If the system remains intact I'm sure he feels he has a better chance. Anyway, that's the gist of the political speculation articles recently."

The dean had gone right to the nerve.

"There have been articles," Green said hesitantly.

Pentecost laughed. "That's a gross understatement. The papers and magazines have been full of them. But, as I say, fortunately I've studied the issue very carefully. I doubt if the briefs or oral arguments would be as definitive as my own studies on the matter. So you see, I can honestly say how I would expect to vote on that issue, since I am already completely informed." He smiled. "Convenient, wouldn't you say?"

"Yes."

"Now if I were to tell you that I believed the states had indeed ratified the constitutional amendment and the Electoral College was no more, I rather think I could count on continuing as dean of this fine law school, don't you?" He laughed again. "However, after due study, I can say that because the two state legislatures reversed their original vote, the amendment was not ratified and the electoral system will stand. If appointed, that's exactly how I shall vote. I presume that answers the burning question?"

"One of them," Green replied.

"How old are you, Jerry?" The dean again idly kicked at a clump of snow.

"Forty-six."

"That was my guess. We're the same age. Interesting, isn't it?"

Green shook his head. "Not particularly."

The dean stopped, forcing Green to stop too. "Look, I have just obtained a huge grant for the law school from the Alesia Fund. I am to found the Samuel Alesia Chair for Administrative Law. The man who is appointed to that post will automatically be tenured. In other words, he will serve for life."

"I'm familiar with tenure."

"This job goes a bit beyond that. The grant is made contingent upon that feature. It's a means of insuring independence, a specific demand by Mr. Alesia. So, even in the face of the shifting sands of academic politics or funding, the man or woman who occupies that chair has an absolute umbrella against the stormy future, so to speak."

"So?"

The dean did not resume walking. He stood there, his hands clasped behind him. "You are a partner in one of the nation's finest law firms, I realize that. And, based on that, I have a rough idea of your income, which I hazard goes beyond being merely substantial. I suspect that you may have aimed for that partnership in the same way I aimed to become head of a great law school."

Green made no reply.

"At our age, despite success, men sometimes look for a change in career. Isn't that so? I have seen that in so many of our contemporaries."

"The middle-age syndrome. There have been articles written about it."

Pentecost beamed. "Yes. Now I rather suspect you were sent down here for more than the mere purpose of asking one simple question. The state national committeeman here is a dear personal friend of mine. The question and answer could have just as easily been handled through him. Therefore, I surmise, there's an additional purpose."

Green began walking, forcing the dean to resume.

"Jerry, I know you've talked to the university's president about me. I know also you've talked to some of the faculty. I understand you even spoke to our resident weasel, Malcolm Whittle. Judging by all that effort on your part, I think the White House is looking for some sort of personal appraisal by you. Am I correct?"

Green walked on a bit before answering. "They want an appraisal. I imagine this is being duplicated by others who are looking at other candidates for the job. A great deal rides on who is selected for the Court. The President has to be sure that the person has the ability to fight his or her way through the Judiciary Committee. And he needs to know the stand on the electoral question, of course. But in addition, he has to have some general appreciation of the character of the candidate."

"And that's your job?"

"I'm just part of it. I suppose they'll take my report and add it to the other information they have about you and make a judgment from there."

The dean pursed his lips and blew through them, then smiled. "I suspect you are a most competent lawyer, but you really are a rather poor liar."

"Liar?"

Pentecost nodded. "A strong word, I admit. But you weren't plucked out of Harley Dingell and made Special Counsel to the President just so your observation could be made part of a collection of other material. That doesn't stand to reason, and you know it."

"I rather resent. . . ."

"Why don't we drop all this pretense, Green. My fortunes probably stand or fall on what you say. Don't deny it, there's no tape recorder playing here."

Green again hesitated before replying. "My personal assessment will carry great weight, or so I'm told."

"Or so you're told? Modesty is such a becoming virtue, isn't it? Well, you asked me about trading cases, didn't you? You know as well as I that to question me about how I might dispose of a case is highly improper. But I answered it, did I not?"

"You did."

"Then who is the greater sinner, Mr. Green? Who is less worthy of confidence? The man who answers the improper question, or the man who asks it?"

Green laughed despite himself.

"So here we are, you and I, a couple of very dishonorable fellows, trading away a significant portion of the country's constitution for the promise of a job. Isn't that what it amounts to?"

"That's one way of looking at it."

"Ah, of course, never give the opponent a point, right? I tell you, sir, that's the only way to look at it. You can, in all good conscience, report that since I answered the question in expectation of appointment, I do not possess the necessary integrity to perform the job. If you did that, do you know what would happen?"

"I think I do," Green said, trying to keep the sudden irritation out of his voice.

"No, you don't, not if you're becoming angry about it. The gentlemen who sent you, the President included, are politicians, not civics teachers. They'd laugh at your naivete."

"I think you're wrong."

Pentecost sighed. "You know, you look like me. We are the same age. I suspect we even think alike. That's why I'm speaking to you quite openly, something I usually tend to avoid. But you're an intelligent man, and I know this is a high stakes game, at least it is for me. I want that damn job very much. Sure, I'd like to be in a position where I could tell you to go take a jump, to protest the impertinence and impropriety of your questions. But if I did that, your people wouldn't take me for a man of integrity, they'd take me for an imbecile. Look at it from my point of view. If there was a good and valid reason for me to go the other way on the Electoral College case, if it was truly against my conscience, I would tell you so, believe me. But what's really at stake in that case? It's a mere political question. No one will be denied due process, no fundamental rights will be destroyed. So as worldly gentlemen, in good conscience, you can ask it and I can answer it. Had that occurred to you?"

Green looked at Pentecost. The blandness had gone. There was real animation in his face now, a hard-eyed salesman moving in to close a deal.

"When I proposed this law school, the most powerful man in the legislature, then and now, was State Senator Jacob Rock." Pentecost turned and gestured toward the law school building, jutting above all its neighbors. "You know how I got that? A knowledge of human nature, that's how. Jacob Rock is a wealthy man, a millionaire several times over. Self-made in every way. He had only an eighth-grade education. Now I suspected he just might be touchy about that. I gently raised it with him and he was painfully defensive. To make a long story short, I arranged for him to take certain tests in general subjects and political science here at the university. I had to twist a few arms but Senator Rock is now a graduate of this university. All quite aboveboard and legal. He's well read and he easily passed all the exams. And getting him that degree is the thing that swung the law school. He was grateful, and you've seen the result."

"What are you getting at?"

"A bribe."

"Pardon me?"

"Oh, I could substitute a host of nicer words, but it would remain a bribe, nevertheless."

Green stopped. "What the hell are you talking about?"

"A knowledge of human nature, just as with Senator Rock. The way I figure it, Jerry"—it was the first time he had used the name with ease— "you took that White House stint because you aren't completely satisfied with your lot in life. It's a guess, but I think maybe you aren't so happy with good old Harley Dingell, or perhaps they aren't happy with you. It happens. In any event, if you put in a good word for me, I'll see you get that professorship in administrative law. You'll take a hell of a cut in income, but we do pay better than all other American law schools, so you won't live in poverty by any means. You'll be away from the strife of Washington and back home. A nice happy lifetime job, no stress, no cares. As a bribe it really isn't much, but it's the only thing I can think to offer you."

"You certainly throw words around loosely."

"Or truthfully," Pentecost snapped. "Don't you think I could just as easily put my arm around your shoulders and tell you of the great need this school has for a man of your background and experience. I could do that, hell, I do that all the time. But you're an intelligent man, you'd know that no matter how sugar-coated, it would still be a bribe. So what's wrong with the truth?"

"Would you write your decisions in such a candid manner?"

The dean laughed. "No. Never. The truth is a very dangerous weapon and should be used most sparingly. I would follow the lead of my predecessors on the Supreme Court and take several pages to say in very long words what could easily be condensed into a sentence. I won't embarrass the President or you, don't worry."

"Well, I suppose that's it then," Green said, stopping and turning. "I've made my improper inquiry, you've made your improper response, and thrown in a bribe to boot. I would guess we have gone as far as we can about the nation's business. Shall we go back?"

The dean slapped him on the back. "When you walked into my office today I thought to myself that you were a man I could really talk to. What's your decision?"

Green looked at the rising prow of the law school in the distance. "I'll have to give it some thought. That doesn't mean my report will be unfavorable. But it doesn't mean it will be favorable either."

The dean looked puzzled. "Is there something additional I can do for you?"

Green was about to answer no, then the germ of an idea popped into his mind.

"Maybe there is. Do you know much about the other cases coming before the Court?"

"We subscribe to a service that keeps the school up to date. Needless to say, in the last few days I've studied it very carefully. Always be prepared, as the Boy Scouts say."

"What would be your position on the Marchall case?"

Pentecost frowned. "The antitrust case? Is the President interested in that?"

"I suppose you might say he was pro business." Green paused. "I'm informed Harley Dingell will offer the oral argument on behalf of Marchall."

The dean smiled broadly. "Well now, I'm pro business myself. I rather think the Marchall company can count on my vote."

Green nodded. "Out of curiosity, how would you go on the rational suicide issue?"

"Is the President interested in that?"

"Not that I know of," Green replied.

"Well, I have no strong feelings one way or the other. What does the press call the nun involved, Sister Death? Well, we put animals out of their misery, I suppose we can extend the same courtesy to our fellow man on occasion. I would probably vote to acquit the nun."

"And the affirmative action case, the one about the police department?"

"Again, just curiosity?" Pentecost asked.

"Yes."

The dean walked along silently for a moment. "Again, I have no firm position. If I voted to continue the quota system what harm could it do? It would just make our black cities a bit blacker, right? It's going to happen anyway. A vote in favor would look good to the liberals. Yes, I'd probably vote to enforce racial quotas." He looked at Green. "Unless, of course, it would make a difference to the administration."

"What about the freedom of the press issue. They have a case coming up about press negligence . . . ."

"Ah, I know all about that one." Pentecost beamed. "Does the President have a position?"

"No."

Pentecost chuckled. "Well, if I vote for the nun and against the police, the liberals would love me, of course. On that basis I'd have to vote to stick it to the newspapers, so to speak, just to demonstrate that I was even-handed. That's a decision that would please the conservatives. Actually, the press has too much power as it is."

Green walked along without comment.

"Do those answers upset you?" Pentecost still had the confident half smile on his face.

"No."

"Then I presume your report will be favorable."

Green continued to walk, almost feeling the raw ambition radiating from the man next to him. "If I told you I honestly haven't made up my mind, would you believe me?"

"Probably not. What else do you need?"

Green thought of Regina, of his own life. "I need some time to think," he answered honestly.

*　　*　　*

The dean returned to the law school and Green trudged on toward the center of the campus. Classes were changing and Green again had to weather the trampling herd of bundled students, all rushing, bumping, and converging like rapids in a turbulent river. He floated along with the sea of parkas and woolen jackets, without thought, just walking aimlessly.

He found himself in front of the School of Nursing. He

stopped, half climbing up a mound of snow to escape the passing students.

He wondered if she was inside. It seemed he could almost project Regina's soft features on the side of that building. He dwelled mentally on her large, loving eyes. It had been a very long time since he had a real relationship with anyone. He was no longer open or trusting. Everything in his life was at dagger point, emotions, thoughts, reactions—a constant barter and trade position. He longed to stand unarmed before someone, to feel secure against emotional or intellectual attack. Regina offered that. It wasn't romance that he hungered for, it was the peace of emotional safety. He would have that here.

He surveyed the passing throng of students. Teaching law wouldn't be unpleasant. There would be challenge. There was always that from the emerging abilities of the competitive minds found in any law school. But the challenges would be easily handled. They weren't to be feared, they were to be enjoyed.

Green had always liked the campus as a boy, it still held a fascination for him. It was indeed home. Here he experienced a feeling of safe harbor.

The mass of students also thinned out as they found their destinations. He began to walk again, this time coming to the building that housed his brother's office. Suddenly he felt an overwhelming need to see his brother and talk to him.

The eight-year difference in their ages had been more like an entire generation when they were young. They weren't close. However, sometimes, especially when life seemed most perilous, he had sought out his older brother's counsel. It had been given with a certain disdain, but given nevertheless—short, practical, and usually correct.

Green stepped up the walk into the Anthropology Building and climbed the stairs to his brother's office. He tapped gently on the door.

A woman, who looked like a permanent employee, stopped. "Can I help you?"

"I'm looking for Professor Green."

"Oh, he's at home today. A bit under the weather, I understand."

"Thank you."

There was a pay phone in the building's lobby. He found Hank's number and called. It was answered immediately by Adele.

"It's me, Jerry," he said. "Is Hank well enough to see me for a few minutes?"

"He just got up." There was cold hostility in her voice, but he couldn't determine whether it was directed at himself or Hank. "Just a minute," she snapped. He could hear her yelling.

Another phone clicked into life. "Wha?"

"Hank?"

"Yeah."

"It's me, Jerry. Are you up to seeing me for a few minutes? Your office said you were ill."

"Yeah. I'm hung over. Bad. This important?"

"It is to me."

There was a pause. "Jesus, I feel like shit, but come ahead. At least it isn't catching."

"I'll be there in a few minutes."

Green retraced his route to his car and drove quickly off the campus and up into the winding streets of his brother's subdivision. The house looked different in the daylight.

Adele let him in, her face a stiff mask of resignation. "He's in the family room," she said, pointedly not offering to guide him.

He doffed his overcoat and boots. Adele had gone off somewhere else in the large house. He put the boots on a mat and hung up his hat and coat in the hall closet.

Hank lay in rumpled pajamas on a long sofa in the family room. There was a television but it wasn't on. Jerry Green noticed a framed photograph of their father on the wall, along with pictures of Hank and Adele's children in various stages of development.

Hank had a half-full cup on his chest, held in one huge hand. He was unshaven.

"Come in," he said without opening his eyes. "I just look dead."

Jerry Green sat down in a large chair facing the sofa. His brother raised his head and opened one eye. "Tied one on last night. No Goddamn reason. Adele was on my ass about something, but then she's always on my ass about something. I really don't mind the hangovers after I've had a real good time, sort of paying the piper. But Christ, when you just sit in your own house getting blitzed, it seems unfair to suffer like this."

"Can I get you anything?"

"No. This is a Bloody Mary I'm drinking. My stomach isn't rejecting it so it looks like I'll make it. I may not want to, but it appears that way." He opened the other eye, half raising his head. "If you want some coffee or anything, you'll have to ask Adele. She isn't talking to me."

"I'm all set, thanks."

"Well, Jerry, what's your problem? You said it was important." Hank raised his head and slurped at the cup. The tomato juice left a red ring along his upper lip.

Jerry Green wanted to pour out the whole story, his conflicting emotions and the conflicts of his life, but as he looked at his brother he could see that Hank was still slightly drunk. In his state, Hank's advice would be a very weak reed to lean upon. Suddenly he felt very foolish.

"You might say it's a personal problem."

"Ah, trouble with your new old lady, eh?"

"That's part of it."

Hank slurped at his drink again. "Man, that's part of any married man's misery. But you won't get much sympathy out of me. Christ, this is your second marriage. You'd think you would have learned from the first. At least I have that comfort. If I ever get divorced, or if the good Lord in his wisdom swoops down and deprives me of my wonderful Adele, I'll have the good sense not to repeat the mistake. You should have thought of what you were doing. First times don't count, anybody can make a mistake. It's repeating it that's stupid."

"On that basis, there's a lot of us stupid people around."

"Oh sure, you can give me that old loneliness horseshit, everybody uses that one, but it's just an excuse. Getting married again is the result of either lust or romance, usually a combination of both. It robs people of their intellect, their moral courage, their basic integrity, and their common sense."

"You and Adele really must be having a swell time of it."

His brother smirked. "Won'erful, just damn won'erful. See, I carp at you but I don't have the courage to get out. Ya know why?" Hank was slurring his words.

Jerry Green shook his head.

"Because I'm afraid I'd do the same damn silly thing you did. Shit, some wide-hipped blonde with big blue eyes would make me think I was a young stud again. I know I'd fall for the whole bit: the romance, the sweet talk, the beautiful music that will go on forever. That's a bunch of shit. The music and romance stops pretty damn quick. Nobody in the real world lives that way." He sipped his drink. "At least Papa had the guts to stay out of it again after Ma died. That's one thing that's constant, at least to me. When I'm in trouble I always think of Pa and his courage."

Jerry Green said nothing.

"We were blessed with a great father," Hank continued. "I never really understood how much shit he had to eat as a professor. Christ, it must have been much worse for him, being Jewish."

"You're Jewish," Green reminded his brother.

"I mean like it was in the old days. Hell, they called me the 'Flying Hebe' in high school, remember?"

"Sure."

"Whoever thought that up meant the tag to hurt. But I turned it around on 'em. I adopted the thing, made it a gag, something to be proud of. It worked out pretty good. But those were different days.

"Being Jewish must have made it tough for Papa." Hank shook his head and laughed. "That's all changed now. Crap, now half the faculty up here are into some weird religion or other, the other half are flaming atheists. You go to some of these faculty things and you meet everything from nudists to snake worshippers. Yeah, it's a lot looser now."

"You don't sound as militant as you used to."

Hank snorted as he slowly sat up. "I think my head's going to explode." He paused and blinked his eyes. "I'm okay," he said, mostly to himself. "Yeah, I don't give a shit about that ethnic crap anymore. Big deal. Those of my kids who do get married are going to marry shiksas anyway. We celebrate Christmas now, did you know that? And I mean the whole thing, the tree, Santa, outdoor lights, the works. One of these Decembers I expect Adele will put a stable scene out on the front lawn. If you're looking for the headquarters of the Jewish Defense League, this ain't it."

Jerry Green thought back to another time.

Hank seemed to read his thoughts. He looked at him. "Hey, that thing when Pa died, I think we were both a couple of flaming assholes."

Green knew that Hank was coming as close to an apology as he could expect.

"It was a bad time for both of us."

Hank drained the rest of his drink. "See, I was in Europe. I was doing the whole Jewish bit, first Israel, then the European death camps. You ever see them?"

Jerry Green shook his head.

"Don't. I still have nightmares. Anyway, they have carefully preserved all that shit, the barbed wire, the buildings, the showers, the ovens. We were in Munich when I got your call about Pa being dead."

"I remember."

"Yeah, well by the time we got back, everything was over. I expected that, given the religious thing. But I went nuts when you told me you had the old man cremated. It wasn't you, you see, it was I had just come back from seeing those Goddamned ovens. It was, well, it was like a horrible thing had been done to our own father."

Green nodded. "If I had known your feelings, Hank, I wouldn't have done it. Although Pa did leave instructions asking to be cremated." Both statements were lies.

Hank shrugged. "Hey, what's it all matter anyway? You thought you were doing right, I thought I was doing right, and it split the family in one angry instant. I don't think that was exactly the way our old man would have wanted things to turn out."

"I agree."

"I wanted to talk to you about it the other night, but I just couldn't find a way to bring it up."

Green nodded. "I felt the same way."

"Good, then that's over."

"Adele is still angry."

Hank shrugged. "Listen, sport, she's always angry. You know women. She was in Europe along with me. She didn't trust me there alone. Anyway, the camp thing affected her too. But as you know, women never forgive nor do they forget. That's something I can't change."

"I can live with it."

"If we see you once in a while, she'll get over it."

"Probably."

Hank stood up. "God, I feel terrible." He quickly sat down again. He took a cigarette from a pack on the table and lit one. "Before you decide to divorce the broad you married, you ought to bring her here for a visit. I'd like to be able to say that I at least met all my brother's wives." He grinned. "Any other problems beside domestic?"

Jerry Green shrugged. "You spoke of integrity and courage a

while ago. I have a job to do and I suppose it will come down to just that, whether I have basic moral integrity, and maybe even courage."

Hank laughed. "That's heavy stuff to lay on a drunk." He blew out some smoke. "But I'll tell you what, Jerry, you can't go wrong if you just follow one rule."

"What's that?"

"Figure out what our old man would have done, then do it. If there was one person in this wide world who had both integrity and courage, he was it. The older I get, the more I appreciate that. Man, he had to take a lot of crap, and he had to use his noodle, but he just didn't merely survive, he had dignity. Right down to the day he died he had dignity. And courage. I never knew him to be afraid, did you?"

Jerry Green shook his head.

"Anyway, that's your big brother's advice: figure out what the old man would have done then follow his example. You can't miss, believe me."

Jerry Green saw the conviction burning from his brother's reddened eyes. He meant every word, and believed it. All these years had just increased his faith. Hank had never found out, and it would destroy him now if he knew. He had conferred a kind of saintliness upon the memory of their father.

Jerry Green stood up and extended his hand. "Watch the drinking, Hank, it can catch up on you."

His brother grinned up at him. "You try being married to Adele for a while, then I'll take your advice." He started to get up, then sat back down. "Listen, I'd walk you to the door, but I don't think I'd make it."

"I'll let myself out. If I don't see her, square it with Adele, okay?"

"Going back to Washington?"

"Maybe. I don't know yet. I'll let you know."

Jerry Green quickly retrieved his coat and boots. He didn't

really want to see Adele or have to do any additional explaining. He hurried out to his car and sped away, spinning a bit on the slick pavement.

Hank Green had been in Europe when it happened. Jerry Green had been in Washington. Hank was teaching at Penn State. They saw their father infrequently. Both men believed he had a full life at the university. Green fought the car out of another spin and realized he was going too fast. He felt his eyes fill with tears. He was surprised, he thought he was over it after all these years.

Dr. Connolly had called him in Washington and he had immediately flown home. Connolly had been a lifelong friend of his father's and his personal physician. Green vividly remembered every detail of the room where Dr. Connolly had tried gently to break the news to him, to tell him the actual facts. He already knew his father was dead. A heart attack, Connolly had told him that over the telephone. But it wasn't true. His father was dead all right, but he had poisoned himself. A lonely old man, with practically no teaching duties—professor emeritus was his title—his father had an office, someplace to go, but that was about all. So he had ended it. The note was in his handwriting. "There are no more dreams." That was all, just five words. Old Connolly had certified the death as cardiac arrest despite the obvious evidence of suicide. Jerry Green, the smart young Washington lawyer, quickly had his father's body cremated, partly to conceal the ultimate sadness of the suicide, but more importantly, to protect Dr. Connolly, who had acted out of kindness.

When Hank arrived the next day, he had gone berserk, and a yelling, screaming fight had ended their relationship as brothers. But whatever neglect their father had suffered, at least now his memory was enshrined forever in Hank's household.

The blare of a horn behind him angrily informed him the signal light had turned green. He drove on, blinking away the tears in his eyes.

He found it difficult to concentrate. He thought of his brother's advice, what would Pa do? Kill myself, he wondered, instantly ashamed at the thought. He remembered his father, a kind, gentle man with soft eyes. The eyes seemed to melt into the eyes and the face of Regina. Romance was never real, that's what Hank had said—maybe he was right, but he could be wrong too. Then he thought about the dean, and it seemed in his imagination as if his own face was looking back at him. There was a knowing look in those eyes, a look that said I know what you're going to do. But were those his own eyes, or the dean's?

He pulled into his motel's parking lot. He was headed for his room when he noticed that the motel's cocktail lounge was open. He went in, hung up his coat, and took a seat at the small bar.

There was no one else in the place except the young jacket-clad bartender back of the bar.

"Yes sir?" The bartender looked genuinely pleased to see a customer.

"Scotch and soda."

"Heavy or light Scotch?"

"Heavy."

The young bartender made a graceful movement with the bottle as he poured the Scotch, a sweeping, theatrical gesture.

"Are you a student here?"

"Yes sir. I'm an English major."

"Read much Shakespeare?"

"You bet, it's required," he said, as he deftly added ice and soda to the glass.

"He wrote ghost stories."

"Pardon me?" The bartender snapped out a paper napkin and placed the completed drink before his only customer. He beamed, pleased with his own professional performance.

"Shakespeare wrote ghost stories," Jerry Green said. "Macbeth, Hamlet, Julius Caesar; he had this thing about ghosts."

The young man occupied himself with some busy work behind the bar. "It was probably the times," he said cheerfully. "You know, the end of the Middle Ages, superstition and all that. He was just writing for his audience, that's all."

"Dickens, too," Green said, sipping his drink. "You can't find a better ghost story than old Scrooge and his friends."

The bartender eyed him carefully, obviously wondering if this was just idle conversation or whether he had a drunk on his hands, or worse, a nut.

"You'll find it all through literature, young man," Green said, smiling. "Ghosts populate some of the very best stories." He sipped the drink again. "Even today the paperback racks and the movies are preoccupied with hauntings of all kinds."

"Man by his nature is superstitious," the young man said, now a bit wary.

"Did you ever see a ghost?" Green asked. "I mean it, on the level, did you ever have anything to do with ghosts in any form?"

The bartender's eyes narrowed with suspicion. "No. I'm afraid I don't believe in ghosts."

"How about hauntings? Ever been haunted?"

"Only after too much booze." His was an empty, professional laugh.

"You may not have even realized it," Jerry Green said, finishing his drink. "I've been haunted for years and I've just found out about it." He got up and put a bill on the bar. He winked at the young man.

The wink relieved the tension.

"Keep the change," Green said collecting his coat.

"I hope your ghosts don't bother you too much," the bartender called after him.

"Me too." The words were spoken softly and couldn't be heard by the young man. Green thought again of his father. "Me too," he repeated in a whisper as he headed toward his room and the telephone.

It would be the most significant telephone call of his life.

Chapter 11

Sister Agatha Murphy knelt in the quiet chapel. Only a few other nuns were scattered about in the otherwise empty pews. Sister Agatha Murphy made a habit of spending the hours of the late afternoon in the chapel. However, she was not praying. Not that she didn't pray, she did. She prayed upon arising, at morning mass, at noon, at evening services, and just before she retired. But she didn't pray in the chapel in the late afternoon. Being there served two purposes. First, the other nuns believed she was praying and this external mark of extra devotion shielded her against some of the reproving looks of her colleagues. They, she knew, felt that through prayer she would eventually see the error of her ways and admit to God, and to the Mother General, that she was indeed guilty of murder. The second purpose was to have a nice quiet place, free of distraction, where she could plan her new hospice, the one she hoped to build and operate, providing she was absolved by the Supreme Court.

As she knelt, her eyes fixed devoutly upon the altar's stark crucifix, she planned in exquisite detail exactly how it would be.

In her years of overseas service she often had to do without pen and paper and had been forced to develop her powers of concentration and memory. She used that ability now. Besides, she didn't wish to commit any of her plans to writing for fear that they might fall into unsympathetic hands. She used her precise mind like a steel file cabinet, filing away ideas and thoughts on the efficient use of space, work schedules, and even the right chemical mixtures to send her beloved patients to Almighty God when the pain became too much to bear. She planned it all very carefully.

*   *   *

Herbert Mennen, the man who paid for Sister Murphy's legal expenses, also planned, and at the very same time of day. But he was not quiet, nor contemplative. He was talking loudly on the telephone, as he always did no matter how good the connection. He was discussing his plans with a reluctant funeral director in New Jersey, a man who headed a statewide group of cut-price morticians. Mennen was outlining the probable profits for a mortuary owner who had the good sense to get in on the ground floor and tie in with his proposed system of hospices, and thereby obtain a steady stream of customers for funeral arrangements. As soon as the high court ruled for Sister Death, Mennen told the man, the hospice operation was ready to go, and it would be nationwide.

But the mortician seemed to be resisting, raising the problem of possible local suits and criminal actions, despite a ruling by the U.S. Supreme Court on the legality of assisted suicide. The funeral director didn't believe the states would obey such a ruling.

"You think not," Mennen bellowed in reply. "Listen, let me tell you a true story. That fucking Supreme Court couldn't make up its mind on obscenity, right? So there was no nationwide rule. But they had another fucking porno case before them, but it hadn't come down yet. Anyway, one day I'm walking to a business meeting at a local bank. I happen to walk past a sidewalk kiosk, you know, one of them stands with papers and magazines. Like always, all I see are tits and ass. The whole display was magazine covers, tits and ass in high gloss. Well, I'm in the bank maybe three hours, then I walk back.

"I pass the same kiosk and all the dirty girlie magazines are gone. They had been replaced with sports magazines, that sort of thing. The afternoon papers had come out. They all had the same headline: Supreme Court rules on obscenity. I didn't have to read how they decided, just one look at the change of the magazine display told the whole story.

"See, the government didn't need any cops to sweep those magazines off the stands. The decision was obeyed instantly. It's kinda like that television ad, when the Supreme Court speaks, everybody listens. Of course, a couple of months later they reverse themselves and everything is all tits and ass again. But that's only on obscenity, they go back and forth on that one like a Ping-Pong ball. But you don't have to worry about big issues like rational suicide. If they rule for that nun, that's it. Sure, some local hotshots will raise a little hell for publicity, but they'll cave in. I got an army of lawyers standing by to kick the shit out of anybody who tries to get in the way.

"Look, if we get ready now, we can beat everybody else into the field. I got the organization and the finances. I'm doing you guys a favor, cutting you in. Now's the time to get aboard. You don't want to miss this bus, pal, because there's a lot of money to be made here."

Herbert Mennen had no premonition about another telephone call about to be made in the midwest. Mennen had no time for any kind of abstract contemplation when he was busy selling.

*   *   *

Patrolman Charles Garcia and his partner completed the early shift. Garcia, as he had requested, had a new partner. The man was not a good street cop and had a tendency to rush into potentially dangerous situations, but he was what Garcia wanted, he was white.

It had been a slow day, boring, but it at least insured a minimum of paperwork. This night had been selected by Garcia to do his household bills. He didn't need any more paperwork than that. Doing the bills always upset him.

He experienced a sharp sense of bitterness and frustration as he walked into the precinct and saw several black officers. He knew them. They had less seniority, they were younger and hadn't invested as much of their lives in police work. Soon, depending on the court case, either he or they would be out of work.

All their futures now depended on the color of skin, nothing else. He thought about the mortgage payment, the car loan, the kids' dental work. It didn't seem real that he wouldn't be able to meet his obligations, that he would lose everything, just because he just wasn't dark enough.

Garcia was sufficiently objective to know that he was being affected, that his thoughts and attitudes were becoming predominantly racial. Prejudice, he thought, tended to poison its victim, manufacturing hate. The lash of racial discrimination cut the flesh, no matter what the color, equally deep.

He quickly changed out of his uniform, talking very little with the other men of the shift. They had little in common anymore. It was his job and his career that were on the line, not theirs. And the other officers seemed to be withdrawing from him, as if he really didn't belong anymore, as if he was no longer one of them.

He hurried to his car and headed home. He switched on the radio to catch the news. He knew it would be months yet before the Supreme Court would act on the affirmative action case, but he had started listening to the newscasts, hoping that one day they would announce a favorable decision and he would be saved.

Patrolman Garcia had no knowledge of the importance to him of a telephone call about to be made to the White House.

*　　*　　*

They had got the paper out, and the newspaper now operated with only a skeleton night staff; a few reporters and rewrite men ruled by the night city editor, plus the drama critic whose day began when most everyone else's ended. The pace of operation was very different from the fuss and fury of only a few hours before.

Abby Simmons reread his front page story. The mayor and the city council were at it again with charges and countercharges. To a veteran reporter like Simmons it seemed the story could be reprinted at regular intervals, word for word, because it was always the same. He thumbed through the rest of the newspaper, although he had already read it twice.

Harry Phillips, the managing editor, stalked out of his office, on his way home. He saw Simmons and altered course, walking through the rows of desks until he came up to him.

"What are you doing," Phillips asked.

Abby Simmons looked up languidly. "I am admiring this monument to your art. I am reading this fucking newspaper."

"Ah, Abby, I didn't know you knew that word. Isn't it funny, no matter how well you think you know somebody, you find you can still learn something new about them."

"What's biting you? I'm just sitting here reading the paper. I'm on my own time."

"You're sore because that piece of yours about the bank merger didn't run," Phillips growled.

"I'm not sore. You gave me a nice shot on page one with the story about his honor, the mayor. However, since you bring it up, why didn't you run the merger thing? It was good copy."

"Yeah, it was. But it was marginal news. I have to pick and choose."

"Come on, Harry, it was better news that this shit about the mayor and the council. That happens all the time. A major merger of our largest banks is of general interest."

The editor shrugged. "I checked it out with our attorneys. They think publicity might foul up the transaction. They said if we screwed up the merger and it cost the banks some money, they'd be on us like tigers. Bankers aren't forgiving types. Just try missing your mortgage payment."

"Same principle as the bridge story?"

The editor shrugged. "Yeah, more or less. Under that state law we could maybe get our ass sued. So we don't run the story."

"If you had been on the *Washington Post,* Nixon would still be president."

Phillips laughed. "If that law had been in effect in Washington at the time, the Nixon crew would now own the *Washington Post.*"

Abby Simmons tossed the newspaper into a trash barrel. "That damn bridge is going to fall down, Harry. Sooner or later, it's going to fall. And that's a hell of a lot more important than a bank merger."

"If the Supreme Court knocks that law down, Abby, we'll warn everybody about the dangers of your bridge."

"But what if in the meantime. . . ."

The editor laughed. "Okay, to show you that I'm a man of conscience, I'll tell you what we'll do—we'll run a special series on how to swim. But until the court does something about that fucking law, we're not going to print a thing about your fucking bridge."

"My, but you pick up bad language quickly."

Abby Simmons stood up and pulled on his coat. There was no use in further protest. He had done all he could do. "Come on, Harry, I'll buy you a beer."

Simmons had no way of knowing about the man in the motel, staring at the telephone.

*　　*　　*

Haywood Cross, the managing partner of Harley Dingell, stood up and walked to his window. He looked down at the capital's traffic. He smiled to himself. If Green could pull off the key vote on the antitrust suit, the firm would be sitting pretty, very pretty indeed.

They weren't a large firm, and it rankled Cross that the number of lawyers employed had become at least one yardstick used to measure the importance of a law firm.

If Green could pull it off, and if they got the rush of business Cross expected, they could open branch offices in most of America's larger cities. They would have to staff those branches with attorneys. He smiled. Even foreign offices were a distinct possibility: London, Paris, that would look very good indeed. It was time Harley Dingell got the national recognition it deserved.

Well, he thought to himself, it's all up to Green. But he thought no more about the absent partner.

*   *   *

In the Oval Office at the White House, a red-felt pen checked off the electoral vote totals of the big states. California, New York, Ohio, Texas: he could expect to carry them no matter what else happened. That was the prediction of the private poll. And if he carried those states he would win, but only if the Electoral College remained intact. It would be close. The poll said he would probably lose the popular vote, but win on the basis of the Electoral College results. The big states would win it for him on a block vote basis. After the election he didn't care what the Congress, the country, or the Supreme Court did about the Electoral College issue. But he needed it now and he knew his future would swing on the vote of one justice, a man he would name himself. That seemed safe enough, but only if he was sure the man he put on the Court would make that commitment and honor it.

His red pen once again began adding up the new votes given each state by the new census. He studied the poll projections. No matter how he counted, he was through unless he could protect the Electoral College.

Chapter 12

Jerry Green sat on the bed and stared at the telephone. There was no use in putting off the inevitable, yet he seemed to lack the power to organize his thoughts, as if thinking itself had become an impossible effort.

He looked up from the telephone and glimpsed his own image in the dresser mirror. He studied the man he saw. With a few minor changes he could be looking directly at Dean Roy Pentecost; the same hair, the same face, even the same expression, only Pentecost always looked so sure of himself. The man in the mirror did not possess that inner quality. He seemed to be more puzzled, even lost.

Jerry Green's mind began to focus on the mirror image. He and the dean were so much alike, he could almost persuade himself that he could think in the same pattern. What would the dean do if their positions were reversed?

Pride looked back at him from the mirror. But what kind of pride? That was the question.

The image in the mirror was full of ambition, but for what? Green understood the dean's ambition clearly enough. The man wanted to be on the Supreme Court. If Pentecost believed he had a soul, Jerry Green knew the man wouldn't hesitate a moment to sell it for that prize. But what of his own ambition? He had been offered the choice of two paths. To choose one would mean simply a continuation of his career as a partner at Harley Dingell. At one time in his life that had meant as much to him as the Court did now to the dean, perhaps more. But now? What would it be like to no longer be the "fixer," the workhorse of the firm? How would that compare to being a law professor, living a quiet life, but one that promised love? He could have that here, but he would never find that in Washington. But it indeed was here. And it could all be his; all he had to do was make one telephone call and give the right answer.

The dean thirsted for the canonization of the black robe, the honor of the position. Pentecost was prepared to sacrifice anything to obtain that recognition. Green smiled at his own reflection. And my own honor, he asked himself silently, what about it? How does one weigh honor in making such a choice? He knew the men in the White House trusted him and trusted his judgment. It really wouldn't make any difference if he was right or wrong, only the future could reveal that, but they did trust him. And if he violated their trust only he would know, no one else. It was like the old philosophy question: Is there a noise in the forest when a tree falls but no ear is present to hear it? Is there honor if no one knows about it? Perhaps a belief in God might make a silent sacrifice worth it, knowing that reward was only deferred. Honor, did it really exist anymore? Had it ever really existed, or was the concept itself a product of romance and not reality?

But there were rules, ethics. A man did not range over the earth alone, he existed with others, and in order to live in any peace at all there had to be rules, codes of conduct. Without guides the world would be nothing but chaos. Did the rules still have to be obeyed, even when no one was looking?

But the man in the mirror just smiled, there were no easy answers coming back from the reflecting glass.

Green shifted his gaze to the window. It was getting late. The sky was darkening. It seemed to get darker so much faster in the midwest. The clouds hung heavily above the earth. They moved slowly, looking more like gray funeral shrouds than condensed atmosphere. That thought matched his mood.

What would he tell them?

He again sought out his own reflection in the mirror. In a way, the man staring back at him seemed like a stranger. Green felt he knew more about the dean than he did about the man he saw in the reflection.

If he hadn't met Regina, if he hadn't rekindled in himself a feeling long dead, he could have been completely objective. So what to tell the White House? The question hung in his consciousness. Did he tell them he had met an old girlfriend and couldn't think straight anymore? It would sound stupid, but it would be an honest answer.

Regina was like a dream. He wondered how much he had created, and how much was actually reality. If they did finally end up with each other, what then? Would the dream continue, the walks in the snow, the closeness, or would the sandpaper of everyday living wear away the gloss until nothing remained except a formal arrangement, a treaty to avoid war, no more. That was what he had now. Would it be different with Regina, or was the whole thing just a dream?

Did he owe a duty to the President? Duty, it was a word of many meanings. They had come to him. No favors had been done for him and none promised, except the use of the special counsel title. In fact, it had been made clear that he could expect no more than the title, and that for a short time. No doors would be opened for him, no special advantage would be given, save the illusion of inferred power. But no real power was given, so what, if any, duty had been created?

Jerry Green nodded to the man in the mirror, as if in salute. In a moment he would pick up the telephone and make a decision that would mold American law for years to come. But he didn't know what to say. The call would affect people and cases for many years to come. He stared at the telephone. Considering the part it was about to play in the country's future, the instrument should be removed after his call, bronzed and placed in a suitable museum. What was about to be done merited that kind of memorial.

No more dreams, that had been his father's last message. So if you didn't believe in dreams, then what? Self-destruction?

He sighed and picked up the telephone. It took a few moments to be passed through the levels of White House secretary-sentries and to reach Amos Deering.

"Hello, Amos. This is Jerry Green," he said simply.

"Jesus, it's about time! I not only got the chief of staff on my ass, but the man himself called me in only minutes ago. They're anxious as hell, Jerry. What's the decision?"

Green looked at the man in the mirror.

"You mean on Dean Pentecost?"

"What else? Listen, the man was just saying to me that he hoped you cleared him. Everything has been all wired up and we can expect the nomination to go through smoothly. The man wants to appoint the dean."

"Then why wait for me? Have him go ahead."

"Don't go getting sensitive, sport. The man thinks enough of you that he won't make a move until he hears what you have to say. There aren't too many people whom he regards that highly, believe me."

"Do you want to call me back from your telephone booth?" Green asked.

"No. Piss on it. If someone's tapping, let them tap. Time is running, Jerry. Let's have it; do we go with this guy, or don't we?"

"Do you want details, or just the bottom line?"

"If it was just me, I'd only want the bottom line. But I know the man; he'll want details. I'll make notes, so go ahead."

"If this is being recorded it could prove embarrassing."

"Look, I don't give a shit if this is going out via satellite. We have to know on this, and we have to know now!"

"All right. You have the basic facts. Pentecost is intelligent, street smart politically, and he wants the job."

"Good. But did you pop the big question?"

"On the Electoral College issue? Oh yes. It turns out he's made quite a study of the whole question. He doesn't need the briefs or the arguments to know where he stands."

"And where's that?"

"He believes the constitutional amendment wasn't properly ratified by the states. He will vote to keep the Electoral College, at least on the basis of this case."

"Hot shit! That's all we needed. Baby, you did a damn good job," Amos Deering howled into the telephone.

"Too good."

"What do you mean?"

"My firm, Harley Dingell, has taken up the appeal in the Marchall antitrust suit. I asked him how he would vote on that. He promised that he would vote to sustain my firm's position."

"Hey, that's not what you were sent down there for, sport."

"I know. I asked him about the rational suicide case."

"What the hell do I care about that?"

"You should." Green looked at the man in the mirror. "He promised to vote to free the nun."

"Big deal."

"It is a big deal, Amos."

There was a pause. "So what? People are knocking themselves off all over the place without help of medicine. Don't bullshit me, his attitude on the issue doesn't mean a thing."

"The dean promised to vote for continuation of affirmative action in the police case."

Again there was a pause. "I don't know where the old man stands on that. It could be an important issue. Still, I think generally he'd like it if all that civil rights crap could be cooled down, at least until after the election."

"You're missing the point."

"What do you mean?"

"He promised to uphold the state law making newspapers liable for stories a jury might consider negligent. He is for a firm stand as far as newspapers are concerned. He believes they've been granted far too much freedom, much more than was ever intended by the Constitution."

"Well, as a former newsman, I think that's a crock, but it could help us during election. Hell, what the Court does won't reflect on us. You know the press is after our ass anyway. I think the old man might just like that."

"Amos, you're missing the point."

"Well, Goddamn it, if I am, let me know about it!" Deering's voice snapped with irritation.

The man in the mirror smiled; it was a slightly superior smile, not triumphant, just reflecting the pleasure of secret knowledge.

"Your friend Pentecost was willing to go whichever way I indicated."

"Grow up, Jerry. Of course he was. Damn it, he wants the job. As you say, he probably thought everything you asked was a prerequisite to getting it. You know, that's not exactly unheard of in politics."

"I didn't get his commitment in writing, that's the problem."

Deering again paused before speaking. "Have you been drinking?"

Green smiled. "I had one Scotch, that's all. I'm in full possession of my faculties."

"Then what's this shit about writing?"

Green grinned at the mirror's image. "By the way, he offered me a bribe if I recommended him."

"What?"

"He said he would make me a full professor here at the law school, for life."

Deering snorted. "That's a bribe? Shit, you probably make five times the salary. Come on, he probably just liked you."

This time Green laughed. "No, I'm sure that wasn't the reason." He couldn't seem to tear his eyes away from his own reflected image. "Let me tell you about the dean," he said, looking at himself. "He's a conniving bastard and smart. He has a good head and he knows people. And he has dreams, Amos."

"So?"

"I can read the son-of-a-bitch as if I was looking at him right now. He has the dream of being the swing man on the Court, another Brian Howell, only bigger and better. He's a genius at getting publicity, and he knows it. He'll use that skill to carve a new name into the history of the law before he's through."

"That sounds like a recommendation."

"That's his dream. And anything that might stand in the way of that dream will be crushed, destroyed."

"Oh Christ, Jerry, what's the matter with you?"

The image in the mirror seemed somehow indistinct. "He's not honest, damn it."

"I still think you've been drinking. Look, the President isn't Diogenes, he's not running around looking for an honest man. He just wants a reasonably bright lawyer who can get past the Senate and then sew up the Electoral College thing. Honesty—sure it's nice, Jerry—but it isn't essential."

"Oh, but it is. I told you I didn't get any of this in writing."

"Wouldn't be binding, even if you did," Deering snapped. "You know that."

"Right. Now listen to me carefully, Amos. This is what I want you to tell the President. Dean Pentecost made the necessary commitment, but it's my judgment that he can't be trusted to carry through on it. He will only if it suits his dream for himself, but he is totally without conscience, so he cannot be trusted ultimately to vote as promised."

"How can you be sure?"

"He promised anything, everything. It was as if I were inside his head; he never intends any of it. Once he's sworn in, the slate is wiped clean, as far as he's concerned. Integrity, it gets down to that, Amos. The man has all the qualifications, except one; he lacks basic integrity." Green stuided the man in the mirror, whose face was now solemn. "It's an odd twist, Amos, but if he had basic integrity he would have told me, and the President, to go to hell. Politely, but that's what he would have done."

"And he wouldn't get the job."

"Perhaps not. But it's that very lack of integrity that makes his word worthless. He can't be trusted."

Again there was a pause. "Are you really sure? You're not just pissed off at this guy or something? There's a lot riding on this."

"I'm sure." The man in the mirror seemed different, older. "He has dreams, Amos, and that makes him dangerous."

Deering swore softly. "I'll tell the man, but he won't be happy. He was counting on this guy. The appointment would have looked good and it would have been so easy."

"He can still appoint him. After all, what I said is only my opinion."

"No, I know how he feels about this." Deering's voice reflected his disappointment. "The dean is done for."

"Who's next in line? Judge O'Malley?"

Deering chuckled, but without humor, He sounded tired. "No. He put on quite a show over Howell's coffin. It was straight out of old-fashioned ward politics, and it should have worked, but you know the boss, he likes everything proper. It really pissed him off. O'Malley is through."

"Then who will it be?"

He could hear Deering sigh. "Keep your mouth shut about this, eh? They decided that if the dean was out of it, the job would go to Senator Butler, the junior guy from Illinois. He's an old-school politician and all that, but we can count on him. He doesn't reflect the boss's general thinking, but the Electoral College will be preserved, and the Senate will kiss him all through the hearings, even the chairman; club privilege and all that. It's a compromise, but what the hell, what isn't?"

Green's back ached. He had been sitting on the bed without support. "Sorry it had to be this way, Amos."

"Me too. Well, the old man won't be pleased but he'll value your judgment. See, we all knew you had integrity; that's why we sent you down there."

Green looked at the man in the mirror. "Or did you set a thief to catch a thief?"

Deering laughed. "Yeah, maybe that's really more like it. Anything else?"

"That's it."

"Thanks, Jerry. I'll go in and see the man now."

The line went dead and Green listened for a moment to the dial tone before it occurred to him to hang up.

He glanced at his watch and made a fast calculation. He could make it if he really hurried.

He quickly packed his bags. Then he placed another telephone call, again to Washington.

"Janus Associates," the switchboard girl answered. She sounded annoyed. It was almost closing time.

"Mrs. Green, please."

"Just a minute." He listened to pleasant recorded music as he was put on hold.

"Mrs. Green's office." He recognized the secretary's voice.

"This is Mr. Green," he said. "Is my wife there?"

"She's in a conference down the hall, Mr. Green. I can get her if you like."

"No. That's not necessary. Just give her a message. Tell her I'll be catching a late flight out of Detroit, and that I'll be home tonight." He hung up. That would spare them both an unpleasant scene in case she was entertaining in his absence. It was the civilized thing to do.

He debated calling the managing partner at Harley Dingell. He could tell him that the dean refused to vote for the firm's position in the Marchall case so he had recommended that the man not be appointed. That lie would make him a hero and really cement forever the "fixer" image. To hell with it, he thought, let them form their own conclusions. They were Yale men. He knew that his silence in these circumstances would be interpreted as his having acted to protect the firm.

Hank would be disappointed if he left without saying goodbye, but estrangement from his family was nothing new. He could easily patch that up later.

And Regina? He could call, or he could see her. It seemed the least he could do. But she was the one who had made the rules, she had set the boundaries.

And if he did nothing, as cruel as that might be, she would for him always be the Regina remembered walking in the snow. He would always have the thought of what might have been, a pleasant life, peaceful, secure, and loving. But that was a dream.

But it was his last dream. He would cling to it. He knew what happened when there were no more dreams.